Ace Sleuth, Private Eye

by

Joe Purkey

PublishAmerica
Baltimore

© 2007 by Joe Purkey.
All rights reserved. No part of this book may be reproduced, stored in a retrieval system or transmitted in any form or by any means without the prior written permission of the publishers, except by a reviewer who may quote brief passages in a review to be printed in a newspaper, magazine or journal.

First printing

All characters appearing in this work are fictitious. Any resemblance to real persons, living or dead, is purely coincidental.

ISBN: 1-4241-7403-1
PUBLISHED BY PUBLISHAMERICA, LLLP
www.publishamerica.com
Baltimore

Printed in the United States of America

Ace Sleuth, Private Eye. The detective with an attitude.

Dedicated to our granddaughter,
Sara Beth LaFever

Preface

This is a book of fiction and all the characters are figments of my imagination and any resemblance to actual persons is purely coincidental.

First of all I would like to apologize to my alma mater, the University of Tennessee. No one as stupid as Luther Spenser could have possibly graduated from undergraduate school there, much less law school.

The theme factory episode actually happened when I was in school there, however the student who asked me about the theme factory never got beyond Freshman English 101.

This is my first novel and I tried to be careful with naming my characters, trying not to duplicate any names in the Knoxville phone directory. I intended for Brad Adams to be my main character, but Ace Sleuth just seemed to come to the forefront. He wasn't even in my mind when I started writing.

I mention the Butcher brothers several times in my book. They built the two gleaming side-by-side towers and were riding high until their bubble burst in 1983. Their empire fell like a house of cards with the bankruptcy of their banks in 1983. Jake, the elder brother, even ran for governor at one time. Both Jake and his brother C. H. ended up in federal prison for a few years. Many people lost their life savings in their banks.

I would like to thank the employees at the West Knoxville Branch Library for digging out some legal books for me. I got all the information relating to the jury selection process from the Web Site of Mr. Ervin A. Gonzalez. I would also like to thank my wife Joan and my son Scott for proofreading my book. I would especially like to thank my wife Joan for insisting that I do a better job of describing my characters, namely the female ones. My daughter Dana was very helpful by giving me information on courtroom and medical procedures.

A nationally recognized fellow engineer in the electrical power industry, Mr. Al Hudson, reviewed the draft, and was very helpful with the technical portions of the book.

Prologue

Bradford Adams is a corporate attorney living in Knoxville, Tennessee, who only works about two hours a day in his office which covers one corner of the top floor (twenty-fourth) of the beautiful glass-sided south tower which is now called the BB&T Bank Building. All the Butcher brother banks were taken over by the FDIC in early 1983 after their banks went under. The bankruptcy was so massive and widespread that the FDIC kept a workforce of around five hundred people in Knoxville for years just trying to sort everything out. Billions of dollars were involved. However one good outcome for the city was the addition of two beautiful gleaming glass multistory buildings. The Butcher brothers had each built themselves a monument in close proximity to each other. The first tower is now called First Tennessee Bank Building. Brad's office is located on the upper floor of BB&T bank building, the southernmost building. He has a view of the Women's Basketball Hall of Fame building to the east, and directly on a hill above and beyond is the Marriott Hotel. The hotel has a very unusual shape. Someone said it looked like a Tennessee Valley Authority (TVA) dam, while others said it looked like the box the dam came in. Further to the right, facing southeast, and about two miles away as the crow files, is Island Home Airport. The airport is used mainly by small and company-owned planes. Brad had never seen an airport that close to the center of a city before. He can watch the planes take off and land. Directly across the street to the south, a stone's throw away, stands the old Andrew Johnson Hotel building (no longer used as a hotel) where Hank Williams Sr. spent his last night alive in 1953, dead at twenty-nine. Farther to the south and across the beautiful Tennessee River is the Baptist Hospital Complex which plays a large part in this book. Looking southwest he has a view of the beautifully arched Henley Street Bridge over the Tennessee River. While in college, Brad had a view of this bridge from his dorm room and often thought how beautiful it would be if the city would put lights on the arches. His view past the bridge is the imposing University of Tennessee football stadium (Neyland Stadium) which seats in excess of 105,000 people. This is extremely important to Brad because he spent many Saturdays playing fullback for the Volunteers in the '70s. On game days the Tennessee Vol fans come to the game by plane, boats, trains, buses, vans, and cars. The people who come in boats are called the Vol Navy. There may be several hundred boats that are tied up to the dock and several rows of boats tied to the docked ones. To get to the shore the boaters have to climb over the tied-up boats. They may have to cross over up to ten boats to get to shore which is just a short distance from the stadium. It is not uncommon for the fans to take a drink or two and party as they stop and talk to the owners of the boats which they are crossing.

Thirty degrees to the right of the football stadium is the structure called the Sun Sphere, a 150-foot-tall structure with a seventy-five-foot-diameter gold ball sitting on top. It is not unlike a golf ball on a tee. This is another benefit from the Butchers. Jake Butcher, the older of the two brothers (the younger brother was C. H.), was instrumental in bringing the World's Fair to Knoxville. The Sun Sphere, like the Space Needle in Seattle, was the focal point of the 1982 World's Fair hosted by the City of Knoxville. The Sun Sphere consists of eight levels with the center level that served as a rotating restaurant and provided a beautiful panoramic view of Knoxville during the fair. Since then it has been sitting idle for most the past few years. After the fair it served for a time as the Tourist Bureau, and was also rented out for parties and wedding receptions. Brad often wondered, as did most Knoxvillians, why someone had not opened up a restaurant up there again, especially in the city known as the town where everyone eats out.

Brad is six foot two and weighs 220 pounds, just ten pounds over his playing weight thirty years ago. As they say in Big Orange Country, "Mark's blood runneth orange." He graduated from the University of Tennessee College of Law two years after his football playing days were over, and has been so successful in his profession that he doesn't ever need to work again if he doesn't care to. Although he is a highly successful attorney, he is not widely known in the city because corporate lawyers seldom get their names in the paper or their faces on TV. This suits Brad just fine. He was much better known back in his football-playing days than he is today. Strangely enough he has never argued a court case before a judge, but this is about to change

Since his wife died two years ago Brad has never remarried although he is considered to be the town's most eligible bachelor. The truth is that he has never gotten over his wife's death. He drives a Mercedes 500 SL sedan and lives in a three-bedroom condo overlooking the Tennessee River.

As far as Brad was concerned, life couldn't have been better until the morning of September 5, 2006. It had been a hectic weekend. The previous Saturday night, September the second, he had attended the UT-California football game at Neyland Stadium along with 106,000 other fans and a dozen of his close friends in his rented sky box on the west side of the stadium. There is a waiting list for these sky boxes, which is pretty amazing, because the cost is $25,000 per year plus the cost of the tickets. If you want a parking space near the stadium, another $1,000 a year is needed. Incidentally Tennessee won the game. To top off the weekend the city had what's known as "Boomsday" on Sunday the third. The attendance for this event makes the football attendance seem puny with over 300,000 people attending. This event is one of the largest fireworks displays in the country. In addition to the normal rocket blasts into the night sky, the arches of the Henley Street Bridge are made to look like waterfalls as the fireworks are directed down toward the water.

Life changed drastically for Brad Adams around 9:00 a.m. on the morning of Tuesday, September 5, 2006. As he normally did, he pulled into the parking garage beneath his office tower, and as he turned the first corner, a figure stepped in front of him and went flying into his windshield before falling to the concrete floor. Brad stopped, jumped out of his car, and at the same time dialed 911 on his cell phone. A man of about forty years of age was lying flat on his back and appeared to be in great pain. He was conscious but said that he couldn't get up or move his legs. Brad was afraid to try to move him, but he put his coat under the man's head to comfort him. The KPD took only about five minutes to arrive with the paramedics from Baptist Hospital only a few minutes behind them. The hospital is only a half mile away (as the crow flies) across the Tennessee River. The paramedics immobilized the victim, placed him in the ambulance, and took him directly to Baptist. After giving a brief statement to the police and promising to be available to them later, Brad got in his car and headed for the hospital emergency room and waited there for word of the victim's condition.

After about an hour, an emergency room doctor with a name tag that read "Dr. Reed Smith" entered the waiting room and inquired if anyone was here concerning the man who was hit by a car. Brad held up his hand and the doctor came over to give him the update.

"We gave the patient a painkiller and he'll probably be out for three or four hours. He said he was in a lot of pain and couldn't move his legs. There is nothing more we can do for him right now but keep him comfortable. We took several x-rays and there appears to be a vertebra somewhat out of place in the lumbar area of the lower back. The number one lumbar vertebra seems to be the one that is causing the problem. It appears to be pushed out a bit."

Brad introduced himself and told the doctor that he had never seen the man until he walked in front of his car in the parking garage beneath his office building a little over an hour ago. "By the way, Doctor, what is the patient's name?"

"I can give you his name and age but that's all I can give you at this time. I don't want this hospital to become involved in any kind of lawsuit because of me. The man's name is Bret Martin, and his ID lists his age as forty-one."

Brad didn't figure there was any more that he could do at the hospital so he left his name, his insurance company's name, and asked the doctor to see that the information got to the patient. Since he wasn't in the mood to work, he got in his car and drove home.

Chapter 1

Brad had hardly settled in at home when the phone rang. It was KPD Officer Collins, who was one of the officers at the parking garage, asking him if he could come down to the police station and sign some papers. Brad said he would be there within the hour.

He met in a small conference room with Officer Collins.

"Can you go over with me again and tell me exactly what happened in the parking garage?" the officer asked.

"There's not a whole lot more I can add that I've not already told you. I was going to work as usual at around 9:00 a.m. and had just made the first turn in the garage, when this figure seemed to jump right out in front of me and come flying into my windshield. I didn't even have time to apply my brakes. I immediately stopped and jumped out of my car and pushed 911 on my cell phone and then went to the man to see what I could do to help. He was conscious and talking, but he said he couldn't get up or move his legs. I didn't want to move him and probably cause more damage, but I did put my coat under his head to make him a little more comfortable. That's all I can remember."

"You need to sign a few forms," said Officer Collins, "which is a standard procedure in cases like these. There will be no traffic citation issued. As you probably know, the KPD has no traffic jurisdiction on private property. Even if we did there would be no ticket in this case because we can find no fault on your part, but I must warn you that I cannot testify to that in court because of that same jurisdiction."

Brad signed the papers and went back home. As he was sitting in his easy chair, he went over the events of the past few hours. It seemed to him that this whole scenario was choreographed, but that didn't make sense. What about the x-rays that showed the damage to the vertebra? That information came directly from Baptists Hospital's x-ray machine. There's no way that it could be doctored. On the other hand he could see where he would be a perfect patsy for this kind of scam. *I'm wealthy and have a good auto insurance policy. I have a routine of going to work at the same time and parking in the same spot. It would not be hard for someone to pick up on this by doing a little legwork.* When he thought about his car insurance he went to his desk and took out the policy. He hadn't looked at it for years, but he did remember that he had a $5 million umbrella policy. The umbrella is designed to cover losses and liability on his home and car, and his office within certain limits. He decided to look at the policy a little closer.

The policy's maximum payout was $5 million but not for a single accident. For a single accident for which he would be liable, the maximum payout for a single individual was $2 million. The policy also stated that the insurance would provide an attorney if required. Brad sat straight up in his chair. He had completely forgotten to notify his insurance agent.

He picked up the phone and called his local agent who happened to be available, a Mr. Frank Wheeler. "This is Brad Adams. I had an automobile incident this morning, and in my confused state, I forgot to call you."

"It's not a big deal, Brad. I just got off the phone with the victim's attorney. Do you have any idea how a man in the emergency room at Baptist Hospital could get in touch with an attorney in such a short time?"

"What is the lawyer's name, and what time was it that he called?" asked Brad.

"His name is Luther Spenser, and he called at almost twelve noon on the dot. He said that Martin has retained him as his attorney. Do you know him?"

"Do I ever? I spent six years going to UT with him from my freshman year all the way through law school." Brad had not seen Spenser for a number of years and he wondered if he still looked the same. He remembered him as being around six feet tall and weighing around 170 pounds with a black pencil mustache that he would have been better off without. Brad thought it made him look more like a crook than he really was. He thought Luther would be a natural as a carnival barker.

"Knowing Luther as I do, I don't think the victim got in touch with Luther, I think Luther got in touch with the victim. I have been told that

Luther has three police-band radios, one in his office, one in his home, and one in his car. He often beats the police to the scene and has been seen handing out his cards to the victims as they lie in the street."

"I have passed this case along to our local claims office and they will be in touch with you in a short while," said Wheeler.

"Thanks, Frank."

Chapter 2

Wednesday, September 6

Brad went back to work on Wednesday following the accident the day before. He had just got his morning cup of coffee when Denise, his receptionist, informed him that a Mr. Charles Nelson from US Auto was on line one.

"Hello, Brad Adams here."

"This is Charles Nelson of US Auto Claims Department, and I have been assigned to handle your case. I will try to handle it locally if at all possible. I don't like having to bring in the big guns."

"How can I be of help?"

"For one thing, do not tell anyone the monetary limits of your insurance policy."

"I figured as much, and I have told no one."

"Good. As you know, we have been contacted by a lawyer named Luther Spenser claiming to represent Bret Martin. So far he has made no demands or suggested a settlement. I understand you went to college with Mr. Martin in the seventies. What can you tell me about the man?"

"Nothing good, I'm afraid. I first met him at the freshman orientation session in September of 1969. I found out later that we had adjoining rooms in the dorm so I got to know him pretty well our freshman quarter. To be honest, he wasn't the sharpest knife in the drawer. I found this out when we were both taking Freshman English 101. At UT during that time, all that English 101 consisted of was theme writing. Some of these students had never written a theme in their life, and I suspected that Luther belonged in this group. My suspicions were confirmed one day when Luther asked me if I knew where the theme factory was located."

"'Did you say theme factory?' I asked him.

"'Yes,' he said. 'Today in class, our instructor said that a lot of us would probably utilize the theme factory to write our themes.'

"I replied, 'Oh! You mean *that* theme factory.'

"I just happened to think at that time of a friend who was sort of a practical joker, and I told Luther that I could put him in touch with a student who could help him. After I left Luther, I immediately went to the dorm room of my friend, Ernest, and filled him in on the theme factory. I then brought the two together and the conversation went something like this:

"Ernest asked Luther what kind of theme he wanted. Did he want an 'A' theme, a 'B' theme, or a 'C' theme? Luther wanted to know what the difference was. Ernest replied that the difference was in the cost, and proceeded to give him the sliding scale prices. I could no longer keep a straight face, so I left them both haggling over the price.

"Luther continued to have difficulty with English, especially with literature. He was probably the biggest Cliff Notes user in school history. I don't think he ever read a complete book in his life. In fact, when we both started our first year of law school, Luther got saddled with the nickname 'Cliff Note' because he spent the entire first week of law school trying to locate Cliff Notes. I remember that he was always trying to copy off someone else's paper whenever he got the chance. We both graduated in 1975 with Luther graduating in the top one hundred percent of his class. In other words, he graduated dead last. Do you know what they call a medical student who graduates dead last in his class, Charles?"

"What do they call him, Brad?"

"They call him Doctor."

"That's a very clever one, Brad."

"Let me get back to Luther Spenser," said Brad. "As we were standing in line to receive our diplomas, I heard the man in front of Luther say to him, 'Luther, if you'll just hop on my back, I'll carry you across the stage. I've carried you this far and I might as well take you all the way.' Traditionally ninety percent of UT law school graduates have passed the Tennessee State Bar exam on the first try, but it took Luther three tries. I never did find out if he took his Cliff Notes with him to the test. I have had very little contact with him since we got out of school, but I did read in the paper several months ago that he had won a $3 million wrongful death suit. It must have fallen into his lap."

"I believe you have told me more than I need to know, Brad."

"I don't think so. You need to know all you can about this man. I know for a fact that he never met Will Rogers. He is not to be trusted. By the way, have you seen the x-rays of Mr. Martin that was taken in the emergency room?"

"Until Spenser makes his next move, I don't think we can get our hands on them unless we get a subpoena. For right now just sit tight until I get back in touch with you in case there are any changes. In the meanwhile don't make any statements to anyone without first checking with me."

Chapter 3

Brad couldn't stand the thought of sitting around doing nothing waiting for the axe to fall. He needed to be ready for what he knew was coming. He got out the Knoxville phone directory and looked in the yellow pages under "Private Detective." The first one listed was "Ace Sleuth, Private Eye."

Out of nothing more than curiosity Brad dialed the number. Mr. Sleuth evidently didn't have a receptionist because he answered the phone with "Ace here."

"Mr. Sleuth, this is Brad Adams, and I was wondering if we could have a little discussion?"

"Sure, Brad, would you like for me to come to your office?"

"Do you know where it is?"

"That's my business to know things like that."

"I think it would be better if I came to yours. Where on Gay Street is your office?"

"It's about ten blocks north and one block past Magnolia Avenue. The address is 209 North Gay. Be careful or you'll go right past it. I don't have a very big front."

"Good. I can be there in an hour. Is that OK?"

"See you then," said Ace.

It was such a pretty day that Brad decided to walk the ten blocks. He was not aware of most of the historic places he would pass on his walk up Gay Street. Gay Street was named many years ago after a street with the same name in Baltimore. Gay Street is the main street in Knoxville although there is a cross street called "Main Street." A few years ago a resident in jest suggested that Gay street be renamed "Straight Street."

There was hardly anyone on Gay Street these days. You could go an entire block and not pass anyone, unlike sixty years ago when there would have been a hundred people milling about on every corner.

The first place that Brad passed was the First Tennessee Bank Building (the building that Jake Butcher built). It was the first of the two. It came out during the bankruptcy hearing that the Butcher brothers were having a party in the building and someone asked what a million dollars in cash looked like. Jake had one of his cronies go to the vault and get a million dollars in currency. When he brought the cash back the partygoers began to pass the million back and forth like passing a football.

The first historic place that Brad passed was the old Bijou Theater. This was once a beautiful movie house that also hosted live performances and stage productions. The theater has since been refurbished and restored to its original splendor.

A couple of blocks farther north he came to the magnificent Tennessee Theater, which was built in the twenties and just recently underwent a $23 million overall restoration to its original beauty plus some. Brad considers it to be the most beautiful theater he has ever seen. It is absolutely thrilling to be waiting for the movie or show to start, and the mighty Wurlitzer organ rises from beneath the floor with the organist already sitting there playing.

Brad continued a short distance to the building that the S&W Cafeteria once occupied. In its heyday there was an organist playing for the customers of which there were many. At peak hours the cafeteria could open up three serving lines, and the food was very delicious.

Brad continued three or four more blocks until he came to the spot where the old variety show of the thirties and the forties broadcast their show to east Tennessee and parts of Kentucky. The show called *The Midday Merry Go Round* featured country music with a sprinkling of popular. The show also had no shortage of comedians. It was aired five days a week on the 10,000-watt radio station WNOX which reached parts of Kentucky, Virginia, and North Carolina. This was a live show of about one and a half hours in length with a live audience. Many people believe that if WNOX had had a 50,000-watt clear channel station like Nashville's WSM, that Knoxville would have been the home of country music instead of Nashville. Many famous county music stars got their start on the show. They included Roy Acuff, Chet Atkins, the Carter Family and their daughter, June Carter Cash, the Homer and Jethro Duo, and Archie Campbell, who gained fame on the country show *Hee Haw*.

ACE SLEUTH, PRIVATE EYE

A couple blocks further Brad smelled the pleasant aroma of roasting coffee from the JFG Coffee Company a half a block away. Next he crossed the Gay Street Viaduct, which is currently being rebuilt over the old Southern Railway tracks with the old train station half a block to the east. There has been no passenger service in Knoxville for fifty or more years. Back then trains were the primary mode of transportation to and from Knoxville. There was always a lot of activity around the train stations. Knoxville, unlike Chattanooga, did not have a Union Station. The other major railroad in Knoxville, The L & N (Louisville and Nashville), had its own depot a couple of blocks west. It had a much prettier one than the Southern Station.

A block further north Brad passed Knoxville's oldest restaurant (Regas). It was opened July 7, 1919, by a by a pair of Greek brothers by the name of Frank and George Regas. The restaurant was originally called the Astor Cafe, but was later renamed The Regas Brothers Café. The café, featuring an eighteen-stool counter and tables covered with white cloths, stayed open twenty-four hours a day. As it grew it was considered by many to be Knoxville's finest restaurant. Back forty or so years ago, Dave Thomas worked there for the Regas Brothers, and went on from there to found Wendy's fast-food chain.

The next stop for Brad was the office of Ace Sleuth.

Chapter 4

Brad entered Ace's office and noticed that he had no receptionist. He found Ace at his desk wearing clothes that looked like they had been discarded by a homeless man. Brad shook hands and introduced himself, and remarked, "Did Goodwill have a clothing sale recently?"

Ace looked to be about forty-five with a full head of hair standing almost six feet tall. He had rugged looks and a fairly good build. Brad guessed that he worked out a few times a week. He was fairly good-looking, but fell a little short of Tom Selleck in the looks department. He had a permit to carry a gun but he seldom did. He liked to live by his wits and avoid trouble as much as possible. He refused to take on any domestic cases such as spying on a cheating husband or wife because they could become very messy.

"Are you referring to my disguise? I am a man of many looks. I wear this one when I want to rummage through garbage cans looking for who knows what. I don't think a cop or anyone else is going to stop a homeless man looking for food, especially in these politically correct times. By the way, I clean up real good."

"Let me tell you why I'm here. But before we get started, how did you know who I was? We've never met."

"It's my business to know people in this town."

"Let me begin," said Brad.

Brad brought Ace up to speed on everything that had happened to him since 9:00 a.m. Tuesday, September 5. When Brad had finished, Ace knew as much about the situation as he did. Brad had already decided to hire him.

"Let me tell you why I need you," said Brad. "I believe I've been set up for a multimillion-dollar scam, and I believe Luther Spenser is smack dab in the middle of it."

"Are you referring to 'Slip and Fall' Spenser?"

"Yes, and he also answers to 'Cliff Note' Spenser. I'll tell you about that sometime."

"Bret Martin is in Baptist Hospital and the hospital will give me no information at all concerning him or his condition. I know absolutely nothing. All I know is his name and age.

"I would like for you to start by putting on one of your many disguises such as an orderly or janitor outfit, and gathering as much information as you can. I would like to have a copy of all the x-rays that were made of him the morning of the accident so that I can have an independent radiologist look at them. Do you think you can handle that?"

"They don't call me Sleuth for nothing. It'll be a piece of cake."

"By the way, is Ace Sleuth your real name?"

"No, I changed it because of my work."

"That's pretty clever coming up with the name Sleuth."

"I didn't come up with Sleuth, that's my real name. I was born to do this job. I came up with Ace so that I would be listed first in the yellow pages."

"Does it work?"

"You called me, didn't you?"

"When can you get started?"

"Is right now soon enough?"

"There is one more thing I forgot to ask. What are your rates?"

"For you they are four hundred dollars per day plus expenses."

"What are your rates for others?"

"Don't ask."

"OK, go to it."

Chapter 5

Ace donned his best suit (his only one), got in his '76 Mustang, and headed across the Gay Street Bridge which ended up right at Baptist Hospital. His Mustang is no ordinary car and he loves it. There is no original equipment on the car to speak of. He has a 300-horsepower turbo high-performance engine that can push the car up to speeds of 140 mph. It also has high-performance tires and all the electronic gadgets one could imagine, including a Global Positioning System (GPS). He pulled the Mustang into one of the parking garages at Baptist and found an empty space on level six and parked. He opened the glove compartment and pulled out a name tag that read:

Dr. Zachary
Vanderbilt Hospital
Orthopedics

He pinned the name tag to his left breast pocket and also removed a stethoscope from the glove compartment and placed it in the right pocket of his suit, making sure a goodly portion was hanging out. He walked up to the receptionist's desk and identified himself and asked for the room number of Bret Martin.

"He's in room 408 East Wing," she replied. "Check in with the fourth-floor nursing station before you see the patient. Take the elevators to your right."

Ace went directly to the nursing station and spoke to the nurse there working the desk. She looked to be about twenty-five years of age and was about five foot five with shiny blond hair and smile that would be suitable for a toothpaste ad. Ace gave her a rating of 9.5 out of a possible 10.

"I'm Dr James Zachary from Vanderbilt Hospital, and I've been retained as a consultant for a patient by the name of Bret Martin. I would like to see him," said Ace.

"I'm Nurse Jones. May I see some identification, Dr. Zachary?"

"Certainly, I'm glad you asked. In this day and time there all sorts of kooks running around." He took his billfold from his pocket and handed his AMA ID card to her.

"Room 408 is the third room down the hall on the left, Dr. Zachary."

"Thank you, Nurse Jones. There are a couple of things you can help me with."

"I'd be glad to, Doctor."

"OK. First I would like to look at his charts, and if possible, get a copy."

"Certainly, Doctor. Is there anything else?"

"I would like to get a copy of all the x-rays that have been made since the patient was admitted to the emergency room on Tuesday. I need these ASAP because I have to catch a plane from McGhee Tyson back to Nashville at 3:00 p.m. I will be glad to pay for them."

"That won't be necessary, Doctor. I have a very close friend who works in x-ray, and I can have those ready for you within thirty minutes at no cost."

"You have been most helpful, Nurse Jones. I'm going to put in a good word for you with the hospital."

"Thank you, Doctor. Just don't mention that I didn't charge you for the x-rays."

Ace walked into 408 and saw the patient lying flat on his back watching TV.

"Mr. Smith, I'm Dr. Zachary, and I've been brought in to consult on your case."

"My name is not Smith. My name is Martin."

"This is room 408, isn't it?"

"Yes, it is."

"Excuse me for a minute," said Ace, as he pulled out his cell phone and pushed a button. "Bill, what was the room number that you said Smith was in? Oh! Five-o-eight. I thought you said 408. Thanks. I'll get right up there."

"I'm sorry to have bothered you, Mr. Martin. Are they treating you well?"

"I can't complain, but I'll be glad when I get out of here and get back to normal."

"See you later. Again, I'm sorry for the mix-up." Ace hung around the nurse's station for several minutes until Nurse Jones had brought him the copies of the chart and x-rays he had requested.

As he was about to leave the hospital through the lobby door, he noticed a sign that read:

Hospital Administrator Office
William Hopkins

Brad walked up to the receptionist and identified himself and said he would like to speak to Mr. Hopkins.

"Just a minute, let me see if he can see you." She came back and told Brad to go on in.

"Mr. Hopkins, I'm Dr. James Zachary from Vanderbilt seeing one of your patients, and I just wanted to let you know how helpful one of your nurses was to me. If it weren't for Nurse Jones in acute care on the fourth floor, I'm afraid I would have had to spend another day in Knoxville at the expense of my Vanderbilt patients. I can't say enough about her cooperation."

"Thank you, Dr. Zachary. I am always glad to get positive comments about our employees. It seems that I always get the negative ones."

"Thank for your time, Mr. Hopkins. I have a 3:00 p.m. plane to catch back to Nashville." They shook hands, and as Ace was walking out the door he thought to himself, *When you're on a roll, you're on a roll.*

As he was returning to his car in the parking garage, he called Brad on his cell phone.

"Are you going to be in your office for the next few minutes?"

"I'll be here at least for the next hour," said Brad.

"I'll be there in ten minutes. I want to fill you in on my hospital visit."

Ten minutes later Ace walked into Brad's office.

"What did you find out?" asked Brad.

"I got copies of all the victim's x-rays and also a copy of his daily chart."

"I would appreciate it if you didn't refer to him as the victim."

"Sorry about that," said Ace.

"What else did you find out?"

"I got a picture of him with my cell phone camera."

"How in the world did you manage that?"

"If I told you, I'd have to kill you."
"Is that it?"
"Well, there is one more thing."
"What's that?"
"Either Martin is a good actor or he's really hurt."
"Why do you say that?"
"Because when the hospital fourth floor fire alarm inadvertently went off, he didn't try to leave his bed."
"Don't tell me you had anything to do with that."
"I will deny it to my dying day."
"Just leave the x-rays and the chart with me, and I'll get them examined. By the way, you did an excellent job."
"Thanks."
"There are two more jobs I would like for you to do next, but before I go into that, I was wondering if you need an advance on your expenses."
"I think a grand would tide me over for a week or so."
"Good, I'll have Denise write you out a check. Keep a running record of your expenses and the man-hours you have spent, and I'll pay you weekly, if that's OK with you?"
"Thanks, that's fine with me. What would you like for me to do next?"
"First, I would like for you to find out all you can about Luther Spenser. I want to know everything about him. I want to know what he has for breakfast, and right down to the brand of toothpaste he uses. I believe he's behind this whole scam. Secondly, I would like to get someone to do a computer check on Bret Martin, if that's his real name. Do you know of a computer whiz who could handle this?"
"I'm sure I can find one."
"Good, get back to me when you come up with anything new."
"You'll be the first to know," said Ace.

Chapter 6

Tuesday morning, September 5

Ace looked up the address of Luther Spenser in the yellow pages and found that his office was located in a low-rent area of South Market Street. He got into his '76 Mustang, drove to the Market Street address, parked across the street from the office, and dialed Spenser's number. The phone was answered by a pleasant-speaking female voice announcing that this was the office of Luther Spenser, Attorney at Law.

"Is Mr. Spenser in?"

"Yes, he is at the moment, but he has to go meet a client shortly. How can I be of help?"

"Thanks, I'll call back later when he's not busy."

Ace didn't mind waiting until Spenser left. He looked at Spenser's window and saw the gold lettering that read "Luther H. Spenser—Attorney at Law" and thought the sign would have been more appropriate if the "at" in the lettering was changed to "out." Ace didn't mind waiting. That was part of his job. He didn't want to see Spenser anyhow. He wanted to see his receptionist.

About thirty minutes later Spenser came out and Ace again made good use of the photo feature of his cell phone. *These little gadgets are amazing,* he thought. He could now take pictures while appearing to be talking on the phone.

As soon as Spenser left, Ace walked up to the receptionist's desk and asked if Mr. Spenser was in. She was around thirty-five and had a bare ring finger. She had shoulder-length brunette hair, beautiful intelligent brown eyes, and stood about five foot six. Ace also noticed that she had a contagious smile. The plaque on her desk identified her as Paula Novak. On a scale from one to ten, Ace gave her a 7.5.

ACE SLEUTH, PRIVATE EYE

"Do you really want to see my boss, or did you come in here just to see me?"

"Why do you ask that?"

"Well, it just seems kind of strange that you would sit out in the street in your car, and come in when the very man you wanted to see just left."

"You got me." Ace thought that he had better be careful around this woman, she was one smart cookie.

"I am glad that you called me first. Why do you want to see me? I don't even know you."

"You don't miss a trick do you? I'll be honest with you, I'm one of those big Hollywood talent scouts you've heard about who goes all over the country looking for beautiful women so that they can make them big movie stars, but don't worry, I don't have a casting couch, those things are too big to get into my Mustang."

"Goody, goody. I've always dreamed of being a big movie star. What is your name, Howard Hughes?"

"No. My name is, believe it or not, Ace Sleuth."

"Is that your real name?"

"No, my real name is Fred, Fred Sleuth. My full name is Fredrick Ulysses Sleuth. I think my mother had a sense of humor."

"I don't think I need to ask you what line of work you're in. Why do you really want to see me?"

"I was just wondering if you had ever dined at Regas."

"A couple of times but not lately."

"Would you like to dine there again?"

"Are you asking me out to dine?"

"If I were, what would your answer be?"

"Are you paying?"

"No."

"Dutch?"

"No."

"I pay?"

"No."

"What?"

"My client pays. How about tomorrow evening at seven?"

"Let me look in my little black book and see what's on my agenda. Oh! I'm sorry. That's the one time out of my hectic schedule that I've set aside to do my nails."

"If I pay for a first-class manicure for you, would you reconsider it?"

"Let me think. Yes. After much thought, I accept your invitation."

"Good. Where can I pick you up?"

"I'm not real crazy about the phrase, 'Pick me up,' but come by here about six-thirty tomorrow evening. I will be working a little late."

"Good, I'll wear my best suit."

"You have a suit?"

"I have a lot of things you don't know about."

Chapter 7

Wednesday evening, September 6

Ace picked up Paula at 6:30 p.m. as planned. He was pleasantly surprised to see how attractive she looked in her dress clothes. He immediately upped her rating from a 7.5 to an 8.5. *She must have kept a change of clothes in the office,* he thought. It was just a short drive to Regas, and when he got there he decided he might as well go first class so he made use of the valet parking for the first time in his life. What the heck. This night was on Brad. The valet gave Ace a skeptical look as he got behind the wheel of the '76 Mustang. They didn't have a reservation because it was Thursday night and most of the Early Bird Special crowd had left, opening up more tables.

When they were seated the waiter appeared and asked for their drink order.

"What do you want, Paula?"

"I would like a glass of wine but I don't know what kind until I know what I'm going to be eating."

"I am going to have the sixteen-ounce prime rib, so I think I will have a glass of Merlot," said Ace."

"Sounds fair to me, I'll have the Maine lobster and white Zinfandel wine."

After the wine was served a waiter appeared and announced that his name was Bruce and that he would be their server.

"Good. My name is Ace, and this is my friend Paula, and we'll be your customers."

Bruce then went into the usual spiel about the daily specials.

Ace stopped him and said that they had already decided what they wanted. "The lady will have the Maine lobster and I'll have the sixteen-ounce prime rib, medium with a pink center. By the way, Bruce, today is my girlfriend's birthday."

Paula spoke up. "But today's not…"

"Paula is a little sensitive about her age, which we will not disclose," said Ace.

From out of nowhere Ace heard a woman's voice say, "Dr. Zachary, what a pleasant surprise meeting you here. Did you miss your flight back to Nashville?"

"How good to see you again, Nurse Jones. Thanks to you I didn't miss my plane, but on the way to the airport I received a call on my cell phone that has resulted in me staying a few more days in Knoxville."

"I just want to thank you for putting in a good word to the hospital administrator. A lot of people make promises they never keep, and I really didn't think you would either since you were on such a tight schedule."

"A man is only as good as his word. I'm sorry, Miss Jones, but I never got your first name."

"It's Jennifer, Jennifer Jones."

"That name sounds vaguely familiar to me," said Ace.

"That's probably because there was a movie star who was popular years ago with that name."

"Let me introduce you to my friend, Paula Novak."

"Glad to meet you, Paula. You're with a good man."

"I know. I'm glad to meet you too, Jennifer."

"If you ever need my assistance at the hospital don't hesitate to look me up, Doctor."

"Thanks, Jennifer."

"Bye."

"Bye."

"Would you mind telling me what that was all about, Ace?"

"I could tell you, Paula, but then I would have to kill you."

After they had enjoyed their delicious dinner, Paula looked up and there came a server carrying a six-inch red velvet cake with a single candle on it followed by six other servers singing happy birthday and clapping their hands. Paula felt like crawling under the table. She decided that she was going to kill Ace when she got him alone. They ate the traditional Regas red velvet birthday cake, and Paula looked at him and said, "Ace, you're something else, but dull isn't one of them."

Ace paid the bill, left a twenty-dollar tip of Brad's money, and gave his parking stub to the valet.

The parking valet brought Ace's car and there went another piece of Brad's money as Ace handed him a five-dollar bill.

Chapter 8

Ace took Paula back to her office and parked his car beside hers in the parking lot.

"Can we talk?" he asked.

"Shoot."

"Do you like your job?"

"It's not too bad, but I'm afraid I may have to quit."

"What's the problem?"

"My last two paychecks have bounced."

"What does Spenser say about that?"

"He says not to worry because he is going to have quite a bit of money in a few weeks. He says that when he gets the money that he will give me back pay plus a hefty bonus."

"Does he say where this money is coming from?"

"I don't have a clue."

"I read in the paper that he won a $3 million judgment a few months back. What happened to all that money? He must have gotten at least a million out of that."

"He got a million and a half of that."

"Is that legal? Are you sure? I thought a third was the going rate?"

"I don't know whether it's legal, but I would think it would be unethical. I am positive how much he got because I drew up the contract and deposited the check in the bank."

"Enough said. What happened to that one and a half million?"

"I suspect that Luther has a gambling problem."

"Why do you think that?"

"He has made several trips to Vegas since he hit the big one. I think Luther likes to think of himself as a high roller."

ACE SLEUTH, PRIVATE EYE

"Anything else?"

"I'm afraid that the Knoxville Utilities Board (KUB) is going to cut off our electricity. We are about four months behind on our bill. There are also many other unpaid bills with very little income coming in."

"What is your salary, if I may ask?"

"I don't suppose it would hurt anything since I'm not getting one anyway. It's $600 per week."

"How are you getting by?"

"I work Friday nights from six to eleven serving at the Copper Cellar Restaurant. It's the one on Kingston Pike, out near West Town."

"How is that working out?"

"I love the work and I make almost as much counting salary and tips as I do at the office, but there is one drawback. I don't like leaving my fifteen-year-old daughter, Lisa, home alone on the weekends. I really haven't decided what to do. If I don't make a decision shortly, I'm afraid one will be made for me. I can see the handwriting on the wall."

"Let me tell you what's been going on. I know you probably think I'm crazy, but you need to know. Have you ever heard of a man by the name of Bret Martin?"

"Yes. That was the man who was injured in the parking lot when he was hit by Brad Adams. He just hired Luther as his attorney."

"I am working for Brad Adams and he believes that the accident was staged to get a big settlement from a wealthy man. I am beginning more and more to agree with him. He believes that Spenser is in it up to his eyeballs, and after hearing about his finances, I can understand why. I think this case is where he is expecting the big bucks to come from."

"Knowing Luther as I do, I can believe that."

"Brad and Spenser were classmates from their freshman class all the way through law school. He told me that Luther had a dishonest streak back then. It's mighty hard for a zebra to change its spots," he said.

"How can I help?"

"Could you get me the dates of Spenser's trips to Vegas and the hotels where he stayed?"

"That should be no problem since I made all the travel arrangements."

"Great. I'll keep you up to date on all that's happening, and I'll also explain Miss Jones."

"Now that I'd like to hear, *Dr. Zachary*."

"When can we get together again?"

"How about coming over to my apartment for pot luck Sunday evening about sevenish? I'd like you to meet my daughter, Lisa. I think she will surprise you."

"I can hardly wait. See you then."

Chapter 9

Thursday morning, September 7

The first thing Ace did when he got to his office Thursday was call Nurse Jones at Baptist Hospital. "Jennifer, this is Dr. Zachary. How are you this morning?"

"I'm fine, Dr. Zachary. It's good to hear from you. How may I help you?"

"If it's not too much trouble I would like to see if you can find Mr. Martin's Knoxville address for me. I would rather you didn't disturb Mr. Martin. He needs his rest."

"No problem, Dr. Zachary. I think we have that information on file. Here it is. He was living at the Downtown Knoxville YMCA. I don't have a room number."

"No problem, Jennifer. You're a lifesaver. Thanks. Maybe we'll run into each other again sometime."

"I will be looking forward to it," said Jennifer.

After a few minutes spent forging a driver's license on his computer and running it through his laminating machine, Ace made the short drive to the YMCA. He parked in the lot behind the structure and entered. A man of about sixty was sitting behind the desk.

"Good morning. My name is Steve Martin. My nephew, Bret, sent me to see if his rent is paid up. He was in an accident Tuesday and is in Baptist Hospital recuperating. He asked me to make sure he is currently paid up and to also pay for another week. He is very conscientious about paying his bills."

"Let me look at my records. Here it is. He was paid up through yesterday, so add a week to that, and it comes to $160. I wondered what had happened to him. Is he going to be OK?"

"He was in an automobile accident, but he should be out of the hospital in a few days. By the way, when did he check in?"

"Let me look in my check-in book. Here it is. He checked in a week from yesterday. That would have been Thursday, August the thirty-first."

"Thanks. Bret should be out of the hospital by the end of the week. He just wanted to make sure that he didn't lose his room here. By the way, I didn't know the YMCA still had rooms to rent."

"We still have a few rooms to rent, but they don't seem to appeal to young people like they used to."

Ace handed the man eight crisp twenty-dollar bills and asked for a receipt, and told the man that Bret also asked him to pick up a few things from his room."

"To let you do that, I'm going to have to see some ID."

"Of course, you can't be too careful these days." Brad reached into his wallet and handed over the newest driver's license in Knoxville.

"I'll let you in the room. It's on the third floor. We'll walk up the stairs. Just lock up when you leave."

"Thanks a lot."

As soon as the man was out of sight, Ace gathered up all the documents he could find and placed them in a plastic bag he had in his pocket. To make it seem more on the up-and-up, he also gathered up a few articles of clothing and placed them in another bag. He then walked back downstairs, thanked the man again, got into his car, and drove back to his office. He could sort out the stuff much better in his office. He made a mental note to call Brad as soon as he got back to his office.

Chapter 10

While Ace was getting Martin's things from the YMCA, Brad called the office of radiologist Roger Kennedy and asked to speak to the man. He happened to be free at the moment and took Brad's call.

"Mr. Kennedy, this is Brad Adams. You probably don't remember me, but I believe we attend the same church. I think we met once at a church function."

"I certainly do remember you, Brad. How can I help you?"

"I have an x-ray that I need interpreted, at your convenience of course."

"I can see you this morning. In my line of work time is not of the essence."

"I can be in your office in thirty minutes if that's OK with you."

"That's good. I'm on the second floor of the Fort Sanders Doctor's Office Building, room 206."

"I'll be there shortly."

Brad walked into the doctor's office twenty-five minutes later.

"Good to see you again, Brad," said the doctor. "Let me see what you have here." He placed one of the x-rays on the light table and studied it for several minutes. He turned to Brad and said, "Do you know this man in this x-ray?"

"I have never met the man, not formally anyway."

"Do you know what kind of work he does?"

"No. All I know is that this man stepped out in front of my car Tuesday morning and is now lying flat on his back in Baptist Hospital."

"Take a look at this x-ray. See this faint line here on his third rib on the right side. That rib has been broken before sometime in the past. In fact, this man has many broken bones. If I had to guess, I would say this man was either a rodeo performer or a kick boxer."

39

"Do you see anything out of place near the first lumbar vertebra in the lower back region?"

"Yes. I see that the first lumbar vertebra there is pushed out a little."

"Would this result in the patient being unable to walk or be in great pain?"

"It's possible, but doubtful."

"Can you tell me if the vertebra damage is recent, or if it is a previously existing condition?"

"Not with any degree of certainty, but I can say that most of these broken bones are old breaks. You can pretty much tell if it's an old break in the rib area because you can see where it's grown back together. It's a different situation in the lower back area with all that congestion of bones and nerves. This man has seen a lot of trauma. I would imagine we would find a lot more breaks if we x-rayed his lower body."

"Thanks, Roger. You've been a lot of help. What do I owe you?"

"You don't owe me anything, Brad. I'm glad if I was of any help. However, I don't think I told you what you wanted to hear."

"You have been very helpful, Roger. Would you be willing to testify for me as an expert witness if this case goes to trial and I need you? I would pay you of course."

"You can count on me, Brad."

"Thanks again, Roger."

"Glad to help, Brad. See you in church."

Chapter 11

Ace was still in his office developing the picture he had taken of Bret Martin in his hospital bed along with the one he had taken of Spenser outside his office. He enlarged them both to letter size and made several copies. He was pleasantly surprised of the quality of the pictures he had made with his cell phone. He was about to call Brad when his office phone rang. He had thought about getting rid of his office phone and just going with his cell phone to cut back on expenses, but he didn't think that Bellsouth would act too kindly on placing his Verizon cell phone listing in their yellow pages. He picked up the phone. It was Brad.

"We need to talk," said Brad.

"We sure do," replied Ace.

"Would you like to come over here to my office, Ace?"

"I'll be there in two shakes of a sheep's tail."

"Fine. Park in the garage under my building and be careful of pedestrians. Bring your parking stub and I'll have Denise validate it for you. That will save you five dollars, no, let me reword that. It will save me five dollars."

Chapter 12

Ace arrived at Brad's office a few minutes later and Denise led him to Brad's office.

"Denise, would you bring us some coffee?" asked Brad.

"Cream or sugar, Ace?" asked Denise.

"Both please, Denise."

"Do you want to start first, Ace?"

"I have discovered so much I don't know where to begin."

"Why don't you start at the beginning?"

"OK. I told you about my little venture at Baptist. I developed the picture I took of Martin and also the one of Spenser. I have blown them up to letter size and made several copies. Here are a couple of copies of each for you."

"Thanks. The quality is very good," said Brad.

"I have become friends with Spenser's receptionist, and as a result, I have discovered some very helpful information. Spenser is flat broke and Paula's last two payroll checks have bounced."

"Paula is it? You're on a first-name basis already?"

"Paula Novak, his receptionist. She said that the electricity is about to be cut off, and that bills are piling up with very little income coming in. Luther is broke flatter than a fritter."

"That means that Luther must be getting desperate to settle. It also means to me that the last thing he wants to do is go to court."

"I agree," said Ace. "He doesn't have the money to hire a competent doctor to testify to Martin's condition in court. He will have to get some fly-by-night quack who he can hire on a contingency basis. You'll chew him up and spit him out on the witness stand."

"You are right. He is in a desperate situation right now and he will do everything in his power to settle out of court."

"Are you going to allow that to happen?"

"No way, Ace."

"If your insurance company wanted to settle the case with no money coming out of your own pocket, would you settle then?"

"I will not allow that to happen. I was not at fault and I will fight tooth and toenail to keep that from happening. The insurance company would probably pay the money and double my rates, and I would be on the black list of every insurance company in the country. No, this booger is going to court, period."

"Brad, I think we have enough evidence in our hands right now to put this phony case to bed."

"No, we're going to court. What else do you have?"

"Paula is in a tough situation right now. With no money coming in from her job, she is working as a server at Copper Cellar on Friday and Saturday nights to support herself and her daughter, Lisa. I would like for you to provide her with the salary replacement of $600 a week so that she can continue with her present job for a few more weeks. She doesn't feel she is being a traitor to Luther because he is not paying her, and she's convinced that Luther is doing something illegal. She has to be very careful so she doesn't get involved in the illegal side of it."

"I think that we can arrange that. Add it to your expenses."

"Speaking of expenses, I need to make a trip to Vegas for a few days," said Ace.

"Why is that?"

"It seems that Luther has made several trips to Vegas lately. Paula believes that's where all the one and a half million dollars from his wrongful death suit went."

"A million and a half, I thought his part was only one third of the three million?"

"It was, but Luther was greedy, and took half."

"What do you think you will find in Vegas?"

"I believe this is where Luther met Martin and hatched up their little plot together."

"Why do you believe that?"

"Because Martin was staying at the downtown YMCA when he ran in front of your car. I went down there and looked around in his room and found some very interesting things."

"Before I forget it," said Brad, "and I wonder why I didn't think of it before, but what was Martin doing in the parking garage in the first place? And where is his car? Is it still in the parking garage? I think we dropped the ball on this one."

"I'll get on that as soon as I leave here," replied Ace. "Let's get back to the YMCA thing. Among the items I picked up there was a stuntman's union card issued to Martin five years ago."

"That clears up a lot of things for me. I had a radiologist take a look at the x-rays you gave me, and he said that Martin had so many broken bones that he suspected he was either a rodeo rider or a kick boxer."

"I also found a Las Vegas address for Mr. Martin. That's the reason I want to go to Vegas. I think that Mr. Martin paid our city a visit at the invitation of Mr. Luther Spenser."

"What do you need for your trip?"

"Paula is looking up all the dates and times Luther went to Vegas. She said he always stayed at the MGM Grand Hotel."

"Luther always did like to go first class."

"I would like to leave Monday morning and stay at the MGM also. I would like to have the use of a credit card and $5,000 in cash."

"Why the cash?"

"I may need to do a little bribery, and the bribees don't like to take credit cards."

"I'll have Denise make all the travel arrangements and get you the cash. She should have everything arranged by this afternoon. She will call you to pick everything up before the end of the day. Are hundreds OK?"

"Fine."

"Keep me informed."

"Will do."

Chapter 13

Friday, September 8

Ace picked up his tickets and cash Friday afternoon at Brad's office and ate a TV dinner at home Friday evening. Saturday he started an investigation into why Martin was in the parking garage in the first place. Surely he wouldn't go in there and stage an accident without having a good reason for being there.

He drove down to the garage to see if he could find out anything. He spoke to the attendant who was working there.

"I was wondering," said Ace, "what happens when a person leaves their car here for several days?"

"Every day around 6:00 p.m., one of us will drive around and note any cars that are still here. We record the license number, and if that vehicle is still here after three days, we have it towed."

"If a vehicle was parked here around 9:00 a.m. this past Tuesday, would it have been towed if it was here more than three days?"

"Yes."

"Could you check your records and see if one has been towed the last couple of days?"

"I don't have to check my records. There have been no tows from here in the last two weeks."

Strange, Ace thought, as he thanked the man and left. Ace had a bright idea. *I will call Miss Jones again. She happened to be working on a Saturday. Luck was still riding with him.*

"Jennifer this is Dr. Zachary again. You don't mind if I call you, Jennifer, do you?"

"I wouldn't have it any other way. And by the way, I recognized your voice."

"I was a little hesitant about calling you again, but you have been so helpful in the past and I need your help again."

"I'm surprised that you haven't returned to Nashville yet. Did you get held up again?"

"Yes. This place is beginning to grow on me."

"How can I be of help?"

"This still concerns Mr. Martin in 408. As you know he was injured in the parking garage of the South Tower, but we don't know what happened to his car. I thought it had been towed, but that's not the case."

"Just how is his car related to his condition?"

"We would like to find his car because Mr. Martin doesn't need to be unnecessarily worrying about the whereabouts of his car in his present condition. We would like to get this cleared up as soon as possible."

"I see. Exactly what do you want me to do?"

"I think the best thing would be to go back and ask him for the make, model, and license number of his car. I would appreciate it if you didn't mention my name when you talk to him. He doesn't need to worry about me on top of everything else he's been going through."

"I understand, Dr. Zachary. Do you have a phone where I can call you back?"

"Yes, you can call me on my cell phone." He gave her the number, including his Knoxville area code.

"Thanks, I'll get back in touch with you as soon as I find out."

"Thank you very much, Jennifer."

As soon as Ace got off the phone he realized he had made a big booboo. The area code for Nashville is different, 615 for Nashville and, 865 (VOL) for Knoxville. He hoped she didn't stop to wonder why a man from Nashville would have a Knoxville area code.

Jennifer called Ace back in about fifteen minutes. "I got your information, Dr. Zachary. It's simple. He doesn't own a car. He said he was picking up a friend's car that had been left there overnight."

"Did he say who the friend was?"

"Aren't you the nosy one? No. I didn't ask."

"Thanks, Jennifer."

"No problem."

Well I guess that solves that problem, Ace thought, *unless of course the car belonged to Luther. There probably never was a car,* he thought.

Chapter 14

Sunday, September 10

Ace took the day off Sunday. He spent the afternoon watching the Tennessee Titans and the Indianapolis Colts' football game on the tube. Ace always has mixed emotions when he watches these two teams play each other. Being a native Tennessean, he wants the Titans to win, but he also likes for Peyton Manning to play a good game. Peyton is an institution all over Tennessee, especially East Tennessee. It was just about two weeks ago that Peyton donated one million dollars to the UT Athletics Department. The Colts won the game as Peyton threw four touchdown passes.

Around 6:00 p.m., Ace got in his '76 Mustang and headed out on I-40 west. Two miles out I-75 south converges with I-40 west and continues that way for about fifteen miles until I-40 veers to right toward Nashville and Memphis and I-75 peels off to the South toward Chattanooga and Atlanta. The traffic on this convergence of these two interstates normally averages 160,000 vehicles a day (almost a third of them eighteen-wheelers), but today (Sunday) it was much lighter. Ace got off about seven miles west of the convergence point on Cedar Bluff Drive, and went two miles north until he ran into Middlebrook Pike. Paula had given him good directions so he had no problem finding her two-bedroom apartment a few blocks away. He pulled into the driveway, parked his car, and rang the doorbell.

Lisa opened the door the door and said, "You must be Ace."

"And you must be Lisa. I'm glad to meet you," said Ace. Lisa stood about five foot four with bright brown hair tied in a ponytail and dressed a little conservatively for a fifteen-year-old, but rather cute, Ace thought.

"Mom's in the kitchen cooking dinner and she wants me to amuse you."

"I'm not so sure I like the way she worded that."

"She said you'd say that."

"Sounds like she knows me pretty well."

"I was just doing my homework before you came in. I have a test in trigonometry tomorrow."

"Where do you go to school?"

"I go to the Magnet School in town."

"Why do you go there?"

"They are strong in math and the sciences, and I'm going to become a medical doctor."

"I like the way you said that."

"How do you mean?"

"You didn't say that you wanted to become a doctor, but that you were going to be a doctor."

"I'm sure of it."

"I bet you are. Do you like trig?"

"Pretty much, but I like physics better'"

"I notice that you have a scientific calculator with all the trig functions at your fingertips. Did you ever hear of trig tables?"

"What are trig tables?"

"Math was my favorite subject in high school and trig was my favorite subject," said Ace. "Unfortunately I didn't take much interest in the other classes. Back then we had no calculators, so to find the value of a trig function for a given angle; we had to look it up in tables. Trig function tables were usually in the back of our trig textbook, but were only given for the whole angle. If you wanted the trig function of twenty-nine degrees and thirty minutes, you had to interpolate between twenty-nine and thirty degrees. This could be very time-consuming. You are very fortunate to be able to get this information by the touch of a button."

Paula stuck her head out and informed them that dinner would be ready in thirty minutes.

"Do you like to play math games, Lisa?"

"When I have time."

"This will only take a minute. Look at your calculator. Do you have a random number button on it?"

"Let me see. Yes, here it is."

"Push the random number button. You'll probably have to push the '2nd' button in the upper left-hand corner first."

"OK, I did it, now what?"

"Square it."

"OK. Now what?"

"Remove the last digit of the result and give it to me."

"How do I do that?"

"I don't mean for you to physically give me the number. Just tell me what the last number is and remove it in your head. After you remove this number you are left with either a positive number or a negative number. Am I right?"

"Yes."

"Now what number did you remove?"

"Five."

"OK. Now what would be the odds of me telling you whether the number remaining is even or odd?"

"Fifty-fifty."

"The number you have left is even. Is that correct?"

"Yes, but you had a fifty-fifty chance of getting it right."

"I will get it right every time."

"Impossible. I'll do another. OK, I'm giving you number six."

"Your result is odd."

"You just got lucky."

Lisa tried ten more times and Ace got it right every time.

"That's amazing, how does it work?"

"It's really very simple. If the number you give me is six, your remaining number is always odd. If the number is anything but six, the number is always even. It works every time for any random number."

"How do you know it works for all numbers?"

"I tried them all. Prove me wrong. How do the experts know that there no two snowflakes alike?"

"What makes that work? Is there something magical about the number six?"

"I have no idea what makes it work, I just know that it does. There may be one exception however. It all depends on whether zero is an even number or an odd number. I think it may be a neutral number. If it's considered an even number then the rule of six has an exception. That exception works like this. If you square a number and the last digit of the squared number is zero, the number remaining after you remove the zero will always be another zero. If this zero is considered to be an even number then that would be an exception to the rule of six."

"Do you have any more little gems?"

"Just one. A few years ago I read in the *Knoxville News Sentinel* that a UT professor had memorized the value of pi to around 25,000 places. Being the wise guy that I am, I shot off a letter to the paper stating that this pi thing was child's play to what I could do. I stated that I had memorized the results all the numbers from one to 121 divided by nine to an infinite number of places."

"OK, smarty pants, what is 110 divided by nine?"

"Twelve point two two two two…the two's go on forever."

"What is thirty-three divided by nine?"

"Three point six six six six…the sixes go on forever."

"How does that work?"

"Take the first example. The closest number to 110 divisible by nine is 108. One hundred eight divided nine equals twelve. Subtract 108 from 110 and that leaves two. Hence the answer: 12.222… Take a look at the second example. The closest number to thirty-three divisible by nine is twenty-seven. Twenty-seven divided by nine is three. Thirty-three minus twenty-seven equals six. Hence the answer is 3.6666."

"**MOM**, where did you get this guy? How do you know all this stuff, Ace?"

"I stumbled onto it while solving math problems that I received in my Emails."

Paula announced from the dining room, "Dinner is served."

"About time," said Lisa. "I'm famished."

Chapter 15

Ace and Lisa sat down at the table and Paula entered the dining room with a casserole dish and said, "I hope you like lasagna."

"I love it," replied Ace.

"Did you two get acquainted?"

"Did we ever?" said Lisa.

"I hope you like the Reunite, Ace."

"One of my favorites," said Ace.

When they had finished the meal of pasta, salad, and bread, Lisa announced that she was going to her bedroom to finish her homework. "I'll leave you two lovebirds alone," she said.

Paula and Ace simultaneously replied, "Lovebirds?"

After Lisa had retired to her room, Paula and Ace sat down in the living room.

"We have a lot to talk about," said Ace.

"Why don't you start then?" replied Paula.

"OK. How in the world did a man as dumb as a tree stump ever manage to win a $3 million settlement?"

"It actually fell into his lap. He was driving toward town about two miles out on I-40 east when a big eighteen-wheeler plowed into the back of a car driven by a woman with her three-year-old son strapped into his car seat in the back. The mother was not seriously hurt, but the son was critically injured. Luther was an eyewitness to the whole thing. He was right beside her in the outside lane and she was in the middle lane. Traffic had been backed up a little and that probably contributed to the accident. The truck was clearly at fault. Luther pulled over to the side of the road and parked and went to the car and helped the woman out. A doctor who was also tied up in the traffic removed the child from the back seat. It was obvious that he had been critically injured and that there was not much the doctor could do for him. The mother was going crazy and wanted to hold her baby but the doctor wouldn't allow it. Luther took the woman in his arms and tried to console her. Within about five minutes a Baptist helicopter landed and loaded the son. Since Luther was hugging and consoling the woman, the paramedics assumed he was the husband, and put them both on the bird. The woman was in such a state of shock that I don't believe she knew what was going on. While the son was in emergency, Luther sat with the woman and kept hugging and consoling her. He gave her his card and made sure she put it in her purse as he got her phone number. After about two hours, a doctor came out and informed them that he had done everything humanly possible, but it was no use. 'He's gone,' he told them.

"Because of the attention and concern that Luther showed, the woman was an easy mark for him. He called her the next day and asked her if there was anything that he could do to help her. 'Just call me if you need anything at all,' he told her. A few days later she called him and told him that the trucking company had been in contact with her and she wondered if he would be kind enough to be her attorney.

"The case was slam dunk. The insurance company offered $2 million right off the bat. Luther felt real proud that he got it bumped up to $3 million. I don't believe a good attorney would have settled for less than ten.

"I typed up the contract for the normal lawyer's fee of one third and Luther had me retype it and change it to one half. I don't think the woman knew what she was signing. I felt real bad about taking advantage of someone like her, because she was still in a state of shock and grief. Luther was very irate when he went back to I-40 east to retrieve his car and found that it had been towed. I don't think he had the seventy-five dollars to get it out."

"Good old Luther."

"Now it's my turn. What about Jennifer?"

"It's really not very complicated. Brad asked me to go over to Baptist and try to get a copy of Martin's x-rays and anything else I could get my hands on. I put on my doctor's suit and name tag, making sure my stethoscope was visible in my right coat pocket. I entered the lobby and asked for Martin's room number.

"Jennifer just happened to be the fourth-floor acute care nurse. I told her I had been hired as a consultant on Martin's case and I needed to see him. I also asked her to get me a copy of his chart and all his x-rays."

"Didn't she ask you for identification?"

"Of course."

"What did you do?"

"I showed it to her. I can manufacture all kinds of ID's and diplomas and laminate them so that an expert would not be able to tell the difference from mine and the real McCoy. I left her station and headed for Martin's room and pretended like I had made a mistake and had come to room 408 (his room) instead of 508. I then pretended like I was making a cell phone call, but instead I took his picture."

"You devil you."

"There's something bothering me about Jennifer, but I can't put my finger on it," said Ace.

"There's something bothering me about her too," said Paula. "She's in love with you, Ace, and I can understand why."

"No. I don't believe it's that at all. I first noticed it the other night when I introduced you two and she said to you that I was a good man. Why would she make a statement like that when I had just met her that one time? I called her again today and asked her if I could call her Jennifer, and she said she wouldn't have it any other way. She found out that Martin didn't own a car. He told her he was retrieving a car for a friend."

"I still say she's in love with you, and now it sounds like you're in love with her."

"I do get a feeling of love but it feels more like a father-daughter love. After all, I'm old enough to be her father."

"You don't think that she could be your daughter, do you?"

"There is an absolute zero chance of that," said Ace.

"I don't think she wants you for a father anyway. I think she loves you."

"She may, but for all we know, she may already be married. I feel so bad about taking advantage of her like that. It seems like that every time I have to make contact with her, I have to tell her another lie. I think I'll confess everything to her the next time I talk to her."

"You're all heart, Ace. When will I see you again?"

"Not for three or four days, I'm afraid. I have to fly out to Vegas at nine in the morning to check on Luther's great adventure. I think that's where he and Martin met. Thanks for getting me the dates he stayed at MGM, that's where I'll be staying also. You have my cell phone number if you need me. By the way, give me your home phone number in case I need to call you after hours. I have a little something for you," said Ace, as he handed her an envelope.

"What is this?"

"That's your salary for the coming week."

"I don't accept charity."

"That is not charity. Brad wants you to stay with Luther for at least the next few weeks, and he's afraid you may have to quit and get another job to pay the rent."

"He's probably right."

"I'll see you as soon as I get back."

"Be careful. I'll miss you," said Paula.

"Likewise," said Ace.

Chapter 16

Monday, September 11

Brad drove Ace to McGhee Tyson to get his Delta flight to Las Vegas which had a one-hour layover and change of planes in Atlanta. There is a saying in this neck of the woods that you can't go to hell without first going through Atlanta. Brad made sure that Ace got on the plane after telling him he would pick him up on his return.

When Brad returned to his office Denise told him that Mr. Nelson from the insurance company had called him and would call back at eleven. It was presently 10:45 a.m., giving him time to look at a few documents and enjoy his morning cup of coffee.

Nelson called back at eleven on the dot and Denise connected him. "This is Brad Adams," he said.

"This is Charles Nelson of US Auto. I'm the local claims officer. We talked last week."

"Yes, I remember. How can I help you, Charles?"

"Martin's lawyer, a Mr. Luther Spencer, has filed a claim regarding your accident and is asking for $3 million. The home office has authorized me to make a counter offer of $1 million. What are your thoughts on this?"

"Have your people done any investigation at all into this case, or do they just have money lying around that they don't know what to do with?"

"What do you mean?"

"I have performed a very vigorous investigation on this case and found that Martin's lawyer, Luther Spenser, is flat broke and would probably settle for $10,000 right now. I hope you haven't paid any of Martin's medical bills."

"I'm not sure, but if we have, I'll put a stop to that immediately. How is it possible that Spenser is broke? Didn't he just win a $3 million settlement a few months back?"

"Yes, he did, but that's all gone. It seems that Mr. Spenser has a major gambling problem. He has squandered away all that dough."

"That certainly puts things in a different light, Brad. What do you suggest?"

"I want him to sue me in a court of law where I can vindicate myself. I have gathered enough facts to convince me that I was set up. This whole thing was staged. Did you know that Martin was a former stuntman?"

"I certainly didn't. I'll see that you get one of our best attorneys."

"I've decided to represent myself. I am an attorney as you know."

"You know the old adage, don't you, Brad, that states that a man who acts as is own attorney has a fool for a client?"

"I don't put a whole lot of stock in adages. There is another one that states that a grand jury would indict a ham sandwich. I believe that they would indict a baloney but not a ham sandwich."

"Don't you think we will be taking a big chance with some of the types of people these tort lawyers like to pack the jury with?" Nelson asked. "We might even get a billion-dollar judgment against us considering some of the awards I've seen in the papers."

"I know exactly what you mean," said Brad. "I have heard it said that the ideal jury for them is a mixture of eleven men and women with an average eighth-grade education with one liberal college professor thrown in just to make it fair and balanced. It doesn't seem reasonable to me that a juror with an eighth-grade education should be allowed to sit on a jury and try to determine if a brain surgeon made an error on the operating table. I honestly believe that a slick slip-and-fall lawyer could convince some of these jurors that the earth is flat."

"I agree with that one hundred percent."

"You think the world is flat?" (*I think that I've been around Ace Sleuth a little too much*, thought Brad).

"You know what I mean."

"Sorry, I don't think you have to worry about a billion-dollar judgment. Your company is only liable for two million tops. Besides, I believe I may have a solution to prevent uneducated people from being selected on a jury civil case in the first place."

"How do you intend to do that?"

"I would rather not show my cards just yet."

"OK, I'll call the home office and fill them in on what you've told me. I am going to recommend that we make no offer whatsoever, but I don't know how it will go over, better than a lead balloon, I hope. Those big boys at the home office are so accustomed to working with big money, that another million here or there is not a very big deal. I'll let you know what they say."

"Thanks, Charles. I don't think we'll have too long to wait. When Spenser finds out there is no Santa Claus, I expect a lawsuit within a week. He needs money desperately."

"We'll have to see. Let's stay in touch."

Chapter 17

Monday afternoon, September 11

Ace boarded the Delta flight at Atlanta for Vegas and got a window seat in business class. He had always been a wise guy even when he was in his teens. As the plane was getting ready to taxi to runway, Ace thought back to 1978 when he was only eighteen years old. He had won a tour of Europe by selling more newspapers than any other high school student in Knoxville.

He was seated in an Air France 747 at Kennedy Airport in New York when the French-speaking pilot announced in English that they would take off in a few minutes along with the information on the flying time and landing time in Paris. He also said that the weather would be good for the trip. He then repeated the same information in French, and the elderly lady sitting next to Ace had not understood the announcement in French, so she inquired of Ace what the pilot had said. "He said," replied, Ace, "'I have never flown a 747 before, but I'll give my best shot.'" Ace had to restrain her from getting off the plane.

A few minutes later he was joined by a man in a three-piece suit who was around six feet tall and a little on the heavy side. He was sporting a little goatee. "Good morning," said Ace. "My name is Ace Sleuth from Knoxville. Have a seat."

"Glad to meet you. My name is Christopher Newcastle from New York City. Where are you headed, Ace?"

"I'm going to Vegas. How about you?"

"I'm going to LA. By the way, what type of business are you in, if I may ask?"

"You may ask, but why don't we play a little game and try to guess each other's occupation?"

ACE SLEUTH, PRIVATE EYE

"I can see that you are a people person like me, Ace. Now let me see, a private detective would be too obvious with a name like Ace Sleuth. I'd say that you were a timeshare salesman. Am I close?"

"Not very. I really am a private eye," said Ace, as he took his PI license and showed it to Christopher.

"What line of work do you think I'm in, Ace?"

"Let me see. I would guess that you are either a psychiatrist or a psychologist."

"Amazing, I am a psychologist. Do you see that man on the right side of the plane four rows up sitting in the aisle seat?"

"Ace looked at the man and said, yes, I do."

"Let's see which one of us can get the closest to what his profession is."

"OK," said Ace, "but how will we know?"

"I'll go over and ask him, Ace. What do you think he does?"

"Right off the top of my head I'd say he is a fertilizer salesman," said Ace. "What do you think he does, Christopher?"

"I think he is a banker, Ace. I'll just go up and ask him."

Christopher walked up to the man and introduced himself and explained that he and his seat mate had a little game going trying to guess people's profession, and asked him if he be so kind as to tell him what he did for a living.

"Who is the seat mate?" the man asked.

Christopher pointed back to Ace who put a finger to his lips as the man looked back, Christopher didn't see the gesture.

"I'm a fertilizer salesman," the man said.

Frustrated, Christopher returned to his seat and informed Ace that he was right, that indeed the man was a fertilizer salesman. "I'm a little tired of playing games," he said. "I think I'll read a little while." He read all the way to Vegas.

Ace got off the plane in Vegas and the good doctor stayed on board. The fertilizer salesman got off right behind him and said, "What was that all about back there on the plane, Ace?"

"Just playing a little game to pass away the time. Are you going to a fertilizer convention, Ralph?"

"You got it, Ace. How about you; business?"

"Yes. Maybe we'll run into each other out here."

Ace arrived at the LAS (the United States' seventh busiest airport) around 4:00 p.m., having cheated the clock out of two hours on the trip out. He knew he would have to pay back those two hours on the way home.

He followed the signs pointing to "Hotel Busses" and noted that there must be at least five hundred people waiting. He hoped they weren't all waiting for the MGM bus. When it pulled up about fifteen minutes later, he noticed it was empty. Only twenty or so people got on. Twenty-five minutes later the bus pulled up to the MGM entrance. Denise had booked him a small suite, number 917, the first one in which he had ever stayed. *I could get used to this,* he thought.

After he had showered and freshened up he discovered he was very hungry. All he had on the plane were peanuts. *I wonder why Denise didn't fly me out here first class and make it a complete package,* he mused.

He opened the desk drawer to check on the food situation. He was shocked. There were more restaurants in the MGM than in a small town. There were eighteen listed eating places including fine dining, casual dining, and quick eats. Ace chose The Pearl, one of the "fine dining" ones, mainly because of the oysters Rockefeller on the menu. After a delicious dinner, at what Ace considered to be a reasonably priced meal, he went back to his room and called Paula. It was about eight-thirty her time.

"How was your trip?" she asked.

"Great. Brad put me up in a suite here at MGM Grand, and I just ate the best oysters Rockefeller I ever had in my life. There are eighteen full-service restaurants in this hotel."

"I'm envious of you," said Paula.

"I miss you," said Ace.

"I miss you too, lovebird."

"Is Lisa there?"

"Yes."

"How is she on the computer?"

"She's a natural."

"Can you put her on the phone? I have a little job for her."

"Hold on a minute. Lisa, pick up the phone."

"Hello."

"How's my favorite student?"

"Hanging in there."

"How would you like to make a little extra spending money?"

"Is this on the up-and-up?"

"Of course, sweetheart, I wouldn't get you involved in anything sleazy. Have I ever lied to you before?"

"I don't think so, but I only met you that one time."

"You got a point there. Let me tell you what I need. By the way, I'll pay you twenty dollars per hour and let you keep your own time."

"Sounds fair."

"I want you to get on your computer and find everything you can about a man by the name of Bret Martin. I know that he was a stuntman in LA or Hollywood and lived at one time in Las Vegas. I have a Vegas address I can give you. I'm in Vegas right now, and I'm going to rent a car in the morning and try to find out where he lived. See if you can find out if he was ever in a hospital in the LA area. Make a note of all dates, times, and places associated with him. See if you can pull up his name in any of the LA area papers. As soon as you find something get back to me. Paula has my cell number."

"Do you want to talk to her again?"

"No. Just tell her to be a good girl. I'm bushed and I'm going to bed. See you two in a few days."

Chapter 18

Tuesday morning, September 12

Brad picked up a city map in the hotel lobby, stepped outside, and waited for the Enterprise Rental Car (we pick you up) Company to do as they advertised. A driver picked him up and drove the short distance to the rental office where Ace got a car of his own. He got in and headed toward the center of town. The address he was looking for was about a mile north of downtown Vegas. The area was somewhat run down and so was the building at the address.

The building was a two-story structure that looked like a home residence. He knocked on the door and was greeted by an elderly man in some rumpled clothes that reminded him of his homeless outfit.

"My name is Buford Whitehead from Knoxville, Tennessee, and I'm here on a little R&R. Bret Martin asked me if I could pick up the things he left here when he moved out. Do I have the right address?"

"He didn't move out. He skipped out. He left in the middle of the night owing me a full month's rent."

"Yes, he told me he was sorry about that and he wants to make it right. He had to go to Knoxville because his mother was involved in a serious accident. To add insult to injury, Bret was also injured in an auto accident and is in a Knoxville hospital as we speak." Ace thought to himself that it wouldn't hurt anything to throw in a little truth to help the lie along. *I kind of get carried away with myself sometimes,* he thought.

"Well, I'm sure sorry about that, but he owes me $300 rent."

"No problem. Would twenties be all right? By the way, I don't believe I caught your name."

"I didn't throw it, but my name is Sam Pile, and twenties will be just fine."

ACE SLEUTH, PRIVATE EYE

Holding the fifteen twenties in his hand, Ace said, "Could you let me in to pick up his things?"

"Follow me."

Pile led him up to a single bedroom upstairs.

"I can take it from here," Ace said, as he handed him the money. "There are a couple of things I'd like to know. First, do you know what date Mr. Martin left?"

"I sure do, it was rent-paying day, the first of the month, the first of August."

"Do you happen to know where Bret worked?"

"I think it was in one of them den-of-iniquity joints up on that sinful girlie strip."

"Do you happen to know which one?"

"I'm not sure, but I saw a letter come to him that had the letters MGM on it."

"Do you know what kind of work he did?"

"I think he said he was dealing in something."

"Did he say what type of thing he was dealing in? Do you think it was drugs?"

"No, I never saw any drugs around here."

"Thanks, Mr. Pile. I will be out of here in about ten minutes."

Brad looked around the room to see what he could find. Mr. Martin was very messy. Brad looked in one of the dresser drawers and discovered six VCR tapes which he placed in a plastic bag he pulled from his pocket. He also found several pictures of Bret dressed up in cowboy clothes, evidently his stuntman outfits. Ace gathered up all the papers, pictures, and anything else that looked interesting, and put them in the bag and left. He figured he'd sort all that stuff out at the hotel. *Martin must have left in a big hurry to leave all this stuff behind*, thought Ace.

He returned the car to Enterprise and they in turn returned him to the MGM. He decided to rummage through the stuff later. He had other plans for now.

Chapter 19

Tuesday afternoon, September 12

Ace took the elevator down to the lobby went up to the check-in counter and asked if he could see the security chief for the hotel.

"Who should I say wants to see him?"

"Tell him it's Ace Sleuth from Knoxville, Tennessee, and it's important."

"Mr. Brown, I've got a man here who says his name is Ace Sleuth from Knoxville, Tennessee, and that he has an important matter to discuss with you."

"I can't pass up a chance to talk to a man named Ace Sleuth. Send him in."

A bellboy took him to Brown's office and Ace tipped him five dollars.

"Come in, Mr. Sleuth, my name is Lamont Brown, head of security here at MGM Grand. I'm glad to meet you. How may I help you?"

Brown was a black male who looked to be in his mid-thirties. He was about six feet two inches tall and weighed around 210, most of it muscle. He looked like a man who commanded much respect.

"I am a private detective from Knoxville and I represent a wealthy client who was involved in an accident last week. We think he was set up."

"Why do you think that?"

"My client was pulling into his parking garage on a work day at 9:00 a.m. as he usually did, when a man walked right out of the shadows and hit his windshield before falling to the concrete floor."

"Did it kill the man?"

"No, but he ended up in the hospital and is still there. We think he staged the whole thing. The so-called victim was a former stuntman and his lawyer is a very shady character."

"How does that involve me or MGM?"

"The lawyer, Luther Spenser, has stayed in your hotel several times during the last several months."

"Are you referring to High Roller Spenser?"

"He's the one and the same."

"Yes, Mr. Spenser stayed with us several times. He was one of our favorite guests."

"What can you tell me about him?"

"Ace, I have to be real careful about what I say in today's lawsuit-happy climate," said Lamont.

"I agree one hundred percent, Lamont. In my line of work, mum's the word. I know enough about some people in Knoxville to send them up the river for twenty years."

"Tell me about it. I could tell you some things that have happened here that would knock your shorts off. We are very much like a small town of about 25,000 people with our own police force, and I'm the chief of police."

"Do you mind if I ask you how you ended up here?"

"Not at all, I'm proud of my accomplishments. I was a marine in Desert Storm and when my enlistment was up, I took advantage of Uncle Sam by getting a degree from UNLV in criminology, and here I am pulling down seventy-five G's a year plus room and board."

"Do you by any chance need an assistant?"

"Get in line."

"I have a picture I would like for you to take a look at, Lamont. This is of Bret Martin," said Ace.

"He was our dealer at blackjack table three, the table that Spenser played at all the time. Where does he fit into the picture?"

"He is the so-called victim. What can you tell me about him?"

"Let me start at the beginning. When Mr. Spencer first started coming here he would stay about a week at a time. The first couple of times he was winning. I think at one time he was up about a half mil. Martin was dealing and he and Spenser took a liking to one another. It's hard not to like someone when they keep pushing winning chips at you. One day Martin resigned and became sort of an aide to Spencer. I saw Spencer on several occasions peel off a few hundred-dollar bills and give to Martin. He followed Spenser around like he was the Pied Piper. I think Spenser was giving him more money than he was making dealing."

"What happened next?"

"Once we found out that Spenser was a high roller, we rolled out the red carpet for him. He ate it up. Although he had won quite a bit of our money on his first visit, we paid for his second flight out here and picked him up at the airport in a stretch limo. He was in seventh heaven. We put him up in one of our better suites on the penthouse level and gave him a card that entitled him to eat anything he wanted in any of our restaurants at any time. We don't discriminate between winners and losers here; we treat them all the same way. We give them the red-carpet treatment because we know the winners will usually become losers. Even if they don't, we're not upset because we get a lot more customers when we have big winners. What happened next was just as we expected, Spenser started to lose. He stayed on this losing streak until he had dropped close to a million and a half, which was evidently all he had. After he lost all his money we flew him home first class."

"What happened to Martin?"

"When he saw that his money well had dried up he tried to get his old job back."

"Did you give it to him?"

"No. He wasn't one of our better employees. He would call in on sick leave quite often and we would have to call in backups at the last minute."

"Do you pay your dealers well?"

"No, we don't. We don't pay a whole lot more than the minimum wage, but some of the better dealers can make more than that in tips, especially if they have a big winner at their table. One of my dealers got a $5,000 chip as a tip one night, but that's very unusual."

"Do you have any videos of Spenser and Martin?"

"I think I could retrieve them from the archives if you could give me the dates. You can look at them but under no circumstances could I let you have copies and subject our hotel to a possible lawsuit."

"When could I look at them?"

"Give me the dates and I believe I can have them ready by nine in the morning. Give me a call before you come. My cell phone number is 555-5555."

"What strings did you have to pull to get that number?"

"If I told you, I'd have to kill you, Ace."

He stole my line, thought Ace, as he told Lamont he'd see him at nine in the morning.

Chapter 20

Big-spender Ace decided to meander over to the twenty-five-cent "Jacks or Better" draw poker machines. He got four $10 rolls of quarters from the change girl and sat down at a corner machine. He was really more interested in watching people than playing. He considered himself a dyed-in-the-wool people watcher. He tried to guess the occupation of each of them as he looked around. *There goes a banker*, he thought. A schoolteacher passed by followed by a computer nerd. *Watch out, there's an axe murderer coming down the aisle. I see a pickpocket over there bumping into all those people and taking their wallets.* This was much more fun than watching grass grow. Out of curiosity he got up and walked over to the smoking section where his make-believe pickpocket was bumming a light from a smoker. The man pulled out some matches and offered him the light. As Ace got pretty close he noticed the "lightee" take hold of the man's wrist, as if to steady it, but when he removed his hand the man's Rolex watch was gone, slick as a whistle. This guy was no amateur. He followed the man around and saw him bump three more people but the man was so good that Ace couldn't see the actual thefts.

He pulled out his cell phone and dialed 555-5555.

"Security here," said Lamont.

"This is Ace. You better get out here on the floor. There's a crime in progress."

"Where are you, Ace?"

"I'm in the smoking section near the twenty-five-cent slots."

"OK, big spender, I'll be there in two minutes."

Lamont showed up ten seconds shy of two minutes by Ace's watch.

"What have we got here, Ange, a 201, a 304, or 409?"

"We've got a PP-109, Barney."

"What's a PP-109?"

"That's policeeze for a pickpocket."

"Should I cuff him and book him, Ange?"

"You can if you keep that bullet in your shirt pocket, Barney."

"That's enough horse play," said Lamont. "We need to get him into a closed room because we have to handle these cases very delicately. What kind of proof have you got, Ace?"

"See that man over there. He just plucked a Rolex off a man's arm and didn't blink an eye. He's the best I've ever seen. He could take a set of false teeth out of a man's mouth and the man wouldn't know it until he sat down to eat dinner."

"Are you sure, Ace? I mean one hundred percent drop-dead sure."

"Cross my heart. You better nab him quick. These guys hit and run. He'll be in Caesar's Palace ten minutes after he leaves here."

"I'm gonna trust you on this one, Ace, but this must be done behind closed doors," said Lamont.

They took the man into Lamont's office and did a quick search but came up empty.

"What's going on here?" asked the suspect. "I'm going to sue this joint for every last penny it's got. And as for you, O. J., you and your affirmative action job are history."

"He's clean, Ace. Remind me to kill you when we get him out of here, and let's hope he doesn't sue us for the kitchen sink."

"I don't understand, Lamont. I never let this guy out of my sight. I even followed him into the restroom. Wait a minute. Do you have someone who can watch him for a couple of minutes?"

Lamont called a backup security man who showed up in less than a minute.

"Bill, watch his man for about five minutes until I get back," said Lamont.

"Follow me, Lamont," said Ace.

Lamont followed Ace into the men's bathroom as Ace went over to the third stall and lifted up the commode tank cover. In plain sight was a waterproof plastic bag filled with wallets and watches.

"You better lock this up for safe-keeping, Lamont. There are enough prints here to convict him ten times over. They all don't have to jingle like a little old woman to be guilty. We nipped it, Barney."

"In the bud, Ange. I owe you one, Ace."

"No problem, Lamont, but there is one thing that you could do for me. Could you have a VCR sent up to my suite? I need to watch some videos. VCR's are about as hard to come by these days as hen's teeth."

"You got it, Ace. It'll probably beat you there. By the way, have you eaten yet?"

"I forgot all about eating."

"Would you like to be my guest for dinner tonight?"

"What time and where?"

"Seven o'clock in the L'atelier de Joel Robuchon, here in the hotel."

"Sounds like I'll need a tux for that, which I don't have."

"Out here in Vegas, Ace, you can never dress inappropriately. See you there at seven."

"Do you have a road map, Lamont? I almost didn't find The Pearl Restaurant the first night I got here?"

"OK, let's just meet here in my office and we'll go up together. Meet me here around 7:45 p.m."

Chapter 21

It was about 4:00 p.m. when Ace got back to his suite. He had plenty of time to scan the videos. They were all labeled, Ace assumed, by the name of the movie in which Bret appeared. He would fast forward through one until he found some action scenes. He found mostly westerns where the stuntmen were thrown off their horses. He had found nothing of interest until he came to a scene that could have been made in the very garage where Brad and Bret tangled. You could never tell in the movies what the stuntman looked like. They tried to keep his face hidden as much as possible, but you could always go to the credits and find out who they were.

In the scene that interested Ace, the circumstances were almost identical to Brad's situation. In both cases, the victim came in from the passenger side and both incidents happened in a parking garage. The one on the VCR looked almost like a rerun of Brad's encounter with Martin. A half-intelligent jury would throw this case out. Ace made note of the elapsed minute mark on the VCR so he wouldn't have any trouble finding it again. He packed the VCR's away and decided to rest until he met Lamont for dinner.

Chapter 22

Tuesday evening, September 12

Ace met Lamont at his office and they both went to the L'atelier de Joel Robuchon dining room as scheduled, and all at once Ace discovered he was famished. Things had been moving so fast that he had forgotten to eat. He ordered a twelve-ounce filet mignon and Lamont had a full slab of baby back ribs.

"Could you come by my office around eleven in the morning, Ace? We had planned to meet at nine, but it is taking a little longer to check all those dates you gave me and sort out the parts that pertain to your case. I can let you view them, but that's all I can do."

"I can promise you, Lamont, that none of this will ever get back to you or MGM. All I need is just a short clip showing Spenser and Martin together with a verifiable date. I need to show that they knew each other prior to the accident."

"Let me think about it. When do you plan to return to Knoxville?"

"I would like to get back as soon as possible. I was thinking about returning tomorrow."

"Today is Tuesday the twelfth. We have our Gulfstream G200 flying to Washington on Thursday and Knoxville is not out of the way. Have you ever flown on a Gulfstream G200?"

"Not lately. Does MGM own a Gulfstream G200?"

"I'm not sure, but I think we share it with three or four other casinos."

"I hope they don't just serve peanuts on the plane."

"No, they serve jumbo shrimp, roasted cashews, and macadamia nuts, among other goodies."

"I accept your generous offer," said Ace.

Chapter 23

Ace went back to his suite and started to call Paula when he realized it was past 11:00 p.m. in Knoxville. It was too late to call. He decided to summarize everything he had discovered in Vegas and write it down.

Brad Martin had lived in Vegas but he didn't know for how long.

1. He worked as a blackjack dealer at table three at MGM.
2. He quit and became sort of an "aide de camp" to Spenser.
3. He evidently left Vegas for Knoxville. If he had no car, how did he get to Knoxville? Why did he go to Knoxville? Why did he leave a lot of his keepsakes behind? He must have left in a great hurry.

Spenser made four trips of about a week each to Vegas during the past eight months.

Spenser played the blackjack table number three where he evidently met Martin, who was the dealer.

Spenser lost all his money on his last trip about six weeks ago.

He had videos of movies in which Martin was a stuntman.

He hoped to get video clips of Spenser and Martin together.

Not least of all, he felt that he had made a new friend in Lamont Brown.

As Ace lay in bed, he couldn't keep from thinking about Jennifer Jones. It seemed that she had gone far and beyond what would be expected of a nurse he had never seen before. He knew that she had stuck her neck out to help him. *And she told Paula I was a good man when I introduced them at Regas last week.* There was also the way she looked at him, a look of mirth, and at the same time, a look of admiration. She had become an enigma to him. He decided that he was going to confess everything to her the next time he saw her. He knew that he had one final task to ask of her and it would probably be the hardest one yet. She didn't seem to be the least bit suspicious of him asking her not to reveal any of those tasks to

Martin. *Most people would be,* he thought. He hoped that Lamont would have good news for him in the morning. Regardless of what Lamont did tomorrow, Ace had a little surprise for him.

Chapter 24

Wednesday, September 13

Brad met with Lamont in his office at eleven as planned to view the tapes of Spenser and Martin.

"We have some coffee and doughnuts if you're interested, Ace."

"I don't mind if I do," replied Ace.

"I had my man look at all the videotapes associated with blackjack table three during the dates you gave me. He has edited out everything not involving Spenser or Martin. What we have here is a thirty-minute condensed tape that clearly shows that Spenser and Martin know each other. In fact, we even have a tape of Spenser handing Martin money. All the tapes have the date and time imposed in the lower right corner of the video. Would you please run it for us, Arnold?"

They both looked at the thirty-minute tape and Ace was highly pleased. "This is even better than I had expected," he said. "It's too bad that I won't be able to take it back with me."

"Thanks a lot, Arnold, that's all I need right now. I appreciate your effort on this."

"No problem, boss. Call me if you need me."

"Ace, a funny thing happened to me this morning," said Lamont. "As I was walking to my office, I found this manila folder lying in plain sight right out there in the hall in front of my office. It has your name on it. Here, why don't you take it? It evidently belongs to you."

"You know, Lamont, that we live in a small world filled with coincidences. As I stepped into the lobby on the way to your office the first thing I noticed was this envelope lying on the floor with your name on it. Take it. It belongs to you."

"What do you think it is, Ace?"

"I have no idea, but it might be a ringside seat to the Robinson-Gonzales world championship fight at Caesar's Palace next Wednesday night."

"Do you have any idea what one of these little babies cost, that is, if you could find them?"

"I do now."

"How did you pull this off, Ace?"

"I could tell you but then I'd have to kill you. I hope you noticed, Lamont, that there is no way that the tickets could be considered a bribe, which I know you detest."

"Why is that, Ace?"

"Because you delivered my manila envelope to me before I delivered yours. You would have gotten the tickets no matter what."

"Touché, Ace. Your plane leaves the airport at ten in the morning. If you could be in my office at nine we can have some coffee and doughnuts before the limo ride to the airport. By the way, were you serious when you asked me if I needed any help?"

"I'm really not sure, but it wouldn't work out anyway."

"What makes you think that?"

"Well, Barney, I don't think I could ever get used to being your deputy after being the sheriff all those years."

"You have a point there, Andy."

"That's not my real reason though. I have discovered that I have an interest in Knoxville."

"What's her name?"

"Paula."

"See you later, Ace."

"Until tomorrow morning at nine, Lamont," said Ace.

Chapter 25

Ace left Lamont's office and returned to his room. He thought about calling Paula but he didn't think it would be a good idea to call her at Luther's office. He missed her more than he thought possible. It seemed he had been gone for a month rather than a few days. He would like to call Lisa to see what she had found out about Martin, but she was in school.

He had all afternoon and couldn't decide what to do. He had a bright idea. He called the pickup people, rented a car, and headed for Lake Mead and Hoover Dam.

Chapter 26

Wednesday afternoon, September 13

The drive to Hoover Dam took about an hour and Ace enjoyed the quietness, something he hadn't enjoyed for the past two weeks. He thought Lake Mead looked out of place right in the middle of the desert. It seemed a little artificial, sort of like an oasis in the Sahara. Hoover Dam was called Boulder Dam when it was first started, but Herbert Hoover, who was very instrumental in getting it approved, renamed it Hoover Dam when he became president. When President Roosevelt took office in 1933, he changed it back to its original name, Boulder Dam. In 1947 President Harry Truman changed it back to Hoover Dam, and it retains that name today.

He didn't realize that US Highway 93 went directly across the top of the dam and you could drive your car right across it. However all truck traffic across the dam has been banned since the 9/11 terrorist attack. All trucks now have to go downriver and cross the Colorado River at Laughlin, Nevada.

He parked in the parking area and walked into the visitors center and picked up a brochure. He learned that the dam was started in 1931 and finished in 1936 at cost of $165 million. He thought he had read somewhere that there were over a hundred people buried inside the concrete who died during the construction; however this is not true, according to the brochure. Ninety-six people lost their lives in the construction of the dam but none of them are buried in the concrete. The Colorado River provides the water power to turn the massive turbines that drive the generators that produces two billion kilowatts of electricity for Arizona, Nevada, and parts of Southern California. Ace did some quick math in his head and figured that the hydro-electric plant generates up to $2 billion a year in income form electricity. For what it was worth, he learned that there was enough concrete in the dam to pave a two-lane road from Seattle to Miami. The major power users of the dam are as follows:

Arizona—19%

Nevada—23%

Los Angles—15%

The amount of electricity the dam produced amazed Ace. This is almost twice as much as the power produced by one of the largest nuclear reactors. The Colorado River didn't seem that large or have sufficient flow to produce this much power. He took another look at his brochure and found the reason. The dam is 726 feet tall and the amount of pressure exerted on the turbines is tremendous. The pressure on the turbines way down below would be about 230 pounds per square inch.

Ace also learned that the Colorado River is the boundary between Arizona and Nevada.

Ace returned to his car to drive back to Vegas. He decided to call Paula when he got back to his suite. He wanted to hear her voice. *Could he have only been gone three days?* he thought.

Chapter 27

After dropping off his rental car, the pickup people dropped Ace off at MGM, and he went to his suite and called Paula. It was 4:30 p.m. in Vegas, 6:30 p.m. in Knoxville. Paula picked up on the first ring.

"Is that you, Ace?"

"Were you sitting by the phone waiting for my call?"

"Why is it that you always answer a question with another question, Ace?"

"Do I do that?"

"You just did."

"Did I?"

"There you go again. Did you miss me?"

"I called you didn't I?"

"See. That's another question."

"Is it?"

"Ace, you're impossible."

"Am I?"

"Why did you call?"

"I missed you."

"That's sweet," said Paula.

"Don't get mushy on me. Did you miss me?"

"A little bit. Ace, do you know what you are?"

"No, what am I?"

"You're a man of few words."

"You mean sort of like the Tibetan monk?"

"What is a Tibetan monk?"

"That's a monk from Tibet."

"What about him?"

"He was a man of few words. There's a real old, old, joke concerning, him."

"How old is it?"

"It's so old that Milton Berle refused to steal it."

"Who's Milton Berle?"

"How am I going to be able to tell this joke if you don't cooperate?"

"OK. Go ahead," said Paula.

"In Tibet there is this monastery. Everyone admitted must take a vow of silence."

"Give me the details."

"The monk must agree not to speak a word for ten years. At the end of the first ten-year period he gets to speak two words. This vow of silence continues so that the monk gets to speak two more words every ten years."

"How awful," said Paula.

"Well anyway, the monk's first ten years were up and he was called in to speak to the head monk. His two words were: 'Food bad.' Ten years later his two words were: 'Bed hard.' At the end of thirty years, his two words were: 'I quit.' The head monk told him it was probably for the better, because all the time he had been here, he had done nothing but complain."

"That's cruel, Ace."

"I know. I'm coming home tomorrow and I was wondering if you could pick me up?"

"What time?"

"We will be leaving Vegas at ten in the morning, which is twelve noon, your time. I should be in Knoxville around four in the afternoon." *I'm paying back the two hours I cheated time out of on my trip out here*, thought Ace.

"What is your flight number?"

"I am not flying commercial. I'm flying on MGM's jet."

"How did you manage that?"

"If I told you, I would have to kill you."

"I've heard that before somewhere," said Paula.

"I'm going to ask the pilot if he can land the plane at Island Home Airport. That would save you some mileage, and allow the plane to get in and out quicker than it would at McGhee Tyson. I'll be flying in a

Gulfstream G200 and I don't know if the IHA runway is long enough for our plane to land. I'll call you from the plane at least an hour before we land and let you know where."

"I will be breathlessly awaiting your call."

"Is Lisa there? I need to find if she got the information I need."

"She's in her room, I'll put her on. See you tomorrow, lovebird. Phone! Lisa."

"Hello, Ace."

"How did you know it was me?"

"I was eavesdropping on the extension."

"I think you've been around me too much lately," said Ace.

"You said that. I didn't."

"What did you find out for me?"

"Could you wait until tomorrow evening? I have a math test tomorrow and I really to have cram, and besides, I like to look you in the eye when I'm talking to you to see if you are lying."

"You're all heart. How did you know I was coming home tomorrow?"

"If I told you, I'd have to kill you."

It seems like everyone is stealing my line, thought Ace.

Chapter 28

Thursday, September 14

Ace got up around 8:00 a.m., shaved, showered, and got dressed to go check out. Lamont said he would get someone to pick up his luggage. He checked in at the lobby counter and informed them he was checking out of 917. The lady behind the counter checked the computer and told Ace he was all paid up and free to go. *I am going to kill Lamont when I see him,* Ace thought.

He got to Lamont's at almost nine on the dot where coffee and doughnuts were waiting for him.

"You didn't have to do that, Lamont. I'm on an expense account."

"It's the least I could do, Andy. Are you anxious to get back home?"

"Yes, I am, but I must say, this has been one of my most enjoyable trips ever."

"I think you'll have a nice flight home. The plane is very comfortable. There's even a bed if you want to sleep."

"I think I'll be too excited to sleep."

"You'll be riding out to the airport with the pilot and copilot in the limo. You'll be the only passenger on the plane, but there will be a flight attendant on board to fill your every desire."

"What's her name?"

"Her name is Alfred."

"It sounds too good to be true."

Lamont's cell phone rang and he told the caller that Ace would be right out. "The limo is here, Ace." He wished him good luck as they shook hands.

"If you're ever in Knoxville look me up, Lamont."

"Same here, my friend."

Ace reluctantly walked out of Lamont's office to the waiting limo.

Chapter 29

Ace stepped into the waiting limo to find two people already seated.

"I'm Ace Sleuth from Knoxville, Tennessee."

"Good morning, Ace. I'm Michael Kellogg, the pilot, and this gentleman beside me is my copilot, John Kilgore. It looks like we're going to have perfect weather all the way in to Knoxville."

They then shook hands all around.

"I was wondering," said Ace, "if it would be possible for you to land at Island Home Airport near downtown Knoxville. It would be a lot quicker for you to get in and out from IHA than it would be from McGhee Tyson, and it would also be more convenient for me."

"No problem, Ace. I'm familiar with IHA. I flew a bunch of bigwigs in there to a football game a couple of years ago. That place gets pretty hectic down there on football days."

"What time do you think we will get into Knoxville?" asked Ace.

"I figure around three and a half to four hours depending on the winds, so that should put us in there between 3:30 and 4:00 p.m. Knoxville time."

"Would it be all right for me to use my cell phone on the plane? I would like to call the person picking me up."

"That'll be fine. I'll let you know when we get about an hour from touchdown."

"Thanks," said Ace

A few minutes later they were let out at the hangar where the Gulfstream was waiting for them. It was fueled up and ready to go.

Chapter 30

They all boarded the plane and were given immediate clearance to take off. It took only a few minutes to reach flying altitude where the plane leveled off. Ace was amazed at the smoothness of the ride for this size plane. He picked up a pamphlet lying on the desk in front of him and read some interesting facts about the Gulfstream G200. He read that the plane could carry up to ten passengers at speeds exceeding 500 mph at altitudes of 45,000 feet. He also learned that there are several different cabin layouts that could be customized for the buyer. He also learned that the one hundredth plane of this type was delivered just a few months back. He was very glad to see that the plane didn't require a lot of runway for takeoffs and landings.

The pilot announced that if you looked out the left window you could see Hoover Dam. Ace took a look to see how different it looked from 30,000 feet, at which altitude the pilot announced that they were flying. Ace settled in to relax. He had a lot to think about.

He was almost asleep when he heard a voice that said, "My name is Alfred and I will be your flight attendant."

"Are you on this plane just for me?" asked Ace. "I seem to be the only passenger."

"I have been told that you are a VIP and are to be treated accordingly, Mr. Sleuth."

"I appreciate that very much, Alfred," said Ace, as he thought about killing Lamont.

"Would you like to have some eggs Benedict with an English muffin, Mr. Sleuth?"

"I certainly would. Do you have any coffee?"

"Would Starbucks suffice?"

"Very well." said Ace, as he thought it wouldn't take very much to get used to this kind of life. He ate his delicious food and fell asleep. The next thing he heard was the pilot announcing that the plane was one hour out of Knoxville.

Ace called Paula on his CP and she picked up on the first ring. "Hey, lovebird, we'll be landing at Island Home around 3:45. Are you still going to pick me up?"

"You bet your boots I am. I'll see you in an hour."

Ace then called Brad and told him that Paula was picking him up. "I'll call you first thing in the morning and give you an update," said Ace.

The plane landed without incident. Ace shook hands, thanked the crew, and walked to where Paula was waiting for him.

Chapter 31

They walked up to each other, embraced, and had their first kiss.

"I thought we would never have that first kiss," said Paula.

"I was waiting for you to make the first move," replied Ace.

"I just did," said Paula.

"I thought that was me."

"Ace, you're impossible."

"I know. How about us driving across the new bridge, the one that nobody uses, and get a bite to eat at the Marriott?"

"I will if you promise not to embarrass me like you did at the Regas Restaurant."

"Scout's honor."

They drove the two or so miles to the hotel following the road that snaked around the Women's Basketball Hall of Fame, and parked on level two of the parking garage and entered the lobby.

"Isn't this is a beautiful lobby?" exclaimed Paula, as they walked through marble-floored expanse. Above the floor of the lobby there was an open area that must have been seventy-five to eighty feet to the roof covering the entire lobby.

"You could get about four 747's in here if you cut off the wings and stacked them up," said Ace.

"That would be kind of drastic wouldn't it?" replied Paula.

"What would?" asked Ace.

"Chopping the wings off a 747," she replied.

She's been around me too much, thought Ace.

The restaurant in the lobby area had tables back in the enclosed dining room and also some tables in an adjoining area of the lobby.

"Do you want to eat back in the dining room or in the lobby area?" asked Ace.

"Let's eat out here where we can watch all the people go by."

"Sounds good to me," said Ace.

They were seated and shortly a waitress appeared. Paula kept her fingers crossed hoping that Ace wouldn't embarrass her like he did the last time.

Paula ordered a chicken salad plate and Ace ordered a Reuben sandwich.

"Tell me what all you did in Vegas."

"I don't know where to begin, but it was one of the most enjoyable trips I have ever made." Ace told her about the suite, the Gulfstream, about meeting Lamont, and the free accommodations. He filled her in on all that he had found out, and the fact that Luther and Martin knew each other in Vegas.

"I don't want you to feel bad about the situation with Luther. Besides the fact that he is not paying you, he has broken the law and may end up in jail. He will almost certainly be disbarred. I am not going to ask you a lot of questions. I'll just try to dig them out on my own even if I have to put a tail on Luther myself."

"There is one thing I can tell you, Ace. It's not going to be a secret very long anyway. Luther is going to file the civil suit when the courthouse opens Monday. I just got through typing up the papers."

"That's good, Paula. I don't need to know what's in it right now anyway. I can wait until Monday. What have you been doing, Paula?"

"Waiting for you to come back," she said. "I've missed you."

"Ditto," said Ace.

"Still a man of few words, I see."

"Still like the monk."

"Do you like your work, Ace?"

"I wouldn't do anything else, and besides, if I had been doing something else, I wouldn't have met you."

"Good point. Tell me what part of your job you like best."

"Prior to my Vegas trip it was tracking down deadbeat dads."

"Speaking of deadbeat dads?"

"You have a deadbeat dad?"

"No. I have an ex-husband who is a deadbeat dad."

"Maybe we better track him down."

"I don't know where he is. The last I heard of him he was in Memphis, almost four hundred miles away."

"When we put this case to bed let's look into this."

"OK. Why do you like the deadbeat dad cases?"

"It's because of the satisfaction I get from righting a wrong. I love justice and hate injustice. I also like to see the changes in lifestyles it makes in the families."

"Does one case in particular stand out?"

"Yes, it was about twenty years ago. I had only been in business for about a year when a young mother called me about one of these cases. I went over to the housing project where she lived with her five-year-old daughter. The mother was around twenty-five and was holding down two jobs. I felt so sorry for the little girl. She was starved for male attention. Every time I would go over to see the mother, I would talk to the little girl for a while before her mother put her to bed. As soon as I would enter their house the little girl would jump on my lap and hug me as hard as she could. She would cry when her mother would put her to bed and I almost cried too. I decided right then that I was going to track down this no-good bum who had denied this little girl the love of her father."

"Did you track him down?"

"Yes, I did, and when I found him, I must have put the fear of God in him, because he paid the two years' back pay and started making his monthly payments. I told the mother to let me know if he missed any payments. I never heard from her again until after a year she called to thank me for changing her and her daughter's life. She said that they were able to move into a small house and was sending her daughter to a Catholic school. That case meant more to me than any case I've had before or since."

"You're almost making me cry, Ace."

"I did cry, Paula."

As they were leaving the restaurant Paula noticed the beautiful glass-enclosed elevators at either end of the lobby.

"Let's ride the elevators," she said.

"Good idea," said Ace. "I'll go buy the tickets."

"Do you have to have tickets to ride the elevators?" asked Paula.

"Everybody does except for the paying guests. Would you like to go first class or tourist?"

"Do you ever get serious, Ace?"

"Yes. I'm going to get serious right now. This trip which we are about to undertake is very dangerous."

"In what way?" asked Paula.

"It's because of elevator highjackers," replied Ace. "Just last week in Nashville two elevators were highjacked at the Opryland Hotel."

"Who would be stupid enough to highjack an elevator?"

"Luther comes to mind."

"You have a point there."

Ace and Paula decided on the east elevators. They entered the glass-enclosed car, pressed the top button and started zooming up through the vast empty space above the lobby. All at once the elevator seemed to shoot through the roof and they felt like they were out in space. The view was spectacular. They got out and walked around the railing with the view down below of the lobby. They then walked around to the west end of the hotel and took one of the elevators from that end back down to the lobby.

"I really enjoyed that," said Paula. "You see it doesn't take a lot to please me."

"So did I," replied Ace. "I think I enjoyed it because you did. It's like taking a child to the zoo. You enjoy it a lot more than you would by yourself."

"You're sweet, Ace."

"I know."

Chapter 32

It was around 7:00 p.m. when they left the hotel. Paula dropped Ace off at the parking garage beneath Brad's office so that he could pick up his car. He got into his car and followed her home. He wanted to find out what Lisa had found out. He pulled in the driveway behind Paula's car and they both went in.

"I'm going to make some coffee while you two talk. Would you like some, Ace?"

"Yes. If it's decaf. What have you been doing without me around to hound you, Lisa?"

"Studying like crazy," she said.

"Did you find out anything about Martin?"

"The internet is amazing; I Googled it. All you have to do is type in a name and you can find out all sorts of things."

"Such as?"

"Just for kicks I typed in my own name and it showed that I had done math tutoring, which is true. I then typed in Mom's name and it showed that she had donated some flowers to our church in memory of her mother. Who inputs all this stuff and where do they get it?"

"Beats me," said Ace.

"I also typed in your name, Ace."

"What did you find out?"

"If I told you I'd have to kill you."

Why is everybody stealing my lines? thought Ace. "Have you found out anything about Martin?"

"Yes, quite a bit, but most of it you already know. I think what will interest you most is his admittance to LA General Hospital in 1999 for an injury he received while making a movie."

"Tell me about it. Did you find the date and time he was admitted?"

"I have the date. It was July 17, 1999."

"I think that will be enough. How many man-hours did you put in on this?"

"I didn't put in any man-hours, but I did put in seven girl-hours."

"You've been around me too long, Lisa. Were these hours after 5:00 p.m.?"

"Yes, they were. Why do you ask?"

"According to union rules, I'm going to have to pay you double time."

"I'm sure glad I joined the union," said Lisa.

"Get all your information in a nice little package for me and I'll give you fourteen nice crisp twenty-dollar bills."

"That sounds good to me. Have you come up with any more math games?"

"Just one more—do you have pencil and paper? Here goes. Write as equation one, that X is equal to two. Then multiply both sides by X. That's legal in algebra, isn't it?"

"Yes."

"Now subtract four from each side of the equation." When it was finished it looked like this:

$X = 2$

$X^2 = 2X$

$X^2 - 4 = 2X - 4$

"Now factor both sides." Lisa did and came up with equation number four. It looked like this:

$(X + 2)(X - 2) = 2(X - 2)$

"Now I want you to divide both sides by $(X - 2)$. What is the result?"

"The $(X - 2)$ factor cancels out on both sides and I have: $X + 2 = 2$, but that makes X equal to zero and I started out with X equal to two."

"That's right. Do you agree that if two things are equal to the same thing that they are equal to each other?"

"That's what they taught us in math."

"Then you just proved that two is equal to zero because X is equal to two, and also equal to zero."

"How did I do that?"

"Because you just broke the first law of math."

"I did not."

"Yes, you did. The first law of math says never, never, in no way, shape, fashion, or form, ever divide anything by zero."

"I didn't divide anything by zero."

"Look at the equation where you divided both sides by the factor $(X - 2)$, do you see that?"

"Yes, but where did I divide by zero?"

"Right there in equation four. What is the value of $(X - 2)$?"

"Well X was two so $(X - 2)$ must be zero."

"It is and you just broke the law and divided by it."

"It's all your fault, Ace," said Lisa, "you made me do it."

"I didn't hold the pencil in your hand and guide it," replied Ace.

"Will I have to go to jail?"

"That all depends. Is this your first offense?"

"How would I know that? I don't even know what I've done wrong?"

"Ignorance of the law is no excuse, Lisa."

"I still don't know why you can't divide by zero."

"It's because nobody knows exactly what zero is. Write this down. Put any number in the numerator and start dividing by numbers less than one into it. What do you have?"

"I divided by ½ with the number one as numerator and got two."

"OK. Make that bottom number smaller, much, much smaller. What do you have now?"

"I divided one by 1/1,000,000 and got one million."

"Good. Do you see what's happening?"

"Yes. As the denominator gets smaller and smaller, the numerator gets bigger and bigger."

"OK, now keep reducing the denominator until it gets to zero."

"It will never get there will it?"

"No, it won't. What does this tell you?"

"I don't know, maybe it's telling me that we don't really know what zero is."

"I think you're right, but take a look at the numerator and see what's happening to it."

"It keeps getting bigger and bigger."

"Where do you think it will end?"

"I don't think it will ever end."

"You're right and there is a name for this unreachable number, I call it the lazy eight."

"What's a lazy eight?"

"It's an eight lying down, the math term for it is infinity, and infinity is undefined."

"Does that mean that zero is undefined?"

"That's hard to say, but it sure gets fuzzy when you start diving by it. Because one divided by zero could be said to be infinity, and by the same token, one million divided by zero could be also said to be infinity. You know one is not equal to one million. I hope I haven't confused you."

"I guess it all depends on what the definition of is, is, Ace."

"What the definition of is is, is, is, Lisa."

"What the heck, I'm having fun and that's all that matters," said Lisa.

"Zero is pretty well defined for me when I pay all my bills at the first of the month," replied Ace. "Speaking of bills, here are fourteen nice crisp new twenty-dollar bills. Good job, Lisa."

"Nice doing business with you, Ace."

Ace said goodbye to Paula and told her he would be tied up all day Friday and suggested that they get together Saturday and do something.

"At your beck and call," replied Paula.

Ace was tired out so he went home and hit the sack.

Chapter 33

Friday, September 15

Ace awakened Friday morning about eight, feeling much refreshed. He shaved and showered and fixed himself a bagel with cream cheese and strawberry jelly for breakfast. He was dreading what he knew he had to do next. What he had to do next was call Jennifer and lie to her some more. He wished he could tell her what was going on but he felt the timing wasn't right just yet.

He rang her number.

"Hello. Acute care nurse's station, Nurse Jones speaking. How may I help you?"

"Guess who?"

"Dr. Zachary! Are you still here?"

"I can't seem to get away from this place, but I did manage to get away for three days. I just got back in town yesterday afternoon."

"Welcome back. How may I help you?"

"I really hate to ask you to do anything else, but I have no one else to turn to."

"I'll be glad to help, Doctor, just name it."

"There are several things. Could you give me the name of Mr. Martin's attending physician?"

"I'm surprised that you don't already know that, Dr. Zachary, since you were called in as a consulting physician on his case."

"Well, about that, I was actually contacted by Luther Spenser, Martin's attorney, to do an independent analysis of the case. Spenser is going to sue for injuries and these lawsuits can get a little mysterious."

"I understand, Doctor. I have that information right in front of me. The doctor's name is Heinz Mueller, orthopedic surgeon."

"What is the present condition of Mr. Martin today?"
"My chart says NC."
"What does that mean?"
"No change."
"I wonder if you could tell me what happens to a person's personal effects when they are brought into emergency."
"I don't know, but I think I can find out."
"Good. Now here comes the biggie. Martin was injured on July 17, 1999, and taken to Los Angles Community General Hospital. I know this sounds impossible, but I need copies of the x-rays that were taken of him in emergency that day."
"Would you also like for me to give you the winning lottery number for Saturday's drawing?"
"That would be nice."
"Dr. Zachary, I will do my best, and I'll call you as soon as I find out anything. Is there anything else?"
"I think there is but I can't remember what it was. Jennifer, I cannot thank you enough for what you've done for me, but if you can come up with all this I'm going to hug your neck the next time I see you."
"It won't be the first time, Doctor."
Ace was floored. He was more confused now than ever before. He could never remember before being left speechless. He thanked her and hung up.

Chapter 34

Around 10:00 a.m., Ace called Brad's office and Denise answered the phone.
"This is Ace. Is Brad in?"
"Not at the moment, but I expect him in around eleven."
"Would you have him call me when he gets in? I have some work to do in my office."
"I'll have him call you, Ace."
"Thanks, Denise."
Ace drove to his office. He needed to put everything together to present to Brad, and he thought he had better put it all down on paper before he forgot it. He was just about finished when Brad called.
"Glad you got back in one piece," he said. "We need to get together, don't we?"
"We sure do. When is a good time for you?"
"How does one this afternoon in my office sound to you?"
"Sounds good. See you then."
The timing was good for Ace. He still had a little more work to do and still had time to stop and get lunch somewhere. He decided to get a bite at Harold's, which is a Jewish-owned and Jewish-run restaurant on North Gay Street about four blocks south of his office. He liked the Reuben sandwiches there.
He decided to walk down the right-hand side of the street since this was the side Harold's was on. He had been doing some garbage-can sleuthing and was not dressed in his best duds when a panhandler came up to him and asked for a handout. Ace looked at the man and said, "You must be new around here or you would know that I'm working this side of the street. You're going to have to get on the other side." The man apologized and started to go across the street when Ace slipped a five-dollar bill into his hand.

Ace had a delicious Reuben sandwich at Harold's and walked another block south to a business called "Electronics Are Us." He walked in, and the owner came up and asked him if he could be of any help.

"Do you have a debugger?" asked Ace.

"Are you asking me if I have an electronics detection device?" asked the owner.

"That's what I'm after," replied Ace.

"You've come to the right place," said the owner. "I just got in a new one that's supposed to be ninety-nine percent effective in locating eavesdropping devices. Take a look at this."

"It's not very big," replied Ace. "What is the cost?"

"Four hundred and ninety-five dollars plus tax," said the owner.

"I'll take one," said Ace, as he paid for it with cash. When he got back to his office and changed clothes, he got into his Mustang and drove to Brad's office to keep his 1:00 p.m. appointment.

When he walked in Denise told him that Brad was waiting for him in his office. Ace walked back to Brad's office and motioned for him to come out.

"What's up, Ace?" asked Brad.

Ace pulled the device out of his pocket and showed it to Brad.

"What is that, Ace? It looks like a small Geiger counter."

"It's a bug sniffer," replied Ace. "I want to check your office for bugs."

"You won't find anything here. This place is very secure," said Brad.

"Let me check anyway," said Ace. "You come with me but don't say a word."

Ace first checked Brad's desk and surrounding area but found nothing. Next he went into the small conference room just outside Brad's office. He probed around and stuck the probe under the small conference table and got a positive reading. He then looked under the table but couldn't find anything. "Do you have a flashlight?" he whispered to Brad.

Brad silently got one from his desk and handed it to Ace.

Ace took the light, got on his hands and knees, and looked under the table. He came back out signaling that he had found something. He then motioned for Brad to follow him out of the conference room.

Brad followed him back to the reception desk and asked him what he had found.

"I found a bug no bigger than a green pea under a metal brace beneath the table."

"Let's get it out of there," said Brad.

"I have a better idea," replied Ace. "Let's use it to our advantage."

"How do you plan to do that?" asked Brad.

"One of the reasons we're meeting today is to come up with a list of witnesses. That's exactly what we'll do. When we get back into the bugged room, let's start off with the list of witnesses. The ER doctor will be first, the attending physician second, followed by the radiologist." Ace explained to Brad exactly what he had in mind and they rehearsed it a couple of times before entering the bugged room.

They sat down at the bugged table and Brad said, "OK, Ace, let's get started on our witness list. First I would like to call Dr. Reed Smith, the ER physician, followed by the attending physician, Dr. Heinz Mueller. Have you found us a believable radiologist, Ace?"

"Yes, I found a perfect one in California by the name of Malcolm Sanders. He is really talented. He is a bit actor who has mainly acted in plays and consequently is not widely known. No one will recognize him, Brad."

"How good is he?"

"They tell me that he could convince you that black is white. I don't think he will have any trouble making the jury believe him. He rehearses his roles relentlessly until he has them down pat. He is going to tell the jury that Martin's back injury is a preexisting injury, and that he is one hundred percent sure if it."

"How about his credentials?"

"No problem, Brad. I'll just run some off in my office. Where would you like for him to graduate from?"

"I think Vanderbilt sounds impressive," said Brad.

"Consider it done. I'll even make his diploma from real sheepskin that you can't tell from the real thing, and just for good measure, I'll make and laminate an ADA ID card for him. What do you want his name to be?"

"Let me see. How does Dr. Roger Kennedy sound to you?"

"Sounds very believable to me, I'll go with it."

"By the way, Ace, what is this going to cost us?"

"He's not cheap. We'll have to pay him $10,000 plus expenses, but from what I hear, he's well worth it."

"We'll just have to bite the bullet on this one, Ace. Let's continue with the remainder of the list at a later date. I have some other things to do," said Brad. Brad closed the door to the office and he and Ace went back into his office. "Do you think Spenser will fall for this?" asked Brad.

"It has been my experience that the easiest people to con are the con artists themselves," replied Ace.

"Do you think Luther is listening to this bug?"

"I doubt it, but I'm sure his voice-activated recorder is."

"By the way, how do you think the bug was placed in my office?"

"There are a number of ways," said Ace. "Spenser could have slipped a janitor a $100 bill to plant the bug or he could have hired a private eye like me to hide somewhere in this building during the day and pick your lock and place the bug after hours. The PI could leave the building the next morning when everyone is coming to work. He could have hidden in a bathroom or a janitor's closet. It would be a piece of cake for a good PI."

"Good. Now tell me about your Vegas trip. I'm glad to see you back safe and sound," said Brad. "Was the trip worthwhile?"

"And then some," replied Ace.

"Tell me about it."

Ace proceeded to fill Brad in on all the key points. He told Brad that Spenser and Martin not only knew each other, but had become friends, and that he had video clips to prove it. He also told him about the old VCR movies that he found at the rooming house where Martin lived. "We have enough evidence to stop this law suit in its tracks Brad. I just found out that Luther will be filing the lawsuit as soon as the Courthouse opens Monday morning."

"This is good, Ace. I know that Luther is going to be pushing for the suit to go forward as fast as possible and this is what I want also, but I don't want Luther to know that. I am going to act as though I don't. I want him to think that we are not prepared. I want him to go into court as confident as possible."

"You said that the local claims agent, Frank Wheeler, called you Monday afternoon and told you that Luther had called and informed him that Martin had hired him as his Attorney."

"That is correct."

"Luther is lying through his teeth. I have it from a reliable source that Martin was under sedation during that time period."

"Luther will have a hard time explaining that when I call him to the stand."

"You can do that?"

"I certainly can and I will. All I have to do is bring up the discrepancy when the ER doctor, the local insurance agent, and Frank Wheeler testify."

"I bet Luther will wet his pants if he is called as a witness in his own lawsuit," Said Ace.

"He made his bed now he will have to lie in it," replied Brad.

"Ace, I don't know the first thing about civil lawsuits. I am going to get a good lawyer from one of the firms in this building to give me a crash course. I don't even know if you have to have a unanimous verdict to win the lawsuit, but I do know that we still have a lot of work to do. First I would like for you to make a list of all possible witnesses that we will need to call and why we need them. If there's any doubt list it anyway, we can always correct it. Secondly, about a week prior to the trial, I want a tail put on Luther. I want to see where he goes and who he talks to. He's the key to this whole thing."

"I'll handle that, but there's one more thing I would like to talk about," replied Ace.

"Shoot."

"There is a time frame of about a month where Martin is unaccounted for. I have a theory about it, but that's all it is."

"Let's hear it."

"Martin quit his job and became sort of an aide to Luther when he was winning, but when Luther lost all his money, Martin tried to get his dealer's job back but they wouldn't rehire him. He had no money so I think he borrowed money from loan sharks, and when he couldn't repay them, he skipped town."

"Why do you think that?"

"I found out where he lived, and it was obvious that he left in a hurry, because he left a lot of his things behind, including six VCR tapes of movies in which he was the stunt man. I believe these were important to him."

"That's a good point, but what do you think he has been doing the past month?"

"This is only conjecture on my part, but I think he was hitchhiking across the country doing odd jobs and not really knowing where he was going. Somewhere along the way, I think he decided to come to Knoxville and look up Luther. I don't know whose idea it was, but I think they hatched up this scam to get money they both urgently needed. They were both desperate. Martin may have told Luther that he was once a stunt man and had injured his back in a stunt for a movie. He may have told Luther that this would show up on an x-ray. By the way, before I forget it, I had Paula's daughter look up Martin on the computer and she discovered that he was injured while making a movie in July of 1999 and was taken to LA General. I am trying to get copies of those x-ray's to compare to the ones from Baptist."

"You have done some excellent work, Ace. I will get a subpoena of the Baptist x-rays. I don't think it would be a good idea to use our pilfered ones."

"Good point Brad. I think we also need a subpoena to get the list of the contents of Martin's pockets when he went into emergency."

"I'll take care of that Ace. I realize it's a little late, but I was wondering if you had any plans for tomorrow evening."

'What do you have in mind?"

I had a couple of cancellations in my sky box, and I was wondering if you and Paula would like to attend the football game. UT is playing Air Force."

"I can't think of anything else I'd rather do," said Ace.

"Good. If you and Paula could meet here in my office at five tomorrow evening, we'll all go over there together. Let's take the weekend off and see what shakes out Monday. We could all use a little rest. By the way, I read in today's paper that the city is working on a plan to reopen the Sunsphere."

"I think that's a good idea, Brad. I'll see you tomorrow evening. Thanks for the invitation. I know Paula will be thrilled." By the way," said Ace, "here is a copy of my expenses for this week."

"I'll look them over and have Denise write you a check." Ace returned to his office to finish up his work.

Chapter 35

Ace had only been back in his office for a couple of hours when the phone rang.

"Guess who?"

"I recognized your voice, Jennifer. Do you have good news for me?"

"I think so. I got you a copy of the list of items that Martin had on him when he came into ER."

"Great. How about the biggie? The LA General x-rays."

"I have good news. They faxed me a blown-up copy of the lumbar region of the back and they are sending a certified copy of the x-rays by FedEx tomorrow."

"How in the world did you manage that?"

"If I told you, I'd have to kill you."

"That's my line."

"I know."

"Jennifer, we have to talk."

"Do we ever?"

"What time do you get off work?"

"In about an hour," she said.

"Are you free to meet somewhere and talk?"

"I can hardly wait. Where would like to meet?"

"There's a Ruby Tuesday restaurant about a half mile south of you on Chapman Highway. I could come by and pick you up at the hospital, or you could meet me there. Take your choice."

"I'll meet you there."

After he got off the phone he suddenly had a very strange feeling and then he realized what was causing it. Jennifer had called him on his office phone. She also knew he had that little saying of his. *She knows who I am; this is scary.*

Ace couldn't wait to get to the restaurant and see her face-to-face. He beat her there by five minutes. They were seated and the waitress brought them water and the menu.

Jennifer looked Ace squarely in the eye and said, "Oh what a tangled web we weave when first we practice to deceive."

"I'm sorry, Jennifer. I had already planned to tell you everything. I have been feeling like a heel for days."

"Ace, do you remember the last thing you said to me on the phone call before the last one?"

"Yes. I said I was going to hug your neck the next time I saw you."

"Well, hug up, big boy."

"It will be my pleasure."

"I pretty well know almost everything," said Jennifer. "I knew who you were the first day you walked up to my station and introduced yourself as Dr. Zachary with that conspicuous stethoscope hanging out of our coat pocket. You still don't know who I am do you, Ace?"

"I'm sorry, Jennifer, I should remember someone as pretty and as nice as you."

"I'm not surprised or hurt that you don't remember me, I've changed a lot more than you have. Do you remember a little five-year-old girl who used to sit on your lap and hug you as hard as she could?"

"That Jennifer," said Ace said with tears in his eyes. "Are you little Jennifer Kelly? That was twenty years ago."

"I'm the one and the same, Ace. I didn't know what was going on back then. I didn't know until years later that you were working for my mother to track down my dad. I thought you were courting my mother and was going to marry her and be my daddy. I went to bed every night and prayed that you would marry her. Then all of a sudden you stopped coming around. I was heartbroken and too young to understand. I cried myself to sleep every night for a month."

"I am so sorry, Jennifer. I couldn't have possibly have married your mother, I was already married to someone else at that time."

"When I was old enough to understand Mother explained to me what you were doing there. She also told me a whole lot more. She told me that you found my dad and not only got him to start paying child support again but got him to pay the two years that he was in arrears. She also told me that all you would charge her for were your expenses, and that you were responsible for completely changing our life. We moved out of the projects and she was able to send me to Catholic school."

"How is your mother today?"

"Mom is doing great. She has remarried and now lives in Nashville."

"How about you, are you married?"

"I married Scott Jones as soon as I got out of nursing school. He was a helicopter pilot and was killed in Iraq a year ago. He loved his country."

"I am so sorry to hear that, Jennifer. Do you have any children?"

"No. I was afraid to have children. I didn't want my child to go through what I went through. I wish now that I had had more faith in Scott. He loved me and I don't believe he would have ever left me. I wish now that we had had a child so that I would at least have a part of him in my life."

"Do you date?"

"Not very much, I could never find anyone as good as Scott."

"You know, Jennifer, that you are a beautiful woman who could probably get any man you set her sights on. There's someone out there for you."

"Maybe there is. You mentioned when you called me yesterday that you had one more thing for me but couldn't think of it. Have you recalled what it was?"

"Yes, I have. I wonder if you could find out what the current hospital charges are for Martin and if anything has been paid on his bill, and if so, who paid them."

"That should be a piece of cake, Ace."

"I guess you know who I'm working for don't you?"

"I've known from the start, Ace. I didn't come into town on the turnip wagon yesterday."

"There is one thing that bothers me, Jennifer. When you said to me that you would have to 'kill me if you told me' and I said that was my line and you said, 'I know.' How did you know?"

"I was sitting on your lap one day and we were kidding around and I asked you how old you were. Do you know what you said?"

"I must have said that if I told you that I would have to kill you."

"That's exactly what you said."

"Do you know what, Jennifer?"

"What?

"I would be proud to have you for a daughter."

"Do you know what, Ace?"

"What?"

"I'd be proud to have you for a daddy."

"You know what, Jennifer?"

"What?"

"I think it's about time we left this mutual admiration society meeting and ordered something to eat."

"I agree. I'm famished."

"This chicken Caesar salad is delicious," said Jennifer. "By the way, are you still married, Ace?"

"No, my wife didn't like living in poverty, and I was too proud to accept food stamps, so she left me for greener pastures. However there is someone special in my life right now and I suppose that you already know who she is. I've told her about you and she already likes you, and I know you'll like her when you get to know her."

"It's Paula isn't it?"

"Yes, it is. It's hard to believe that we had just met the very same day we ran into you at Regas."

They finished their meal and Ace left a ten-dollar tip and walked Jennifer to her car. "I'm going to hug you again just in case the first one didn't take," said Ace. "Call me when the x-rays come in tomorrow."

"Will do. Bye-bye, Ace."

Chapter 36

Ace has no sooner pulled out on to Chapman Highway when his cell phone rang. "Ace, this is Brad. I hate to bother you but there has been a cancellation in one of my skybox seats and I was wondering if you might like to bring an extra person. The game starts at 7:00 p.m., so we can all meet here at my office at five."

"I have just the person, Brad. Her name is Jennifer Jones."

"Bring her along. The more the merrier I always say."

After he hung up Ace realized that he didn't have Jennifer's home phone number. *Paula should be home by now,* he thought, so he rang her.

"What is it, lovebird?"

"How did you know it was me?"

"Haven't you ever heard of caller ID?"

"Do you have caller ID?"

"Why is it that you always answer a question with a question, Ace?"

"Do I do that?"

"You just did it again."

"Did what again?"

"You just did it three times in a row."

"I did what three times in a row?"

"That makes four times that you have answered a question with a question."

"I'll try not to do that anymore. OK?"

"Ace you're impossible."

"I'll try to be more possible in the future. Is Lisa home?"

"Yes."

"I wonder if I could get her to look up someone in the phone book for me."

"Who?"

"Jennifer Jones."

"Isn't that the mystery girl?"

"Yes, but the mystery is solved. I'll explain everything to you ASAP. Tell Lisa to call all listed Jennifer Jones, all J. Jones, and all two-letter initials Jones starting with a J, until she finds the Jennifer who works at Baptist. Have her call me on my cell phone and give me the number as soon as she finds it."

"Yes, sir."

"Are you doing anything tomorrow evening, Paula?"

"What do you have in mind?"

"I thought we could go up to the Marriott and ride the elevators or—"

"Or, what?"

"Or we could go down to Fort Loudon Lake and watch the submarine races or—"

"You want to watch submarine races at night?"

"It's a funny thing about submarine races, Paula. It doesn't seem to matter when you watch them."

"What was that second 'or' all about, Ace?"

"Or we could go to Neyland Stadium and watch the Vols play Air Force Academy from Brad's skybox."

"I think I'll take what's behind door three," said Paula.

"Good choice. Brad wants us to meet him at his office at 5:00 p.m. and we'll all go to the game from there. Do you want me to pick you up at home or do you want to meet at Brad's office?"

"I'm still not crazy about the 'pick me up' term, but I'll be here waiting. Is four-thirty about right?"

"That's fine. Brad just called and said he had an extra seat and that's why I need to get in touch with Jennifer. I'm going to ask her to come along with us."

"When are you going to explain her to me?"

"What are you doing right now?"

"I'm cooking some delicious broccoli-cheese soup. I'll just dump in an extra cup of water and you can just eat with us."

"Sorry, I can't. I just finished eating, but I'll be there in thirty minutes anyway."

Chapter 37

When Ace got there Lisa had already found Jennifer's home phone number. He called her and she said she would be delighted to go and that she would meet them at Brad's office at 5:00 p.m.

After Paula and Lisa had eaten their delicious soup and salad, they all retired to the den when they were finished.

"I'm going to leave you two lovebirds alone and finish my homework," said Lisa.

"Thanks for getting the number for me, Lisa."

"You're welcome. Good night, all."

"Now do want to explain her to me?"

"Do you remember me telling you about my most fulfilling case and I told you about a little five-year-old girl sitting on my lap? Well, that was Jennifer."

"I understand. She recognized you because you hadn't changed much, but she had changed tremendously."

"She has seen much sorrow. Her father deserted them when she was three and her husband was killed in Iraq after a few short years of marriage. She is a beautiful girl but she doesn't date much because she hasn't gotten over her husband's death. I would like for her to meet someone and finally have some happiness in her life. If it were not for Jennifer getting all the information for me, I doubt if we could win this court case. By the way, she likes you."

"How could she like me, she doesn't even know me?"

"She likes you because I told her that you liked her."

"Why did you tell her that?"

"It's because I want her to like you."

"Why do you want her to like me?"

"Because I like you."

"How much do you like me?"

"I like you a bushel and a peck and a hug around the neck."

"I haven't seen much of that lately."

Ace gave her a huge hug topped by a long hard kiss.

"I hate to eat and run, but I have to go. I'll pick you, oops, sorry, I'll come get you at four-thirty tomorrow afternoon."

He kissed her again and left.

Chapter 38

Saturday afternoon, September 16

Ace picked up Paula at her apartment as planned and drove to the parking garage beneath Brad's office and took the elevator to the twenty-fourth floor. He had given Jennifer the directions to the garage and also Brad's special code number for the elevator. He walked into Brad's office and saw a good-looking man sitting there, and he could tell that he was Brad's son.

"Ace, I would like for you to meet my son, David, from Atlanta," said Brad.

"I'm Ace Sleuth," said Ace, as David eyed him with a bit of curiosity. "I would like for you both to meet Paula Novak."

"I've heard a lot about you, Paula," said Brad.

"Don't believe a thing Ace says," replied Paula. About that time Jennifer walked into the room and all eyes turned toward her, especially David's.

Ace took Jennifer by the arm and said, "I would like for all of you to meet Jennifer Jones, an old friend of mine."

"She couldn't be too old a friend, Ace, judging from what I can see," said Brad.

"Thanks, Mr. Adams, for inviting me," said Jennifer.

"You're quite welcome because I have heard some great things about you. I think that you have saved my financial skin by all that you have done for us. When Ace introduced you I didn't know whether you picked up on the fact that this young man standing beside me is my son, and if you have no objections, I am appointing him as your official escort for the rest of the evening."

"I can't think of any at the moment, Mr. Adams."

"Please call me Brad, Mr. Adams is my dad."

"Thanks, I will." Jennifer then turned to Ace and handed him a letter-sized manila envelop. "This is the information you requested, Ace."

Ace opened it up and found a copy of the LA General x-rays, a copy of Martin's hospital bill to date, and a list of everything that Bret Martin had on his person the night he was admitted to the Baptist ER. Ace looked to Brad and said, "If this is what I think it is, it will be a slam dunk for you in the trial."

"We had all better get down to the lobby; the limo will be there to pick us up in a few minutes," said Brad.

Chapter 39

The stretch limo picked them up and they drove the short distance to the Marriot Hotel and picked up six more of Brad's guests and they were then introduced all around. Within twenty minutes they were dropped of just a few feet from the west-side elevators at Neyland Stadium. They all rode up to Brad's skybox and walked inside. They looked down at the field and it was a complete sea of orange, 105,000 strong. It seemed a long way up from the playing field but that didn't matter a whole lot since the skybox had a fifty-two-inch plasma TV from which they could watch the game, or any other game that was being televised.

Ace and Paula had never seen such a food layout in their lives. "These are the biggest shrimp I've ever seen," said Paula.

"The barbeque ribs and the flowing champagne ain't bad either," replied Ace.

Paula and Ace picked up a plate and gathered some food. "Did you see the size of those cashews, Paula?" asked Ace.

"Yes, they look about as big as a large acorn," replied Paula. They each got their food and drink and sat down, and Paula asked Ace where Jennifer was.

"She and David are cuddled up in a corner over there," replied Ace.

"I think I like her better already," said Paula.

"I knew you would like her. By the way, Paula, do you have any plans for tomorrow?"

"What do you have in mind, big boy?"

"I thought it would be nice if we drove up to Cades Cove in the Great Smoky Mountain National Park and hiked out to Abrams Falls. Then after that we could drive the Little River Road into Gatlinburg and eat somewhere there. Are you up to hiking?"

"I'll give it a try, but no monkey business when you get me out in the woods, Ace."

"On my scout's honor, I won't."

"Were you a member of the Boy Scouts, Ace?"

"Nope."

"Just as I thought."

"I had better come by your house around ten in the morning. Is that OK?"

"Suits me."

"Looks like the game is ready to start, I sure hope the Vols are better than last year," said Ace.

One of the pre-game highlights was when a B-52 bomber came streaking across the stadium at a rather low altitude. There was a tremendous applause from the fans. "It looked as if Air Force had brought their big guns and they almost had enough," reflected Ace after the game had ended.

The Vols did look a lot better than they did last year, but Air Force gave them a fit. They barely squeaked by for a one-point win, and felt very fortunate about that. "We beat California very handily last week," said Ace. "But Florida will give us a good test next week."

After the game they waited awhile for the traffic to thin out, and proceeded to the waiting limo.

Jennifer spoke up and asked who won the game. "I think David did," replied Ace.

The limo delivered them back to the parking garage and they all thanked Brad for a wonderful day.

Jennifer came up and hugged Ace and thanked him for the most wonderful time that she had had in years. "David is going to follow me to make sure I get home safely," she said.

"I like her better and better every minute," said Paula.

Ace took Paula home, and after a long goodnight kiss, drove home.

Chapter 40

Sunday, September 17

Ace picked up Paula at her home at 10:00 a.m. as planned, and headed out I-40 west and turned south on Pellessippi Parkway toward the mountains. He drove past McGhee Tyson Airport, through the town of Maryville, and took US-321 toward Townsend. Driving in the direction that Ace thought was south, the US-321 sign read north. This is not unusual for this is one meandering highway. It is about a forty-five-minute drive to Townsend and five or ten minutes from there to the entrance to Cades Cove.

Cades Cove is lush valley of around five thousand acres that lies on the western edge of The Great Smoky Mountains National Park. It is one of the most popular destination points for park visitors. In 1850, 635 family members and 137 households inhabited this cove. It was incorporated into the Smoky Mountain National Park when it was created in the mid-thirties. There is a one-lane road that encircles the cove within its eleven-mile length. On a busy day traffic along this road is bumper to bumper while crossing streams and sometimes fording them. Deer, wild turkeys, and sometimes black bears may be seen. The thousands of acres that are enclosed are very lush and cattle still graze there.

As you travel the loop you will see a few of the former homes along with a few churches or schools. About halfway around the loop road is an operating water-driven grist mill that is still in operation. Here tourists can purchase bags of stone-ground cornmeal. Just about a half mile before you get to the mill is the turn-off to the parking area at the start of the trail that leads to Abrams Falls. Ace pulled in there for the two-and-a-half-mile hike to the falls. *Did I bite off more than I can chew?* he thought. "Are you up to hiking five miles, Paula?"

"I'll try."

"Good enough. If you get tired we'll stop and rest." Summer vacation was over so there were not a lot of tourists around.

They had walked about a mile and they saw a log that the Park Service had made into a bench, and they both sat down.

Ace looked down and said that he had to make sure his tennis shoe laces were tight.

"They look OK to me," said Paula.

"I'm afraid we might run into one of those black racers."

"Do you mean a black racer snake?"

"No. I'm talking about a black racer bear. Those things are fast, and they don't like people."

"How fast are they?"

"About as fast as a large dog."

"Why haven't I heard anything about them?"

"The Park Service doesn't like to advertise them because it's bad for tourism. It's sort of like the shark situation in Florida."

"If these bears are as fast as you say they are, I don't think you'll be able to outrun them."

"I don't have to outrun them, Paula. I just have to outrun you."

"Ace, do you know what?"

"What?"

"You're full of it."

"I know."

"You're certifiable."

"Yes, and I have papers to prove it"

Ace and Paula still had a mile and a half to go and they were going in the downhill direction. They started out at an elevation of 1,700 feet and that had dropped to 1,500 feet at the falls. This meant that the hike back would be a little more difficult because of the 200-foot rise in elevation.

They arrived at the falls about forty-five minutes later and sat down and rested.

"This waterfall is much more beautiful in the spring when the water flow is about ten times what it is now," said Ace. The waterfall is fifty feet high and drops into a large pool where children like to splash and play.

As they were sitting there resting Paula asked Ace about their relationship. "What do you think about me, Ace?"

"Well, for only knowing you for a couple of weeks, I believe we're spending a lot of time together."

"But do you really like me?" she said.

"Yes."

"Do you like me a lot?"

"Do frogs fly?"

"No. Frogs don't fly."

"If they don't fly how do they get so high in the air?"

"Ace, would you get serious?"

"I'm sorry, Paula. It's been so long since I met anybody I could relate to like you. I think about you all the time and I can't wait to share things with you, but I don't know if you could put up with the likes of me."

"I think I love you, Ace."

"I think I love you too, Paula, but let's wait and see how everything shakes out. You're going to be out of a job in a short while and your boss is going to be disbarred at the minimum, and possibly jailed for perjury. The next several weeks are going to be a strain on all of us, especially you. I know you feel like a traitor working for Luther, but he's not even paying you, and I know he was aware that those two paychecks he wrote you would bounce. He was just buying time. I want you to be extra careful that he doesn't get you to do something that might be unlawful. Just remember that ignorance of the law is no excuse."

"Are you about ready to head back, Ace?"

"I'm ready. I bet we both will have worked up quite an appetite by the time we reach Gatlinburg."

They started back to their car and walked back to the same log bench that they had stopped at on their way to the falls.

"Let's take a short break," said Ace, and they both sat on the log bench. All at once Ace told Paula to turn around very slowly and look at the animal path that led into the woods. Paula turned around and saw a very large brown bird standing in the path not more than fifteen feet from them.

"What kind of bird is that?" Paula asked Ace.

"That is the largest owl that I have ever seen," replied Ace. The owl seemed as interested in the two of them as they were in it. "I better get a picture of this creature," said Ace, "because nobody is going to believe the size of that bird." He then snapped a picture of it with his cell phone.

"What kind of owl is it ace?" asked Paula.

"It is a brown owl that must be close to two feet tall standing there," said Ace. "Let's just watch it and see what it does."

The owl stood there for about two minutes and decided to take flight. Ace and Paula could hear the loud swooshing sound that the owl's wings made in the air as it took off. The downward burst of air from the owl's mighty wings scattered some leaves on the ground beneath as it took flight. "That bird must have at least a four-foot wingspan," said Paula.

"At the very least," said Ace.

It took them about an hour to get back to the parking area from the log bench, and from there, they drove back to the loop road and stopped at the old grist mill a mile or so away. They watched the corn being ground between the two large round stones, and they bought a five-pound bag of the cornmeal. They walked from there down to the old farmhouse that the Park Service had kept up somewhat to show how the people used to live seventy-five to a hundred years ago. They then drove the remaining five miles of the loop road and took the feeder road to the Little River road, and headed east toward Gatlinburg about twenty miles away.

As they exited the park they were instantly in Gatlinburg. Ace asked Paula where she would like to eat.

"What are my choices?"

"There are a lot of good restaurants here, the Open Hearth, the Park Grille, Calhouns, and the Applewood Farm House Restaurant, to name a few, but I have a surprise for you."

"What kind of surprise?" asked Paula.

"Have you ever eaten at the Rel Maples Institute for Culinary Arts at Walters State Community College?"

"What is that?"

"It's a culinary school where the students cook the food and also do the serving," replied Ace.

"Is it near here?" asked Paula.

"It's only about twelve miles from here, and I took the liberty of making us a reservation."

"Let's go for it then."

They drove to the campus and Paula was surprised at the beautiful setting for the community college. The beautiful rolling low hills with the

Great Smoky Mountains in the background painted a beautiful picture. They went in and found that there were already about seventy people waiting for the doors to the dining room to open. After about twenty minutes the doors were opened. They both entered and were seated with another couple and a young student-waiter introduced himself and brought them a menu. Ace and Paula looked at the menu. There was only one choice, but they liked what they saw.

Appetizer
Rissoles d' Oeufs
(egg croquette)

Salad
Lobster Mousse

Entrée:
Tournedos Opera
(Beef tenderloin on tarlet filled w/ chicken
liver surrounded by duchesse potato
Croustades filled with w/ asparagus

Cheese Course
(gourmet cheese delights)

Dessert
Profiteroles au Chocolate
(chocolate mousse filled pate a choux)

"I don't understand exactly what the menu is saying," said Paula, "but it sure made me hungry, Ace." They both enjoyed the delicious food and Paula remarked that she had enjoyed eating there more than any other place she had ever eaten.

After they had eaten, Ace drove the five or so miles to Sevierville and pulled up in front of Temple's Feed Store.

"Why are you stopping here?" asked Paula.

"This is a famous place," replied Ace

"Why?"

"Thousands of couples have been married here."

"Why here?"

"The way I heard it was that Mr. Temple was a justice of the peace and someone asked him to marry them, and he married them right there in the feed store. Word got out and people started coming here to get married. Mr. Temple refused to charge anything for his services, but he would let you drop whatever money you wished in a container, the contents of which was donated to the First Baptist Church of Sevierville. This went on for many years, but I don't know if it's still ongoing."

"Ace, this is the most unique wedding proposal I have ever received."

"In your dreams, Paula," said Ace, as he recalled a local joke that Southerners liked to tell on Northerners of which there was no shortage around Sevier County, especially at this time of year. Around 8 million visitors a year pass through this town. The joke centered on a Northern visitor who had difficulty with the local dialect, and in particular, with the pronunciation of the town of Sevierville. He was in a fast-food restaurant and turned to a local and asked, "Would you please tell me the name of this place, and speak slowly so that I can understand?" The local replied in an overly affected east Tennessee drawl, "Bur-Ger-King."

After a tiring but enjoyable day, they returned to Knoxville.

Chapter 41

Monday, September 18

Ace met with Brad in his office at 9:00 a.m. Monday.

"We need to go over a few things this morning," said Brad. "Luther will be filing the lawsuit right about now. We should be receiving a certified copy of it tomorrow. Here's what we have now.

"I have looked at the stuff that Jennifer dropped off here Saturday. The x-rays appear to me to show that Martin's back injury occurred in 1999 when he was admitted to LA General. I am going to get this verified by my radiologist. I have looked at the list of personal items that were on Martin's person when he entered Baptist ER. Here is what it shows:

    1. A billfold with a social security card and other insignificant papers. There was sixty-four dollars in bills, three twenties and four ones.
    2. A pocketknife and a fingernail clip.
    3. A key with YMCA and the number 201 stamped on it.
    4. Fifty-nine cents in change.
    5. A driver's license from the state of Nevada.
    6. A few pictures.
    7. A Kroger Plus card.

"There were no credit cards or medical insurance cards. His hospital bill as of EOD Friday was $17,568 and Jennifer says he has no hospital insurance. Let me tell you what I think is going to happen. Baptist is going to release him from the hospital forthwith, possibly as soon as today or tomorrow. What I would like for you to do is go to Baptist and see who checks him out. I think it will be Luther. See if they roll him out in a wheelchair or on a stretcher, and see where they take him, which will probably be to Luther's house because neither of them have the money to put him in a motel. After he gets settled in, I want a watch put on Luther's place to see if Martin comes or goes. Also keep an eye on Luther. If you need extra help, hire it.

"In the meanwhile I am going to get my radiologist to look at the LA General x-rays, and I am also going to subpoena copies of both Baptist and LA General x-rays so we won't be working with bootleg copies. I am also going to subpoena the contents list and his final hospital bill. Can you think of anything else we need to do?"

"Not right now, but I think I better get over to Baptist, posthaste."

"OK, let me know the minute they discharge Martin. By the way, I was going over your Vegas trip expense account and I came across an item for a fight ticket for $2,000. What's that all about?"

"I had to pay double face value for a ticket to the World's Heavyweight Championship fight for one of my bribes. Did you also notice that I got a $900 refund on my airline return ticket because I returned on the MGM Gulfstream? Did you also notice that I had a free stay at the MGM, thanks to Lamont Brown?"

"No problem, Ace, I was just curious, and besides, US Auto Insurance will be paying all these expenses."

"Do you really think that they will pay up?"

"I have no doubt about it. Can you imagine what US Auto would do if they saw an article on the front page of the *Knoxville News Sentinel* that read: 'Automobile Insurance Company refuses to reimburse local attorney, who acting as his own lawyer, won the case, saving the insurance company almost a million dollars?' I don't believe I told you, Ace, but US Auto was ready to offer a million dollars to settle out of court. I don't think our expenses will be more than $200,000."

"I see your point, Brad."

"As soon as I get the summons for the trial, I want us to get together and complete the witness list, among other things."

"Will do," said Ace. He then left and headed for his car in the parking garage.

Chapter 42

Ace drove directly across the Gay Street Bridge to Baptist, parked his car, and headed for the fourth-floor nursing station.

"Dr. Zachary, what a pleasant surprise. What can I do for you?"

"For one thing, you could tell me how you enjoyed Saturday evening."

"Thanks to you, I don't remember having such an enjoyable evening in years."

"If anyone deserved it, Jennifer, it's you. What do you think of David?"

"I haven't been as excited about anyone since I met my husband."

"Are you going to see him again?"

"He coming back up for the UT-Florida game Saturday night and he asked me to go with him."

"That sounds serious."

"We have a lot in common. We both are graduates of UT, and we have several mutual interests."

"What line of work is David in?"

"He's a stockbroker in Atlanta. Ace, I want to thank you for inviting me to the game, and by the way, I have really come to like Paula."

"She likes you too. Perhaps she and I, and you and David, could all get together when David is in town and go to Regas, or somewhere to eat. I would like for you to meet Paula's fifteen-year-old daughter Lisa. She's studying to be a doctor."

"I'd love to, but tell me, why are you really here?"

"You know that I only came to see you, Nurse Jones, but now that you brought it up, I was wondering when Mr. Martin is going to be released from the hospital."

"It looks like it will be around nine in the morning."

"Do you know who is going to check him out?"

"It says here that a Mr. Spenser is doing that."

"Thanks, Jennifer."

"You're welcome, Daddy."

Chapter 43

Tuesday morning, September 19

Ace was at Baptist at 9:00 a.m. sharp and positioned himself so that he would have a good view of the door where the patients leave the hospital. It wasn't until about 9:30 that Luther pulled up in a van and parked by the door. A few minutes later Martin was rolled out on a stretcher and laid in the back of the van on a mattress. Ace got a couple of good pictures of Martin with his cell phone before he was placed in the van. Ace was eager to see how Luther was going to get him out when he got home. He jumped into his car and headed for Luther's house to make sure he beat them there.

He parked his car a block away and took up a position behind some shrubs where he had a good view of Luther's house but they had no view of him. About five minutes later the van pulled into Luther's driveway and stopped. Luther got out and looked all around, opened the rear door of the van, and told Martin that the coast was clear. Martin got out and walked quickly into the house, but not before Ace got three good shots of him on his cell phone. Ace thought this would be a good time to try out the movie capabilities of the phone and got about ten seconds of Martin actually walking. *The perps today don't stand a chance with all the technology at our fingertips,* thought Ace. *They leave one strand of hair at the crime scene and DNA can place them there.*

Chapter 44

Brad called Roger Kennedy, the radiologist who had looked at Martin's x-ray's from Baptist, and asked him if he would take a look at the ones from LA General and compare them.

"Bring them over," he said. "I'll be here the rest of the day."

Brad drove the mile trip and parked in the parking garage. He took the elevator to Roger's floor.

"Good to see you again, Brad. What do you have for me?"

"I have x-rays of Martin made in 1999 at LA General Hospital, and I would like for you to compare them with the ones from Baptist for me. You weren't far off when you said he may have been a rodeo rider or a kick boxer; he was a stuntman."

Roger placed the two x-rays side by side on the light board and studied them for a few minutes. "This back injury shown in the Baptist x-ray is definitely preexisting," he said.

"Are there any additional injuries on the Baptist x-ray in addition to the ones on the LA one?" asked Brad.

"No. I don't see anything at all."

"Could you testify in a court of law that Martin suffered no injuries that would cause him great pain and be unable to walk from his run-in with me?"

"Based on these two x-rays, I certainly could."

"Is it OK if I place you on the witness list for the trial? I'll pay your hourly rate plus expenses."

"I would be glad to help you out, Brad."

"There is one other thing, Roger, and I hope you'll go along with me on this. I have indisputable proof that I was set up, and Luther Spenser, who is Martin's attorney, is up to his neck in it. He and Martin knew each other in Vegas and became friends a few months ago. I have movies of them together to prove it."

"Yesterday my investigator and I discovered a bug under the conference table in my office which we think Luther had planted. As a result, we decided to use the bug to supply Luther with some bogus information. We went to the conference table hoping Luther was listening in and went over our witness list. When we came to the radiologist we pretended that you were a made-up witness with phony credentials and were being played by a bit actor from California. I didn't want to spring this on you in court, but I was hoping that you would go along with it. I want to discredit Luther as much as possible."

"I would be happy to help out. I hate injustices as much as you do, and I don't have very much respect for some of these tort lawyers. Do you have any idea what malpractice insurance rates are for a doctor these days? I think that the rates are high because of some of these ridiculous lawsuits. In a lot of cases all you need to show is that someone has been harmed whether there is proof of fault or not. The juries just want to give the victims something for their pain and suffering, and whose deep pockets the money comes from is of little consequence."

"Thanks a lot, Roger. I don't know the exact date of the trial, but I expect it will be in about a month. You will probably be sent a subpoena but that's SOP. Would you mind bringing your diploma with you?"

"No problem, Brad, you can count on me."

"I'll let you know as soon as I know," replied Brad, as he left and returned to his office.

Chapter 45

Wednesday morning, September 20

Ace got into his Mustang and drove the short distance to the parking garage beneath Brad's building and found an empty slot on level three. He took the elevator to the twenty-fourth floor, walked into Brad's office and gave Denise the parking stub.

Brad met him at his office door and asked him how it was going.

"Pretty good, Brad," replied Ace. "A lot has been happening since we last talked. I have been going through Luther's garbage and I've found some interesting things. By the way, is it legal for me to do this?"

"Probably not," replied Brad.

"That's neither here nor there," said Ace, "but let me tell you what I've found. I have also been following Luther around town and he has gone into at least four of those high-interest-rate last-resort loan companies, and each time he has come out looking like he's just lost his best friend. He has maxed out eight different credit cards and is only paying the minimum payments on them. He is two months behind on his house payment and is in danger of being foreclosed on his home."

"Looks like to me that he will want to go to trial ASAP," replied Brad.

"Yes, he certainly will. Martin is still staying with him and I know for a fact that they have no hospital bed for him, nor has any painkiller medication been gotten for him since he left Baptist. I know that they did not give him any pain medicine or a prescription for any when he was discharged from Baptist."

"How do you find out all these kinds this stuff, Ace?"

"If I told you, I'd have to kill you, Brad."

"Keep your eye on both of them for a few days, especially a few days before the trial starts. We should know in a couple of days when that will be."

"Is there anything else, Brad?"

"Not for now. Just keep in touch."

"Before I forget, Brad, there's something I almost forgot to give you."

"What is it?"

"It's before and after pictures. The ones I took of Martin being carried and loaded into Spenser's van from Baptist, and the ones of him walking into Spenser's house about twenty minutes later."

"This is fantastic, Ace. These pictures alone are enough to win my case, but I want to present all the evidence at trial. There will be no settling out of court on this baby."

Ace left Brad's office and took the elevator to parking level three and got out and walked to his car. As he was about to get in he was approached by a young black male who looked to be about twenty years of age.

"I like your car, dude."

"Thanks, so do I," replied Ace.

"I think I'll just take it for myself," the young man said, as he pulled out a switchblade knife with an eight-inch blade.

"Why don't you take one of these newer cars?" asked Ace.

"I want your car. I know what you got under that hood."

"Be my guest," said Ace, as he handed him the keys. *This parking garage is starting to become an unsafe place*, thought Ace.

The young man got into the car, closed the door, and turned on the ignition switch. At the same instant, the doors and windows locked, the horn starting blowing, and the lights started flashing. Ace took out his cell phone and dialed 911 and then knocked on the car door and said, "Hey, dude, how do you like my car now? Smile, you're on candid camera," Ace said, as he took a couple of shots with his cell phone.

The police arrived in just under three minutes. Ace gave them all the particulars for their report as he got the young man's name from them.

Ace returned to his office and put the pictures on his computer and emailed them to the *Knoxville News Sentinel* along with the perps name and all the particulars. The best one of the two pictures was on the front page of the next day's *News Sentinel* and was picked up by the AP and was in newspapers across the country. Ace felt he got a million dollars' worth of free advertisement. He returned to his office and as he sat there he got to thinking about what he was going to do when this job was over. He had been working full-time on the Martin case and ignoring other jobs. He thought that the picture on the front page of the paper might help. *Maybe the phone will start ringing.*

He returned to the office the next morning and had just sat down to a cup of coffee when the phone rang. It was Brad.

"Good morning, Ace. I've got some news."

"Shoot."

"We have a trial date. Both Luther and I have agreed on Monday, October 23. The trial date came open and Luther jumped at it. I told the judge that the twenty-third was much too early for me to get all my evidence together, and I would like a later date. She said that if we didn't go with the twenty-third that we would have to wait until after the first of the year. Luther had a fit. He definitely didn't want to wait. I told the judge that I might not be able to get all my evidence together before the trial, and that I might not get some of it until the trial was under way. I told the judge that if Spenser would let me introduce my evidence whenever I got it, even if it was during the trial, that I would agree to the earlier date. Spenser jumped at the deal. I felt like the rabbit being thrown into the briar patch. I tried to seem a little disappointed and I think Luther bought it."

"Sounds good. Do you think we need to go over the witness list again?"

"I'll get back to you in a few days on that. However, there is one thing that you could do for me. I don't feel comfortable with going into court and showing Martin's movies using his own pilfered VCR tapes. You have a list of the movies. Just see if you can get Blockbuster or The Movie Gallery to order them for you. I doubt very much if they have any of them in stock."

"I think I can handle that. We might be able to get them on eBay."

"Good. I'll be in touch."

The minute that Ace hung up the phone rang again.

"Ace here."

"Guess who?"

"How in the world are you, Lamont?"

"I'm hanging in there, how about you?"

"We're going to trial October 23 and thanks to you, we've got a ton of evidence, but it looks like Martin is going to walk."

"How is that possible, Ace?"

"He is going to get up out of that hospital bed and walk straight to the clink, Lamont."

"Nipped another, didn't you, Ange?"

"Right in the bud, Barn."

"Did you know that you made the *Las Vegas Review-Journal* with that carjacker?"

"I knew that the AP picked it up, but I wasn't sure what papers carried it."

"By the way, Ace, do you still want that job?"

"I would love to, but I still have my interest here."

"By the way, how is Paula?"

She is doing well but she's between a rock and a hard place. She works for Spenser. That's how I met her in the first place. As you know Spenser is flat broke and hasn't paid her in a month if you don't count bad checks. I think I'm going to ask her to quit."

"Is that all you're going to ask her, Ace?"

"What do you mean?"

"Does she know how you feel about her?"

"I think so."

"Have you told her that? Women like to hear these things. They're not mind readers you know?"

"You're right, Lamont, I'm going to tell her right away."

"I'll make a deal with you, Ace. If you get married the MGM will put you both up in a suite plus your plane fare."

"How does the security chief at MGM pull that off, Lamont?"

"If I told you I would have to kill you, Ace."

"When we get married I would like for you to come to the wedding, Lamont, and be my best man."

"I'll see if I can work that out, Ace. Till then, take care."

"You too, Lamont."

Chapter 46

Wednesday afternoon, September 20

Ace called Paula at her office and asked her if she would like to go out to eat around seven.

"I'd love to," she replied.

"I'll be by your place at seven on the dot," replied Ace.

He rang her doorbell at seven on the dot and Lisa answered.

"Hi, lovebird, how you doing?"

"OK, I guess. Is Paula ready?"

"She's running a little late. She'll be ready in about ten minutes."

"I'll just talk to you then. I wonder if you would do a little job for me on the computer?"

"What kind of job?"

Ace handed her the list of the six movies that Martin had played in and asked her if she could order them on the computer.

"I can check. How do you want me to pay for them?"

He gave her his credit card number and told her to charge the movies on it.

"Do you want it on DVD or VCR?" asked Lisa.

"Get them on VCR, if at all possible," replied Ace. "There are some other things we will be showing on VCR tapes. By the way, the pay rate is the same as your other task."

"Sounds good, do you have any more math gems?"

"As a matter of fact I do have one. This church has one hundred members comprised of men and women. The men always put ten dollars each in the collection plate each week and the women always put in five dollars each. One Sunday half the men didn't attend. How much was the offering that Sunday?"

"You haven't given me enough information, Ace."

"You have all you need. Just think about the problem and use a little of your ingenuity, which I'm sure you're full of."

"Ace! You just violated the First Law of Prepositions."

"What's that?"

"Never use a preposition to end a sentence with," laughed Lisa.

"Do you know that your First Law of Prepositions is an oxymoron?"

"Why do you think I laughed, Ace?"

"I didn't know there was such a law, Lisa."

"If I'm not mistaken, Ace, I believe it was you who told me that ignorance of the law is no excuse, when you accused me of breaking the First Law of Algebra. What goes around comes around, Ace."

"Will I have to go to jail?"

"Well that all depends. Is this your first offense?"

"I'm not sure, but I know for a fact that Winston Churchill didn't go to jail when he broke that law."

"Who's Winston Churchill?"

"He just happened to be the Prime Minister of England, that's all."

"No wonder he never went to jail, with all that political pull he had. What did he do, anyway?"

"He just happened to break that law five times over in one sentence," said Ace, "when he quoted the little boy who had just gone upstairs to go to bed and his father took up a book to read to him. The little boy took one look at the book and said, 'Why did you bring that book that I didn't want to be read to out of up for?'"

"I'll try to remember that one, Ace. I'll get back to you on the movies and also the math problem."

About that time Paula came into the room and announced that she was finally ready. Ace thought she looked like a million dollars. He upped her to a 9.0 on the spot.

"Where do you want to eat?" asked Ace.

"How about Bravo's on Bearden Hill. Do you like Italian?" asked Paula.

"Everybody likes Italian," said Ace. "Do you want to go with us, Lisa?"

"And spoil you two lovebirds' dinner?" replied Lisa. "You two have fun. I have mountains of work to do."

Chapter 47

Wednesday evening, September 20

Ace drove the five miles to Bravo's atop Bearden Hill on Kingston Pike with a view of the Smoky Mountains. The restaurant is beautiful with broken Roman columns rising up around the spacious dining room.

"I read in the paper about your little escapade with the carjacker, Ace."

"Let's talk about you, Paula. How is it going with Luther? Has he paid you lately?"

"Still no pay."

"What does he say about paying you?"

"He says he still expects to come into big money soon."

"I think you need to quit the job, Paula. He is going deeper and deeper in debt and is in danger of losing his house. I think Brad could use you in his office, at least until the end of the trial. Then I think he could find you a job with one of the firms in his building."

"I think you're right, Ace. When should I quit?"

"Today is Wednesday. Why don't you tell him in the morning that Friday will be your last day of work? You don't need to give him any longer notice. Just tell him you can't afford to work for free any longer."

"That's what I'll do," said Paula.

"I'll check with Brad. I'm sure he will want you to come in first thing Monday. He is going to have a lot of work to do because the trial starts October 23. Are you ready to order, Paula?"

"I'm famished, let's eat."

Paula had penne pasta and Ace ordered lasagna.

"What are your plans for Sunday, Paula?"

"What do you have in mind, big boy?"

"I thought it might be fun to go somewhere for Sunday dinner and a drive over to Buffalo Mountain."

"Where is Buffalo Mountain?"

"You go through Oak Ridge and cross the mountain and I think it's somewhere close to Oliver Springs. I'm not exactly sure, but I'll look it up before we go."

"How many buffalo do they have there?"

"They don't have any."

"Then why are we going?"

"To see some of the largest wind turbines in the world, that's why."

"You really know how to show a girl a good time, Ace."

"I think you'll enjoy it. I've have always wanted to see the turbines ever since they were installed a couple of years ago. Where do you want to eat, Paula? Do you have any suggestions?"

"How about Puleo's on North Peters Road? They have a real varied menu, and it's right on our way."

"Why don't I come by your place around eleven so that we can get in before the Sunday crowd?"

"That will work for me. Now why don't we talk about us? How do you feel about me, Ace?"

"I think about you all the time, Paula. I didn't tell you this before but I made a good friend in Vegas, and he would have offered me a good job working for him at the MGM Grand, but I told him I had an interest in Knoxville. He asked me what her name was and I said Paula. He called me earlier today and asked about you."

"You can be so sweet sometimes, Ace. You know that I'm in love with you, don't you?"

"That works both ways, Paula."

"I can't believe it, Ace, but I think you just said that you loved me for the second time."

"I can't believe it either," replied Ace. "You won't believe the proposition that my friend Lamont of the MGM Grand made me on the phone today."

"Tell me about it."

"He said if you and I got married that the MGM would fly us out and put us in a suite free of charge."

"I can't believe this is happening to me, Ace. I don't deserve you."

"Paula, you're the only woman I've been serious about since my wife walked out on me nineteen years ago. After this trial is over why don't we get married and take Lamont up on his offer?"

"You know what, Ace?"

"What?"

"I love you, you big hunk, and I proudly accept your offer of marriage."

They both enjoyed their dinner and stayed at the restaurant two hours after they had eaten enjoying a couple of glasses of champagne. Ace then drove her home.

Chapter 48

Thursday morning, September 21

Brad called John Sawyer, a lawyer friend of his in the same building in which he worked, and asked him if he could give him a crash course in civil law.

"I have a couple of free hours after lunch," he said. "Do you want me to come to your office?"

"That would be perfect, John. It's real quiet here. Is one o'clock OK with you?"

"I'll be up there at one, Brad."

John was probably a few years younger than Brad, and had quite a bit of experience in civil law.

They sat down at the small conference table in Brad's office, avoiding the bugged one in the conference room.

"Let's get started," said John. "One of the most important parts of a civil trial is the jury selection. I think that you will find that the jury makeup is probably the most important part of a civil lawsuit. In civil cases, guilty beyond a reasonable doubt goes out the window. All that is needed for a judgment in the plaintiff's favor is preponderance of the evidence for him. What that means is that if the majority of the evidence favors him, the jury can vote in his favor. Sometimes even the evidence doesn't seem to matter. A good tort lawyer will wheel a victim in, who looks like he is on his death bed, to whip up sympathy among the jurors, and it works more times than not. A really big problem with some of these juries is that it is that they are a lot like a loose cannon. You have no idea what kind of monetary awards they might come up with. You need to get the most highly educated people you can on the jury, but try to avoid liberal types, such as people with a sympathetic agenda. As you probably remember from law school, the process of questioning potential jurors is called voir dire.

"The purpose of voir dire is to select jurors who are unbiased and to eliminate the ones who may be prejudiced against you. In your case the opposing attorney will try to get jurors who are poor and uneducated, and who may have a bias against rich people like yourself, or some real liberal types, who think that someone who has suffered injury must be compensated by the nearest deep pockets.

"In Tennessee and Knox County a civil jury is made up of twelve jurors. An agreement between the opposing attorneys will decide if a unanimous or an agreed-on majority will determine the outcome of the judgment in the case.

"You can eliminate any potential juror for cause if it is evident from your questioning that he or she may have preconceived ideas that would prevent them from reaching a fair and impartial verdict. In addition you can eliminate four potential jurors by peremptory challenges here in Tennessee. You can use this challenge for any reason. If you just don't happen to like the looks of a juror you can reject him or her by using this peremptory challenge.

"You should treat each juror with respect, especially the ones you dismiss for cause. The court cannot swear in a juror until the jury has been accepted by both sides, or until all challenges have been accepted.

"The court may name one or two alternate jurors in case a regular cannot make it. These jurors will have to be approved by both sides also.

"Each side has the right to conduct a reasonable examination of each juror orally during voir dire. The court will probably determine the order in which each side may examine each juror, or they may let each side take turns going down the jury list until the proper number of jurors have been selected, or a second list of jurors have to be brought in because too many were rejected for cause or by preemptory challenges.

"You may ask each juror his occupation, his habits, his acquaintances, associations to which he belongs, or any other factors or experiences that indicate any bias on his part.

"The following persons can request to be exempt from jury duty if they have received a notice to report for jury duty. They are: attorneys, CPA's,

PA's, physicians and clergy, all acting professors or teachers of any college, school, or institute of learning, and pharmacists.

"The trial will be held in the civil division of the circuit court in the City-County Building.

"Each side will be allowed an opening statement to present their case and to reveal the amount of money being sued for. As soon as you get the jury list it would be a good idea to do a computer check of each one. Make sure that there are no convicted felons on the list or anyone who may belong to organizations that have a tendency to be anti-establishment or anti-business. You know what these organizations are.

"Become familiar with each juror and remember their first names as well as their last, but always call them by their last name preceded by Mr. or Mrs. or whatever the case may be. Discuss with them the case at hand. Explain that you are representing yourself and tell them exactly what the case is about. Tell them the names of witnesses you plan to call and the issues in the case.

"You may ask questions of the entire people on the jury panel and have a response by a show of hands. A good question to ask by this method is: Do any of you know any of the parties to this case or any of the witnesses or either attorney? It would be a good idea to rehearse with someone you know and have him play the part of a juror.

"You may ask a prospective juror how he feels about lawsuits. Are there too many, and are the awards excessive, etc.

"Do not quarrel or try to change a juror's beliefs, just expose any bias or prejudice that you uncover. Explain to the person whom you reject for cause, that it is not a reflection of their integrity, but you don't want to put them in a position where they s might have to vote against their own principles.

"Make eye contact with each juror and watch his facial expressions. Sometimes you can tell more about how a person thinks by his facial expressions than by the words he speaks. Have someone help you and make notes and get their impressions of each juror.

"In your particular case, I would ask each juror if he would make a monetary award to the plaintiff if the trial showed that the defendant was in no way at fault in the accident even though the plaintiff may have suffered debilitating injuries. That's all I have, Brad. Do you have any questions?"

"I may have when I see the jury list, John. How much do I owe you?"

"My rate is $500 per hour, but for you my work is pro bono. I will keep your IOU in my hip pocket in case I need some corporate advice in the future. However, there is one thing."

"What is that?"

"If you ever have a couple of spare seats in your skybox, I'm available."

"How about the Tennessee-Alabama game October 21?"

"That would be great. I'll be bringing my wife, Shirley."

"Good. I've met her before. You can meet us here at my office two hours before the game, and we'll ride over in a limo. I don't know exactly what time the game starts but I know it's an afternoon game. I guess the starting time will depend on the television people."

"See you then, Brad."

"I really appreciate it, John."

"Don't mention it, Brad."

As soon as John left, Brad called Ace and asked him if he could come over around 3:00 p.m.

"I'll be there," said Ace.

Ace showed up on time and asked him what was up.

"I just want to go over a few things before the weekend. First, I want to finalize our witness list. Here's what I have so far."

"First I want to call Mr. Frank Wheeler, who is the local agent for US Auto. Secondly, I want to call Dr. Reed Smith to the stand. He was the ER doctor who treated Martin. Thirdly I want to call Luther himself to testify. He is going to perjure himself when he answers my first question. Fourth I want to call Martin's attending physician at Baptist, Dr. Heinz Mueller, and if Luther does not have Martin testify, I'm going to call him. Can you think of anyone else that we should call?"

"Don't you think you should call the radiologist, Dr. Kennedy?" replied Ace.

"Of course, he completely slipped my mind. If you think of anyone else let me know, we can always revise the list."

"I'll let you know," replied Ace.

"Do you know of anyone who could work for me here in the office until the trial starts?"

"I certainly do. Paula is quitting Spenser Friday, and she could use the work until she finds something permanent."

"I need for her to look up all the people on the jury list and find out everything she can about them. Can she handle that?"

"That would be no problem for her. Can she start Monday?"

"Sure thing. Have her report to my office at 9:00 a.m. and I will have Denise make arrangements for a parking spot in the garage for her."

"I don't think I told you this, Brad, but when I took Martin's picture walking into Spenser's house, I also tried out the movie feature on my cell phone. I didn't want to tell you about it until I was sure that it worked. This morning I transferred the movie to the hard drive on my computer and then transferred it from there to a CD. We now have a ten-second clip of Martin walking real fast."

"That absolutely cinches our case, Ace. Now I want to see Luther disbarred and Martin go to jail. I also believe Luther will end up in there with him."

"Is there anything else, Brad?"

"I can't think of anything else right now, but keep in touch."

"Will do. See you later," said Ace.

Chapter 49

Sunday, September 24

Ace picked up Paula at eleven and backtracked a couple of miles to get to Puleo's Restaurant. They beat the Sunday rush by about an hour. They liked the extensive menu consisting of about half Italian and half old-fashioned southern cooking. They had a very enjoyable meal. They finished their lunch and headed to Buffalo Mountain via Oak Ridge. As they were driving through the Atomic city of Oak Ridge, Ace was reminded of a story he heard about what happened in Oak Ridge back during the forties, when the top-secret Manhattan Project was in full swing. The project was so top secret that most of the congressmen in Washington had no idea what was going on in Oak Ridge, Tennessee. All most of them knew was that a lot of money was being spent there, so a few of them formed a little group, and came down to do some investigation. They were being escorted around to preselected places when they came upon a man working at a lathe. "What are you making?" one of the congressmen asked him. "A dollar and a quarter an hour," he replied.

They continued on to Oliver Springs toward Buffalo Mountain, which was about ten miles north of Oak Ridge. As they were driving across the mountain, Paula remarked, "You know, Ace, I don't believe that there is any place in the country that is as pretty as east Tennessee in the fall. The beautiful red leaves of the maples, and the bright yellow ones of the hickories combined with the evergreens, present a marvelous picture."

"I agree," said Ace. "And the view of the Great Smoky Mountains to the south, and the Cumberlands to the north are just icing on the cake." About that time Ace spotted a sign along the road that read: "Adam's Apples." "I've got to stop here, Paula," he said.

"Why?" Paula asked.

"Because there is a story here, and I want to hear it."

Ace pulled to the stand at the side of the road and noticed many other people had the same idea. Business was booming at Adam's Apples establishment. Ace noticed several baskets of fresh apples and the adjoining orchard of several acres nearby. He also noticed a teenage boy stirring a copper kettle of apple butter sitting over a bunch of burning wood coals. *If you've ever smelled the fragrant aroma of fresh apple butter being made in this fashion you would never forget it,* thought Ace. He also noticed another teenager hand cranking an old-fashioned apple cider mill.

He and Paula walked up to the gentleman who appeared to be in charge and said, "My name is Ace Sleuth, from Knoxville, and this is my girlfriend, Paula Novak." Paula was grinning from ear to ear at these new strange-sounding words.

"Glad to meet you. My name is Henry Adams."

"How's business, Mr. Adams?" asked Ace.

"It's real good now," replied Henry.

"Hasn't it always done this well, Henry?" asked Ace.

"No, it hasn't, but thanks to my wife Ethel, my business has tripled since I changed it to Adam's Apples."

"How did that happen, Henry?"

"Well, it was kind of funny, but one day Ethel looked at me and said that I had a cute Adam's apple. I had never thought of an Adam's apple as being cute, but I said to her: 'That's it.'

"'What's it?' she asked.

"'Adam's Apples will be the new name for our fruit stand.' That was a year ago. I wish we had thought this name up twenty years ago."

"We would like to buy some of your products, Henry."

"Look around and help yourself," he replied. "If you need any help, let me know."

Ace spotted some baskets labeled "select apples," and saw three different kinds. The apples must have weighed a pound each. He and Paula got three each of the golden delicious, red delicious, and winesaps. They also got two quarts of apple butter, a gallon of cider, and two glasses of cold cider along with two hot fried apple pies for dessert. Ace and Paula were both glad that they had made this stop. They got into their car and drove the remaining five miles to Buffalo Mountain.

Both Ace and Paula were shocked at the size of the wind turbines. There are fifteen new ones which are 260 feet tall with 135-foot-long turbine blades, and three older ones which were 213 feet tall and 75-foot turbine blades. "The structures for the large turbines are as tall as the BB&T Bank Building where Brad has his office," said Ace. "I looked all the information up on TVA's web site, Paula. The large wind turbines are rated at 1.8 megawatts at a wind speed of twenty mph, and the three smaller ones are rated at sixty kilowatts each. All of these turbines together generate enough electricity for 3,780 average homes."

"What if the wind speed is fifty mph instead of twenty-five mph?" asked Paula.

"I would imagine that you would get around 3.6 megawatts, or twice as much as the rated power of each the big turbines," replied Ace.

"How do they make the electricity?" asked Paula. "The blades don't seem to be spinning very fast?"

"They make fifteen revolutions every minute," replied Ace.

"Why do they move so slowly?"

"I believe it is to keep the noise the blades make to a minimum. The tips of those blades are moving at a speed of 145 miles per hour, and the faster they rotate, the more noise they make. They don't want them to sound like a helicopter. The electricity is made when the wind blows and turns the turbines, which are connected to a rotating shaft. The shaft in turn spins the generator, which makes the electricity. Just because the blades are rotating slowly doesn't mean that they aren't doing much work. It's the load on the blades due to the amount of electricity the generators are producing that is the important thing. The wind provides all the energy for this power."

"What happens if the wind isn't blowing?" asked Paula.

"Then you get no electricity," replied Ace. "In fact the turbines are only operated when the wind velocity is between ten and fifty-five miles per hour."

"Why is this?"

"Because at winds speeds below ten mph there is not enough force on the blades to generate any significant electricity, and above fifty mph the force is on the blades is too great."

"Why is that a problem?"

"I'm not real sure, but here is what I think. The turbines blades have a tremendous amount of surface area and when the winds get above fifty-five mph, the force on the blades becomes so great, that there would be a danger of toppling over the whole 260-foot structure."

"How does shutting down the turbines help? It looks like there would still be the force on the blades."

"You are absolutely right, Paula. What I think they would do is feather the blades to cut down on the force."

"What is feathering the blades?"

"It's like a propeller-driven airplane. When a multi-engine plane loses an engine the propeller stops turning, and instead of helping the plane along, it is now resisting the air and causing a backward and a sideways force on the plane. If something isn't done about the engine, the plane could crash."

"What do they do?"

"They do a maneuver called feathering the engine. The pilot will turn on a switch which will cause the blades to rotate ninety degrees on their shafts until the leading edge of the prop is facing the direction in which the plane is traveling."

"So you think that's what they do here?"

"Probably, but I imagine that they might be able to rotate the entire assembly without rotating each blade. They may even have a computer that does this automatically. They may even have a computer that automatically adjusts the pitch of the blades to provide optimum power production efficiency at various wind speeds."

"You just lost me there, Ace."

After a most enjoyable day, Ace and Paula drove the forty or so miles to her apartment. Lisa was doing her homework as usual. "Did you two lovebirds have a good time?" she asked.

"We had a wonderful time," replied Paula. "I'm going into the kitchen and make some coffee and see if I can find some dessert; I'm starved."

"Did you find out anything about the list of movies I asked you to look up, Lisa?"

"Yes, but it wasn't easy. Some of those VCR's were deep in the archives, and I had to pay extra to get copies of them."

ACE SLEUTH, PRIVATE EYE

"That's not a problem. Were you able to get them all on VCR tapes?"

"Yes, they're all on VCR's and they will be here tomorrow by FedEx."

"Have you worked the little church problem I left with you?"

"Yes, I did, Ace. That was kind of a sneaky problem, wasn't it?"

"Kind of, I suppose, but it's the kind of a problem that makes you think."

"It did that alright. I tried all the algebra I knew, but I couldn't solve it going that route. Finally I just took a guess at the number of men who didn't attend and plugged it in and came up with a total collection of $500. I then tried a different number of men and also came up with $500 for the collection. I found out that the number of men could be any number."

"You're right. Lisa, because the women always gave five dollars and the men always gave ten dollars, half the men not showing up made the average collection for the one hundred members five dollars each."

"Coffee and cake is now being served," said Paula, as she placed them on the table. "I need to go back in the kitchen and get the cream and sugar."

After they had finished their desserts, Ace gave Paula a big kiss and reminded her to check in with Denise at Brad's office at nine tomorrow morning. "I'll be there to greet you, because I need to go over some things with Brad while I'm there."

Chapter 50

Monday, September 25

Paula showed up at Denise's desk at 9:00 a.m. sharp and Ace was already there. Brad showed up a few minutes later and explained what he wanted Paula to do.

"I have fixed up an office for you down the hall," exclaimed Brad. "You will have your own computer and telephone. I am going to give you a copy of all my notes on my lawsuit case so that you can get up to speed. I want you to know as much about this case as I do. If you need any help getting set up on your computer just get Denise to help you. You will probably want to put in a personal password for your protection. All of our computers are tied together and connected to a printer down the hall next to the copy machine.

"We will be getting a jury list of about twenty-five or thirty people in a week or so and I would like for you to do a computer check and find out all you can about each juror. I want you to know every witness on both mine and Luther's lists and anyone even remotely associated with this case. Go over to the City-County Building and find in which room the trial will be held. I would like to know the seating capacity of the room and see how much standing room is available. I have a feeling that this is going to be a well-attended trial with standing room only once it gets under way.

"I am going to pay you twenty-five dollars per hour for the time period for which you work, which as a minimum, will be until the end of the trial. Is that OK with you, Paula?"

"It certainly is, Mr. Adams," said Paula.

"It's OK for you to call me Brad, Paula. When your work is finished here, I'll try to find you a position with one of the law firms in this building. I just won't have enough work for you after the trial is over. I'll only be working two days a week myself when this thing blows over."

"I understand, Brad, and I really appreciate the work you're giving me now."

"Fine, Paula, just let me know if you need anything at all. Get Denise to get you a parking garage pass."

"I think she's already working on it," said Paula.

"Well, I guess you're ready to go to work, I'll just get out of your hair." Paula left Brad and Ace to themselves.

"How are David and Jennifer getting along?" asked Ace.

"I really think it's serious, Ace, I haven't seen him as excited since before his wife was killed. He has a little spring in his step that I haven't seen in some time. I'm glad that you brought Jennifer along to the game that night. David told me the story about you and Jennifer when she was only five. She thinks a lot of you, Ace. She told David everything you did for her and her mother, evidently at the expense of your own marriage. That's a very touching story, Ace."

"I know that it certainly touched me to see their life changed completely," said Ace.

"David is taking her to the Tennessee-Marshall football game Saturday," said Brad.

"How is our witness list, Brad?"

"I think that now would be a good time to revise it," said Brad.

"Here's the way I think it should be for now:

>Dr. Reed Smith, the ER doctor
>Frank Wheeler, the local insurance agent
>Luther Spenser
>Heinz Mueller, the attending physician at Baptist
>Roger Kennedy, radiologist
>Bret Martin, the plaintiff

"If Luther doesn't put Martin on the stand, I'll call him and cross-examine him myself," said Brad. "Can you think of anyone else we need to call, Ace?"

"No, but I imagine you would like for me to make sure that we have all the electronic equipment available to show our videos and CD's. I'll also bring along all the still pictures I have taken."

"It sounds like we have all the bases covered," said Brad.

"Have you found out who the trial judge is going to be?" asked Ace.

"Yes, it's going to be Judge Elizabeth Robinson, AKA Beno Robinson."

"Why is she known as Beno?"

"Just wait and you'll find out at the trial. By the way, I want you to be at the trial every minute and if either Luther or Martin, or any of Luther's witnesses leave the courtroom for any reason, I want you to follow them, even if they only go to the bathroom."

"I've got you covered, Brad."

"Good. Stay in touch and let me know if either Luther or Martin make any suspicious moves."

"Will do, Brad. See you later."

Chapter 51

Monday, October 2

Brad called Paula into his office and informed her that the jury list had come in. He gave her a copy as follows:

Knox County Circuit Court—Division 2
Panel 1 10/21/2006–10/25/2006

Brenda Callaway, Baptist Hospital
Randolph Carter, Engineer
Sydney Cook, T Dot
Logan Cooper, Knox City Schools
Hubert Conroy, Pilot Oil
Leonard Crawford, Wendys
Brandon Davidson, Retired Professor
Clarence Hadley, UT
Georgette Jones, CAC
Claude Jordan, Construction
Jane Landrum, TVA
Grace Medford, Maid
Melvin Morris, WalMart
Kim Odell, Homemaker
Leroy Owens, Self-Employed
Melissa Pace, City of Knoxville
Vincent Palmer, Retired
Jack Percy, ORNL
Kevin Puckett, Construction

Stephen Riley, UT
Rueben Silver, Self-Employed
Samantha Smith, Homemaker
Mort Smith, UPS
Ellen Somerset Pellissippi, State CC
Katherine Vance, UT Medical Center
Richard Washington, KUB
Buford Williams, Unemployed
Rethal Williams, TN State Welfare
Mary Young, Teacher, Knox Ct.

"Paula, would you take this list and see what you can come up with? I don't expect very much, but whatever edge we get will be to our advantage."

"I'll get right on it, Brad," replied Paula.

Chapter 52

Monday evening, October 2

Around seven Paula got a call from Jennifer.
"Paula, this is Jennifer. I want to apologize to you and Ace for the way I acted at the UT-Air Force game a few weeks back. I was enjoying David's company so much that time just got away from me."
"I understand," said Paula. "Love can do that to you sometimes. It must have been love at first sight."
"I think it really was, Paula. I have never been affected that way before. Another reason I wanted to call you was to tell you what a fine man Ace is. Did he ever tell you how I knew him?"
"Last week he told me that the most satisfactory case he ever had was one of his first. He said he got money from a deadbeat dad for a mother and her five-year-old daughter. The money included two years of arrears and he also got him to make regular payments on time every month. Ace didn't realize that you were the five-year-old girl when he told me though. You must have made quite an impression on him, because he really liked that little five-year-old girl."
"Did he tell you that the only charges he billed us for were his expenses? He worked for free, Paula. You better grab hold of him and never let go."
"I love him, Jennifer, and he just told me that he loves me. We plan to marry after Brad's trial is over."
"I'm so happy for you, Paula."
"Thanks for those kind words, Jennifer. I'll be honest with you, I was jealous of you before we met even though Ace told me that his and your relationship was more like a father-daughter than between the opposite sex. What is your relationship with David?"

"I really think I'm in love with him, Paula, I never thought I would find anyone else after my husband Scott got killed. David and I have so much in common. My husband was killed in Iraq and David's wife was killed by a drunk driver. Neither of us has done any serious dating since our spouse's death. Their deaths were only two months apart. I do believe that David also loves me. Maybe we can have a double wedding. I want Ace to give me away if I get married."

"That would be great, Jennifer. I'm so glad that you've found someone."

"Ace told me that I should meet your daughter, Lisa. They must get along very well."

"They do seem to have a good relationship. They both like math and the sciences. Why don't we all get together the next time David comes into town?"

"He is coming in on October 21 and I am going with him to the Tennessee-Alabama game, but I hope to see him before then. I'll let you know."

Chapter 53

Thursday, October 5

Brad called Paula into his office for a discussion.
"Are you pretty much up to speed on this case, Paula?"
"I think so. I knew pretty much what was going on when I was working the other side of the fence. I have been going over the jury list and everything is pretty much as it seems to be on the list."
"Is there anyone on the list who we may want to question first?"
"I think Richard Washington would be a good one to open up with. He is a thirty-two-year-old African American and is an electrical engineer with KUB, and engineers have traditionally made good jurors. They are very good at sorting out the facts from the rhetoric."
"That sounds like good advice. Is there anything else?"
"Brandon Davidson is a retired sociology professor from a Michigan community college who moved here about five years ago. If he is honest in his answers, I believe you could probably get him dismissed for cause."
"Good. I think I know just the questions to ask him. Are there any other suggestions?"
"Rueben Silver is listed on the list as self-employed. He owns a successful local retail store and Randolph Carter is a mechanical engineer at TVA. I can't be a hundred percent sure, but I believe there are at least seven African Americans on the jury."
"That's good to know because when I OK Richard Washington for the jury, Luther will be afraid to dismiss him without alienating the other African Americans on the list. You've done a good job on the jury list, Paula; just keep digging and let me know if you come up with anything new. That's all I need for now."

"I'll keep you informed, Brad."

As soon as Paula got back to her desk the phone rang. The voice said, "Guess who?"

"President Bush?" replied Paula.

"Close but no cigar. What are your plans for the weekend?

"I have to work at the Copper Cellar Friday night, but I think I can get away Saturday and Sunday. What do you have in mind?"

"I thought we could drive down to Chattanooga and spend the night, go sightseeing Sunday, and then drive back that evening."

"I would love to, but I don't like Lisa staying at home alone all night. I'll see if she can spend the night with a girlfriend. What time do you want to leave?"

"How about nine Saturday morning. We could stop at McDonald's and get some coffee and a breakfast sandwich. By the way, have you ever eaten at the old Union Railroad Station in downtown Chattanooga, I think it's called The Chattanooga Choo- Choo."

"No, but I've heard about it. I've always wanted to eat there."

"Good. We'll eat there Saturday night."

Chapter 54

Saturday, October 7

Ace showed up at Paula's at 900 a.m. on the dot. When he rang the doorbell Lisa came to the door. "How's the lovebird?" she asked.

"Looking forward to a nice weekend," replied Ace. "Did you find someone with whom to spend the night?"

"Yes, I did, but I'm a big girl now, and I see no reason why I couldn't stay here by myself."

"Why don't you just put your studies aside for one night and you and you friend just kick up your heels and have a good time. Stop and smell the roses."

"I may just do that, Ace, and you take good care of my mom."

"I love your mother, Lisa, and we plan to be married after this trial is over."

"I would be honored to have you for a father, Ace."

"And I couldn't ask for a better daughter, Lisa."

About that time, Paula came out of the bedroom with her suitcase and said she was ready to roll. "We'll be back Sunday afternoon, Lisa. Take care."

"I love you, Mom."

"And I love you too."

They both got into the Mustang and drove to the McDonald's on Cedar Bluff Drive where they ordered a couple of breakfast biscuits and coffee to take with them. There was a senior citizen standing in line in front of them who ordered a bacon, egg, and cheese sandwich along with a senior coffee. He paid the young female waitress, and when she handed him his order he looked at her and said, "What's wrong with you? I didn't order this bacon, egg, and cheese sandwich. I ordered a sausage and egg biscuit? Do you just give people what you want them to have?" The young girl, almost to the point of tears, apologized and placed a sausage and egg biscuit on his platter, and the man walked off with both biscuits, while only paying for one.

Paula looked at Ace. "Did you see that?" she asked.

"I certainly did," said Brad, as he turned to the young girl and told her that she had not made a mistake. "That old codger either has Alzheimer's disease, or he just conned you out of a free breakfast biscuit, and I'm betting on the con."

The young girl looked a little relieved, and Paula said, "It takes one to know one."

"You got that right, babe," said Ace.

The drive to Chattanooga normally took about two hours, but Ace decided to stay on I-40 to Kingston and take scenic State Highway 58 west to State Highway 68 east. They were still on I-40 west as they approached Kingston, when Paula noticed a large plant with a lot of smoke stacks located on the bank of the Clinch River, just a few hundred yards from the interstate. "What is that?" she asked. "Do they burn coal here? I see some big coal piles."

"That is TVA's Kingston steam plant and they do burn a lot of coal here, Paula."

"Why aren't they operating the plant right now?"

"They are," said Ace. "Only the two large stacks are in use. They replaced the nine smaller ones which are no longer in use."

"I don't see any smoke."

"That's because they use electrostatic precipitators to remove the particulates, but there are invisible gases coming out that you cannot see. There are some harmful ingredients in these gases that TVA is working on right now to reduce. They are in the process of installing scrubbers to reduce sulfur dioxide (SO_2). This work will be completed by the year 2010 at a cost of $500 million. In addition all nine units are equipped with catalytic combustion systems which will reduce nitric oxide (NO_x) emissions by ninety percent."

"Why are all those fishermen in boats fishing in the same area?"

"That's because the fish like to feed downstream of the plant."

"Why is that?"

"I think they like the warm water that is discharged from the plant."

"Why does the plant discharge warm water?"

"All power plants that generate steam have to use a tremendous amount of water to condense the steam back to water when they have extracted all the energy they can get out of it. They use the same water over and over again."

"Why don't they just use the water from the river to make steam?"

"Because the water used to make steam must be very pure and free from any minerals or mud particles. Only pure distilled water is used and it is very expensive to make, so special care is made to lose as little of this water as possible. A small amount of this pure water is lost due to small leaks and is continuously being replenished. The pure water never comes into contact with the raw water from the river. The river water runs inside thousands of small tubes where the steam is exhausted over the outside of the tubes, and the cooler river water inside the tubes causes the steam to be condensed back to water. It's a continuous cycle."

"How do they get the water from the river?"

"There are huge pumps upstream of the plant. These pumps pump raw river water through the tubes of the large condensers and back into the river downstream. The water picks up about ten degrees of temperature as it passes through the condenser tubes and is discharged back into the river downstream of the plant where you saw all those fishermen."

They then took Highway 58 west and had driven about twenty miles when they came to State Route 68. Ace took a right turn and drove about ten miles where he crossed the Tennessee River. Paula looked up noticed two huge hyperbolic towers a mile or so in the distance.

"What are those?" she asked.

"Those are cooling towers for Watts Bar Nuclear Plant."

"Why is only one of them running?"

"That's because only Unit-1 was ever completed."

"Why wasn't unit-2 completed?"

"TVA ran out of money because Unit-1 cost about twenty times to build as the original cost estimate for both units."

"How much did Unit-1 cost?"

"I think I read somewhere that it cost around $7 billion, or to put it another way, twenty times as much as it cost to build the World Trade Center in New York."

"When are they going to finish Unit-2?"

"I don't know, Paula, but I just read in the paper a couple of days ago, that TVA is looking at spending $2 billion to get Unit-2 in operating condition. It has been sitting there idle for over thirty years."

"Why do they need cooling towers?"

"They don't need them at all. In fact, using the cooling towers causes the nuclear plant to produce less electricity because they make the plant less efficient. TVA was forced to install them. At the time they were told it was to protect the fish from the warm water that is discharged from the plant."

"That doesn't make sense, Ace. I thought the fish loved the warm water back up at Kingston."

"They do. You can even see the fisherman there on the hottest day of summer. I think someone dropped the ball by not informing the fish at Kingston Steam plant that the warm water was harmful to them."

"Does the Watts Bar plant heat up the water a lot more than Kingston does?"

"No, it doesn't heat it up near as much with the cooling towers and it also wouldn't heat it up near as much without them. If Unit-1 didn't have the cooling towers, it would only heat the water less than ten percent as much as the Kingston Steam Plant does."

"Why is that?'

"The nine units at Kingston Steam Plant produce about one and a half times as much electricity, and discharge one and half times as much heat to the Clinch River as Watts Bar-1 discharges into the Tennessee River. All this heat from the Kingston Steam Plant mixes with the water flow in the Clinch River, which has only ten percent of the flow of the Tennessee River at Watts Bar. It's the mixing of the warm water coming out of the plants with the river water that determines the river water temperature. If the river water temperature at Kingston in the Clinch River is raised by five degrees then the water temperature in the Tennessee River at Watts Bar would be raised by less than one half of a degree."

"Are you telling me that we are spending millions of dollars a year to keep from heating up the Tennessee River around one half of a degree?"

"It appears that way, Paula, however, that's only true if you mix the water with the entire river. There could be a few warmer spots. TVA didn't initially design Watts Bar to have cooling towers. They wanted to put in diffusers to mix the warm water going in with more of the river water rather than just dumping into the river in one spot, but this got shot down by the all and knowing. It seems once again that the squeaky wheel got the grease. You can go a couple of miles downstream and the river water temperature is practically back to normal. So what's the big deal anyway?"

"What is the temperature of the water coming from the Watts Bar Unit-1 plant?" asked Paula.

"It all depends. I'm not sure just how the Watts Bar plant works. There are two ways it could operate. One way is to just pump the river water through the condenser tubes and on through the cooling towers and on to the river after the water has been cooled. The second method is to pump the river water through the condenser tubes and then to the cooling towers where it is cooled and falls into a basin at the bottom of the towers. This cooled water in the basin is continuously pumped back through the condenser tubes and is used over and over again. Using this method about one percent of the water is lost in the cooling tower due to evaporation. And using this recirculation method, there is never any of this cooling water going back to the river, and consequently, there would be no elevation of the river water temperature. I'm not sure which method is used at Watt Bar.

"If there were no cooling towers at Watts Bar the river water going through the condenser tubes would pick up about ten degrees. Just how much the river water would be heated up depends on how much of the warmer water mixes with the river flow. If it mixed with the entire river flow it would probably only raise the river temperature less a half of a degree. There is one thing for sure. No portion of the river can be raised more than ten degrees."

"Then why doesn't the Kingston plant have cooling towers?"

"It was built before the days of 'enlightenment,'" said Ace. "Those cooling towers cost tens and tens of millions of dollars each to construct, and the upkeep on them must be tremendous, and to top it all off, the cooling towers use up a lot of electricity to operate, causing the plant to be less efficient."

"It seems stupid to me. Why do we have them?"

"I believe it is a combination of state and federal regulations. I also believe it is purely political a thing and was dreamed up by a bunch of extreme environmentalists, who then convinced the powers that be that it would be a good thing. I have never seen any studies on how the warm water adversely affects the fish, and I doubt that one exists. By the way, Paula, don't tell anyone what I've just told you about the differences between Kingston and the Watts Bar plants."

"Why not?"

"I'm afraid that the all-knowing powers that be will force TVA to install cooling towers at Kingston."

"Why don't the TVA engineers try to do something about it?"

"Engineers are a laid-back bunch. As a rule they just do what they are told and generally don't like to rock the boat, but they know that cooling towers are a waste of money. I heard a joke about two TVA engineers talking and one of them said to the other, 'I have some good news and some bad news. The good news is that terrorists blew up one of the Watts Bar cooling towers.'

"'What is the bad news?' the other one asked.

"'They blew up the Unit-2 tower,' he said.

"Ronald Reagan once said, 'Tear down this wall, Mr. Gorbachev.' We need someone in this country with some clout to say, 'Tear down these cooling towers, Mr. President.'

"Let's get back to the engineers who work in these nuclear plants. They do have their lighter moments," said Ace. "I heard the following firsthand story from an engineer who worked at Watts Bar nuclear plant. An engineering intern from Tennessee Tech came to Watts Bar to work during the summer, and the engineer to whom he had been assigned told him that he was going to take him into the upper portion of the reactor building while the unit was operating. It is completely safe to go into the upper portion of the building while the unit is operating. The young intern asked about the safety aspects of entering the reactor building. 'It's perfectly safe as long as you don't stay in there a long time,' the engineer said. 'Do you see Jack sitting at his desk over there?'

"Jack was a middle-aged engineer who was probably in his mid-fifties and looked ten years older. He appeared to be a drinker who had lived a hard, fast life, and looked as though he hadn't taken care of himself. He had a few splotches of hair that looked like it was hanging on for dear life, and to top it off, he was missing a couple of front teeth.

"'What about Jack?' the intern asked.

"'He spends a tremendous amount of time in the reactor building. It's hard to believe that he is only twenty-nine years old.'"

"That's really funny, Ace."

"Do you know what, Paula?"

"No, what?"

"I just got to thinking about it, and the environmentalists are correct when they say that the warm water harms the fish."

"Ace, you just got through preaching to me about how useless these cooling towers are, and now you do an about face. What's going on here?"

"I just wanted to say that the fish are harmed because more fish are caught and eaten from those warm waters."

"That's very funny, Ace."

Ace turned around on State Highway 68 and headed west to I-75 south to Chattanooga. They arrived in Chattanooga about an hour later. Ace got off I-75 and drove downtown and pulled into the Hotel Courtyard by Marriott where he had made reservations.

They got unpacked, settled in, and discussed what they would do until dinner that evening.

"Do you have anywhere that you would like to go, Paula?"

"I've heard a lot about the aquarium," she replied, "but I've never been there."

"Then let's go there," said Ace. "After that how would you like to ride the incline to the top of Lookout Mountain?"

"I would like that very much. I remember doing that when I was a child and I really enjoyed it."

"Good. Let me know when you are ready to go," said Ace.

They had a very enjoyable afternoon seeing the aquarium and riding the incline, after which time they went back to their hotel and rested until 7:00 p.m. They then walked the short distance to the Union Station Restaurant. They were settled in at their good window seat when their waiter showed up. He said, "My name is Mark, and I will be your waiter."

"I am Paula and this is Ace, and we will be your customers," Paula said, "and by the way, today is my boyfriend, Ace's, birthday."

For the first time in his life, Ace was speechless.

"It's payback time," said Paula.

"I guess now we're even," replied Ace. "What would you like to eat?"

"I think I would like the six-ounce filet mignon with a glass of champagne," replied Paula. "What are you having?"

"I think I'll have the twelve-ounce T-bone with a Caesar salad and a glass of Reunite."

After they had eaten the main course it seemed to Ace like the entire restaurant staff came marching out of the kitchen clapping their hands and singing happy birthday. For the first time in his life, Ace felt embarrassed.

After dinner they walked back to the hotel and spent the night.

Chapter 55

Sunday, October 8

They both got up around eight-thirty and went down to the lobby and had the buffet breakfast. Paula looked over the table at Ace and said, "I love you, you big hunk. You have made my life complete."

"I love you too, Paula. Did you know that I have never seriously dated anyone but you since my wife walked out on me? I was heartbroken at the time, but now I'm glad it happened. Do you have anything in particular that you would like to do today, Paula?"

"I'm open to suggestions," she said. "Is there anyplace that you would like to go?"

"Yes, there is. You must think that I'm nuts because of some of the places I have taken you, but I have a fascination for all types of electrical power generators. There is one of these facilities a twenty-minute drive away, that is very unique, and many people thought TVA was crazy to spend all that money building it."

"What is it?" asked Paula.

"It's called Raccoon Mountain, and it is a pumped storage generating unit."

"What's so unique about it?" asked Paula.

"Why don't we just drive down there and I'll show you what it looks like," said Ace.

They arrived at the plant thirty minutes later and Ace began explaining the operation of the facility to Paula.

"TVA built this huge reservoir atop Raccoon Mountain that has 528 acres of water surface. This reservoir is about a thousand feet above the much larger Nickajack Reservoir which is at the base of the mountain. It holds a lot of water, which when released through a tunnel and piping, drops 990 feet to underground turbines that can operate for twenty-two straight hours while generating 1,600 megawatts of electricity. That's almost 900 times as much as one of the large wind turbines we saw at Buffalo Mountain."

"Where does the water come from that's in the reservoir on top of the mountain?" asked Paula.

"The same turbines that run the generators are reversed to act as pump motors to pump water from the Nickajack Reservoir back up to the reservoir on top of the mountain."

"What powers the turbine motors?" asked Paula.

"Electricity provides the power," replied Ace.

"Let me get this straight," said Paula. "The water falls down from the top of the mountain and turns the turbines that drive the generators that make electricity. What happens to the water after it goes through the turbines?"

"It flows back into Nickajack Reservoir," replied Ace.

"So after the turbines use the water pressure to make electricity, then the electricity is used to pump the water back up on top of the mountain. Isn't something lost in the process?"

"Yes, there is. The turbines acting as pumps are only about eighty-five percent efficient, so there is lost power. The generators are not one hundred percent efficient either."

"No wonder a lot of people thought TVA was crazy," said Paula. "It looks like they are going around in circles."

"There is a method in their madness," replied Ace. "At times of peak power loads, TVA has to either buy expensive power from other utilities or run their gas turbines to generate it. These turbines are very expensive to operate. What they do is pump up the water to the top of the mountain when power demand is down quite a bit, such as after midnight or when they have lots of electricity available. Then in the peak demand times they can generate 1,600 more megawatts of power instantly. That's fifty percent more power than one of TVA's giant nuclear plants."

"But aren't nuclear plants unsafe?"

"That seems to be the general consensus around the country, but that's not the case at all. In fact, nuclear power is safer overall than coal-burning power plants when you consider the miners killed and the others who die from black lung disease. Did you know that a coal-burning power plant emits more radiation to the atmosphere that a nuclear plant does?"

"How is that possible, Ace?"

"For all practical purposes, a nuclear plant emits no radiation at all, but a small insignificant amount occurs naturally in coal which is released to the atmosphere when the coal is burned. I have done quite a bit of research on operating nuclear plants and I cannot find a single case of anyone being injured or killed from radioactivity in an operating nuclear plant in this country, and many of them have been operating for over fifty years. It seems to me that the people who speak out against nuclear power are much less informed than those who understand it."

"Why then do I see all this negative reporting in the newspapers and on television portraying nuclear power as unsafe?"

"I believe it's partly politics and partly the ignorance of the general public. No one seems to want to take the time to investigate things to find the truth. It also seems to me that the news media takes great pleasure in reporting anything negative about nuclear power. A while back I saw an article in the local paper that had a heading that read: 'Two men killed in nuclear accident in Japan.' When I read the article I found out that the two men were killed in a nuclear plant, but it was in the non-nuclear part of the plant. In my opinion this is irresponsible reporting, but I don't blame the local newspaper, they just picked it up from the Associated Press or one of the other news suppliers."

"Why do you think the news media does this?" asked Paula.

"I think it's a mind-set against nuclear power. It seems to me to be an abnormal fear, a paranoia that has existed ever since we dropped the first atomic bomb. I once had a golfing friend who had an abnormal fear."

"What was his fear?" asked Paula.

"He said that he had a deadly fear of hitting the golf ball over the green."

"What's so abnormal about that?"

"He said that he had never hit a golf ball over a green in his life."

"That's funny, Ace."

"Let me tell you what happened near Watts Bar Nuclear Plant just a few weeks ago," said Ace. "TVA announced that they thought that they had detected a small leak in the reactor coolant system and dutifully notified the proper authorities as required by federal regulations. It turned out to be a false alarm, because there never was a leak. In the meanwhile one of the local surrounding counties made the decision to close all their schools. I really don't know what they were thinking, but I am sure that a lot of the students were much closer to the nuclear plant went they went home. This type of knee-jerk reaction is a result of ignorance on the part of the school officials, but I blame the anti-nukes in this country and the news media for printing all the garbage that these groups send to them. Even if there had been a reactor coolant leak at the plant, there would have been no danger to anyone standing right outside or leaning up against the reactor building. The reactor building is a cylindrical concrete building with three-foot-thick walls. Just a few feet inside the reactor building is the containment vessel. This vessel is also cylindrical and is constructed of one-inch-thick steel. There is no way that any radioactivity could have made it out through these two barriers. We need to better educate the public on nuclear power, because they will never understand it by reading the newspapers or by watching TV.

"I believe that some of these people who oppose nuclear power actually expect one of the nuclear plants to go off like an atomic bomb, however, this is impossible. I read a story several years ago about a Dr. Ramussen who was a nuclear expert at MIT, and who was also a proponent of nuclear power. The article stated that Dr. Rasmussen was being interviewed by some reporters who asked him how many people would be killed during a nuclear plant accident. He said that maybe two or three people would be killed. This answer didn't satisfy the reporters. 'We're talking about the big one,' they said.

"'What big one?' he asked.

"'The one where thousands and thousands would be killed, what are the odds of that?' they asked.

"'Let me see,' he said. 'Suppose that one Sunday afternoon in New York, two fully loaded 747's are flying over the city and they collide with each other and fall to the earth. One of them falls into Yankee Stadium which is filled to capacity, and the other one falls into Shea Stadium in Flushing Meadows, which is also filled to capacity. Many thousands of people would be killed. The odds of a nuclear plant accident killing this many people would have about the same odds as the accident I just described.'

"If we had never dropped that first atomic bomb and had discovered nuclear power as a way to generate electricity with zero pollution, everyone would be extolling its virtues," said Ace. "Did you know that more than 800 people in this country are killed by electricity every year, and it doesn't matter whether the electricity was generated by fossil or nuclear fuel? I can guarantee you that if only one person was killed in a nuclear plant by radioactivity in this country that it would be on the front page of every major newspaper and there would be great pressure to shut down all nuclear plants, yet you seldom see anything in the papers about any of the 800 people killed by electricity. I think there is paranoia among the press and nuclear power. It's sort of like waving a red flag in front of a bull.

"Did you know that the nuclear reactors only have to be refueled once a year and only one third of the fuel is replaced? The other two thirds is just moved around in the reactor core? One pound of uranium fuel provides a million times as much energy as a pound of coal does."

"Are we building any new nuclear plants now?"

"No. It has become too expensive because of all the unnecessary restrictions put on the industry by environmental agencies and the Nuclear Regulatory Commission (NRC), however; TVA is spending almost $2 billion to get Browns Ferry unit one back on line. That unit will add around 1,200 megawatts to the TVA system."

"Why would these agencies impose unnecessary regulations?" asked Paula.

"I think NRC wants to build nuclear plants that are one hundred percent safe, which is impossible," said Ace, "and I think it's because of political pressure and the negative reaction to anything nuclear around the country. In my opinion, this country will eventually go to nuclear power, but I'm afraid we're going to see electrical shortages before the public wakes up to the truth."

"That makes sense to me now about how the pumped storage works, and I now understand a lot more about nuclear power. Can we go down into the power station and see that part?"

"Not anymore, not since 9/11. People used to be allowed to ride the elevator down the 1,000 feet to where the turbines are located, but for now we will have to be content to just see all that in the brochures that have been provided us here in the visitor's center."

"Did you ever go down in the elevator, Ace?"

"Yes, I did back when it was first opened," replied Ace.

"Nine-eleven has created a lot of problems hasn't it, Ace?"

"Yes, it has, Paula. There are a lot of people in this evil world who would dance in the streets if all Americans were blown to kingdom come."

Ace and Paula had already checked out of their hotel, so after a most enjoyable weekend, they drove back to Knoxville.

When they got to Paula's apartment, Ace followed her in to make sure she was safe and found Lisa studying in the living room.

"How did you two lovebirds make out?" she asked.

"I'm not sure I like your choice of words," laughed Paula.

"We had a great time," said Ace. "How's your homework coming along?"

"I am just about finished up, Ace. Do you have any more brain teasers for me?"

"I have just one. It may seem impossible, but it's really quite simple when you examine it thoroughly."

"Shoot."

"If you drill a hole through the center of a sphere and the remaining volume of the sphere is 113.07933 cubic inches, what would be the length of the hole and the size of the sphere?"

"Are you kidding me, Ace? That seems impossible to solve."

"You can do it. I have faith in you."

"I think you have more faith in me than I have in myself."

"Do it. You'll feel good when you do. I guess I had better be going, Paula. Thanks for a wonderful weekend. I'll see you in the office in the morning."

Chapter 56

Friday, October 20

Brad called everyone in his office to go over all the details before the trial coming up Monday the twenty-third.

"It looks like Luther is only going to be calling two witnesses. He has Dr. Reed smith, the ER physician, and a Dr. Felix Upshaw, who I suppose, is his expert witness on back injuries. He does not have Martin on his list. Do you know if this so-called expert witness has arrived in town yet, Ace?"

"If he has, he has made no contact with Spenser. I've been sticking to him like flypaper," replied Ace.

"Just keep on tracking him and let me know the minute that Upshaw shows his face. Has Martin been out of Luther's house since he left Baptist?"

"No, I'm pretty sure he hasn't. Luther has seen to that."

"Has any medicine or a hospital bed been delivered to Luther's house?"

"No, definitely not."

"Do you think that Martin is taking any pain medication?"

"No, I'm sure he isn't. He didn't take any pills with him when he left the hospital, and Dr. Mueller didn't prescribe any for him when he was discharged."

"Is there anything else we need to go over before Monday's trial? Paula and I have got the jury list in pretty good shape and I have turned in our witness list to the court. If there's nothing else, let's all meet back here at 8:00 a.m. Monday and we'll all walk the block to the City-County Building."

After they had all left, Brad got on the phone and called the editor's office of the *Knoxville News Sentinel*. The editor's secretary answered.

"This is Brad Adams. There is going to be a civil lawsuit, *Martin versus Adams*, starting Monday at 9:00 a.m. on October 23 in Knox County Circuit Court—Division 2. It would be worth your while to have a reporter cover it."

"Won't the first day just be the jury selection?" the secretary asked. "We don't normally cover that portion of the trial."

"The jury selection portion might well be the most important part of this trial," replied Brad.

"I'll pass your information along to the editor," she said.

"Thank you," said Brad, as he hung up. *It looks like the trial is finally here,* thought Brad.

Chapter 57

Monday, October 23
Day one of the trial

Brad met with Ace and Paula for coffee and doughnuts and to check last-minute updates.

"I have one tidbit of information," said Ace. "Dr. Upshaw arrived in style in our fair city last night around 9:00 p.m.. Spenser picked him up at the Greyhound bus station and took him to his house where he spent the night."

"It sounds like a cozy arrangement with the lawyer, the victim, and the expert witness, all under the same roof," said Brad.

"It should make it very convenient for the good doctor to perform his examination of Martin," replied Ace.

"If he performs one at all," said Brad.

The three of them left the office and walked the block to the City-County Courtroom. The first thing Brad noticed was that the *News Sentinel* had sent a reporter.

It would be about twenty minutes before the trial got underway so Brad decided to have a talk with Luther about the jury arrangement.

"How's it going, Luther? I haven't seen much of you since college."

"It's going pretty good, Brad. I'm sorry about this lawsuit thing, but my client has been badly injured through no fault of his own, and he deserves restitution."

"I wouldn't worry about that, Luther. I can assure you that Martin will get everything he deserves. What I wanted to talk to you about is the voting of the jury. It is up to you and me to agree on the kind of majority vote we want. Do we want a unanimous, a simple majority, or somewhere in between for the jury to arrive at a decision?"

"What would you like to do, Brad?"

"I naturally would like to see it unanimous, but I would settle for eleven-one. What do you want?"

"I was thinking more along the lines of nine-three," said Luther.

"I'll settle for a ten-two break, Luther," said Brad. "If we can't agree the judge will automatically set it twelve-zero." Brad had no idea what he was talking about but he knew Luther didn't either.

"Since you put it that way, I'll go along with the ten-two," said Luther.

It was now time for the trial to begin. Brad heard this deep authoritative male voice of the bailiff instructing everyone to take their seats and be quiet. After everyone had settled down he announced: "Hear ye, hear ye, the Knox County Circuit Court—Division 2 is now in session, the honorable Judge Elizabeth Robinson presiding." She was a rather good-looking woman who had just turned forty-seven. Brad thought she was very attractive with her brunette shoulder-length hair and full lips, but he also knew that she could be one tough cookie.

"Good morning, ladies and gentlemen," said the judge. "This is a court of law and we will all conduct ourselves accordingly. I have some ground rules that I will now go over:

    1. There will **be no** talking by the spectators in my courtroom.
    2. There will **be no** magazines, newspapers or books.
    3. There will **be no** cell phones.
    4. There will **be no** radios, including the one with headphones.
    5. There will **be no** sleeping.
    6. There will **be no** getting up and moving around or leaving. If you leave my courtroom, you will not be allowed back in.
    7. There will **be no** distractions or unusual clothing, such as low-cut dresses, in my courtroom.
    8. There will **be no** outbursts, laughter, or applause.
    9. You will remain seated at all times unless instructed to do otherwise.
    10. There will **be no** food or drinks in my courtroom.
    11. Finally, there will **be no** gum chewing in this room.

ACE SLEUTH, PRIVATE EYE

Ace was taking all this in and he now understood why the judge was known as "Judge Beno."

"It is now time to select the jury from our pool of thirty or so," said the Judge. "Have the two attorneys arrived at a decision on how the jury voting will proceed?"

"Yes, we have, Your Honor," said Brad. "we have decided on a ten-two vote to arrive at a decision."

"It is so recorded. Is there anyone here on the jury list who feels that they would be unable to serve on this jury?"

An elderly gentleman held up his hand.

"What is your name, sir?"

"Vincent Palmer, Your Honor."

"What is your reason for you not being able to serve, Mr. Palmer?"

"I have a hearing problem, Your Honor."

"Very well, you're excused, Mr. Palmer."

He cupped his hand to his ear and said, "How's that, Your Honor?" (There was laughter in the courtroom.)

The judge replied in a loud voice, "I said that you were excused, Mr. Palmer."

"Thank you, Your Honor," he said, as he left the courtroom.

"Is there anyone else who cannot serve? If not, we will begin with the jury selection. Why don't you go first, Mr. Adams?"

"I would like to question Mr. Richard Washington first," said Brad. "Good morning, Mr. Washington, how are you today?"

"I'm fine, sir." Brad noticed that Richard was a good-looking young African American man who bore a slight resemblance to Denzel Washington.

"Good, I only have a few short questions for you. It says on my jury list that you work at KUB. In what capacity do you work there?"

"I'm an electrical engineer, sir."

"Where did you get your degree?"

"From the University of Tennessee, sir."

"Do you belong to any type of organization, Mr. Washington?"

"Yes, I belong to ASEE."

"Just what is that, Mr. Washington?"

"It's the American Society of Electrical Engineers, sir."

"Thank you very much, Mr. Washington. This juror is acceptable to me, Your Honor," said Brad.

"Do you have any problem with this juror, Mr. Spenser?"

"No, Your Honor," said Spenser. (Brad knew that if Luther had kicked Washington off the jury that he would have alienated everyone of the other six African Americans on the list).

"Very well, we now have one juror and only eleven to go," said the judge. "It's your turn, Mr. Spenser."

"I would like to question Mr. Sidney Cook, Your Honor."

"Mr. Cook, it says here that you work for TDOT. Would you mind telling the court what TDOT is?" asked Spenser.

"It's the Tennessee Department of Transportation."

"What do you do there?"

"I am a mechanic and I am responsible for keeping all the vehicles in good running condition."

"Have you ever served on a jury before, Mr. Cook?"

"No, sir."

"Do you think that a man who has been injured for life through no fault of his own should be compensated?"

"Yes, I do."

"This juror is acceptable to me, Your Honor."

"Is this juror acceptable to you, Mr. Adams?" asked the judge.

"I would first like to ask him a few questions, Your Honor," said Brad. "Have you read anything in the newspapers about this case, Mr. Cook?"

"Yes, I have."

"Do you know the amount of money being asked for in this case?"

"Yes, sir, the amount is $3 million."

"That's a lot of money, Mr. Cook. Do you know how much a million dollars is?"

"Yes, sir."

"Do you know how many thousand-dollar bills it would take to make a million dollars?"

"Yes, sir."

"This juror is acceptable to me, Your Honor," said Brad.

"It's your turn again, Mr. Adams," said the judge.

"I would like to question Mr. Brandon Davidson, Your Honor."

"Mr. Davidson. It says here that you are a retired professor, what subjects did you teach, and where?"

"I was a sociology professor at a community college in Michigan."

"Let me ask you a hypothetical question, Mr. Davidson. Suppose a man was driving down I-40 west one evening just after dusk and another man had just pulled over to the side of the road because one of his tires had blown out. He decided to put on the spare tire himself and took the spare out of the trunk. As he turned, he was not paying attention, and walked into the side of a car that was going within the speed limit. He was knocked about ten feet into the ditch and as a result of his injuries he was paralyzed for life. The man driving the car stopped as soon as he could and dialed 911. He then walked back to see if he could be of any help. My question to you is this. Do you think the man who was injured deserves compensation?"

"Of course he does, he will never walk again."

"And who do you think should pay this compensation?"

"The driver of the car that hit him or his insurance company should."

"Let's take this hypothetical case one step further. Suppose the man's insurance company refused to pay because the driver wasn't at fault, and the injured man hires a lawyer and sues the driver and his insurance company. Now suppose the jury awards the injured man $5 million. Does that sound about right to you considering the extent of his injuries?"

"Yes, that sounds fair to me."

"Now further suppose that the man being sued only has a $500,000 policy, and he is left owing $4,500,000 through no fault of his own."

"The driver should have had more car insurance," he said.

"Do you drive, Mr. Davidson?"

"Yes, I do."

"How much car insurance do you have?"

"I object," shouted Spenser.

"Overruled," said the judge. "Answer the question, Mr. Davidson."

"I don't know exactly," replied Davidson.

"I have one more hypothetical question for you, Mr. Davidson. Suppose that you were the driver of the car that the man ran into?"

"That would be most unfortunate."

"I appreciate your honesty, Mr. Davidson, and your compassion for the victim, but I don't believe the court system was designed to provide compensation for a victim at the expense an innocent man. The innocent man would then become the victim. I reject this juror for cause, Your Honor," said Brad.

"The juror is excused. You may leave, Mr. Davidson. You're up now, Mr. Spenser."

"I call Mr. Buford Williams," said Luther. "Mr. Williams, it says here that you are unemployed, is that correct?"

"Yes."

"I'm sure a man of your caliber will be able to find a suitable job. Let me ask you one more question. It's the same question I just asked Mr. Cook. Do you believe that a person who has been injured in an accident through no fault of his own, and will probably be in a wheelchair for life, should be compensated for those injuries?"

"Yes."

"This juror is acceptable to me, Your Honor," said Spenser.

"Do you have any questions of this juror, Mr. Adams?"

"Yes, I do, Your Honor. I am going to ask you a similar question to the one Mr. Spenser just asked you, Mr. Cook. Do you think a person driving a car and is abiding by all the rules of the road, and a man runs out in front of him and is injured, should be compensated when the driver was in no way at fault?"

"I think somebody should compensate him."

"Let me ask you another question. Do you believe that people should be responsible for their own actions?"

"In most cases I do, but there are always exceptions to be made."

"Suppose someone is struck by lightning. Who is supposed to compensate him? Is it the person who owns the property he was standing on?"

"That's not a very likely case."

"Very well, Mr. Williams. I see a lot of fast-food restaurants with posted signs for workers. Have you applied for work at any of these places?"

"I ain't gonna flip no burgers, man."

"Flipping burgers is an honorable profession, Mr. Williams. A lot of people have put themselves through college flipping burgers.

"I am going to ask you the same question I just asked Mr. Cook. Do you know how much a million dollars is?"

"I just know that it's a lot of money."

"Do you know how many thousand-dollar bills it would take to make a million dollars?"

"I have no idea."

"I would like to dismiss this juror for cause, Your Honor," said Brad.

"Explain your reasoning, Mr. Adams," said the judge.

"Your Honor, if a juror is going to decide how many million dollars to award a plaintiff, he or she should at least have some idea of what's being awarded. If he is going to be handing out thousand-dollar bills, I would like for him to know where to stop when he gets to a million."

"I agree. This man is dismissed for cause," said the judge.

"Your Honor, I'm going to be asking every juror that very same question I just asked Mr. Williams. In order to save the court's precious time, I would like to get a show of hands to answer yes or no to that question."

"I'll allow it," she said.

"Thanks, Your Honor. I would like for every juror who has not already been accepted to answer this question: If you know how much a million dollars is in thousand-dollar bills, raise your hands." Fourteen hands went up.

"The ones of you who did not raise their hand are dismissed and may leave the court room," said Judge Robinson.

Twelve of the jurors got up and walked out of the courtroom but the newspaper reporter beat them all out. He had a deadline to meet.

Brad and Spenser spent most of the morning and were able to able to come up with ten more jurors from the fourteen remaining plus two alternates. Brad had to use only two of his four allowed peremptory challenges, and the jury now looked like this:

1. Brenda Callaway
2. Randolph Carter
3. Sydney Cook
4. Logan Cooper
5. Jane Landrum

6. Melvin Morris
7. Kim Odell
8. Kevin Puckett
9. Jack Perry
10. Rueben Silver
11. Samantha Smith
12. Richard Washington

"We now have a jury," said a relieved judge. "We will now swear them in. Let's take a lunch break and meet back here at 1:00 p.m."

After lunch when the jurors were all sworn in, Judge Robinson made her charge to the jury panel.

"I believe that we have empanelled a very enlightened and fair-minded jury. I want each of you to take this task very seriously. We probably won't get into the meat of the trial until tomorrow, but I would like for all of you to bring a note pad and pen with you then. It is very important to take notes because there will probably be too much testimony to recall once you get into the jury room. The trial could go on for days. In civil cases such as this, reasonable doubt is not required to arrive at a decision. What is required is what the preponderance of the evidence shows. In other words, if the majority of the evidence favors one side or the other, then you should vote accordingly. The two attorneys have both agreed that a ten-two jury vote which will be required for a decision. A unanimous vote is not required for civil cases as it is in criminal cases. I want each juror to vote with his brain and not his heart. Look at all the facts and separate the facts from the rhetoric. If you find that damages have occurred, I want you make awards that are consistent with the damages.

"The first thing I want you to do when you get to the jury room is to elect a foreman. As soon as you do this, I would like to be informed as to your selection. If you have any questions at all during the trial, feel free to ask them. Also, if you cannot agree on a verdict, let me know. Are there any questions? If not, we will now hear opening statements from the attorneys. You may go first, Mr. Spenser."

"Thank you, Your Honor. My client, Mr. Bret Martin, through no fault of his own, was struck by Mr. Brad Adams' car in the parking garage beneath the BB&T Bank Building on September 5, 2006, where Mr.

Adams works. Mr. Adams was driving in a reckless manner when he ran into my client, throwing him to the concrete floor and causing permanent and painful injuries. He will probably never walk again. I have an expert witness who has examined Mr. Martin and he will testify to this. Thank you, Your Honor."

"It's your turn, Mr. Adams."

"Thank you, Your Honor. Let me say first, in case some of you may not know, I am acting as my own attorney. You have probably heard the old adage that a lawyer who acts as his own attorney has a fool for a client." There was a small outburst of laughter in the courtroom.

"Order in the court," said the judge. "Continue, Mr. Adams."

"Thank you, Your Honor. I would like to tell my side of the story. At 9:00 a.m. on September 5, 2006, I was pulling into the parking garage beneath the BB&T Bank Building where I work, like I have done almost every working day for the last twenty years. I was driving no more than ten miles per hour when this figure came out of the shadows and jumped into my windshield. It seemed to me like the whole thing was planned to extort money out of me."

"Objection, Your Honor," screamed Luther.

"Overruled. Mr. Adams can state what his thoughts were at the time. The facts in the case will come out in the course of the trial. Continue, Mr. Adams."

"Thank you, Your Honor. I just want to say that I intend to prove to the jury that my suspicions were correct. I will be calling several witnesses to verify to that. That is all I have, Your Honor."

"I want to thank everyone for the orderly fashion in which this trial has proceeded," said the judge. "I am going to adjourn for the day. We will all meet back here at nine in the morning. Court is adjourned."

After the court broke up Brad, Ace, and Paula met in a brief huddle in the hallway.

"How do you think it went?" Brad asked.

"I think we probably have one of the most intelligent juries that has ever been empanelled in a civil case," replied Ace.

"I agree," said Brad. "Can either of you think of anything we need to do before tomorrow morning?"

"I'm sort of curious as to how they are going to handle Martin," said Ace. "Although Spenser does not have him on his witness list, he will still have to bring him in because he is on your witness list."

"That's true," said Brad. "I don't think you need to stake out Luther's house. We'll see Martin when they roll him in. Let's all meet at my office at eight in the morning for coffee and doughnuts." Brad left to go back to the parking garage to get his car.

"We'll see you there," said Paula and Ace.

Chapter 58

Monday evening, October 23

"What are you doing this evening, Ace?" asked Paula.

"What do you have in mind, big girl?"

"I thought I might throw a couple of pizzas in the oven. Are you game?"

"Count me in," said Ace. "Let's walk back to the garage and get our cars and I'll follow you home." It was about 5:00 p.m. when they got into their cars and drove the nine miles to Paula's.

Lisa was there as usual doing her homework when they walked in.

"I'll go put the pizzas in the oven," said Paula.

"That was a bear of a math problem you gave me, Ace," said Lisa.

"Did you solve it?" he asked.

"Yes, but I thought I never would. Let me make sure I understand the problem. You wanted to know the length of hole drilled through the center of a sphere, and also the size of the sphere, if the volume of the remaining material in the sphere was 113.09733 cubic inches?"

"That is correct, what is your answer?"

"The length of the hole is six inches, and the size of the sphere is any sphere larger than six inches in diameter."

"You are exactly right, Lisa, but wasn't it real simple to solve?"

"It was real simple to solve once I had enough gumption to look up the formula in a book of tables. If X is the length of the hole, the remaining volume is equal to pi (3.1416) times X^2. I knew the remaining volume so all I had to do was solve for X. That took all of five seconds. It doesn't matter what the size of the sphere in which the hole is bored, the remaining volume is the same for all spheres having a diameter larger than six inches. It can even be as large as the sun."

"I'll give you an A+ for that, Lisa."

"Thanks a lot, big spender."

Paula announced that the pizzas were ready. She had also prepared a salad to go along with the pizza. When they were through eating, Lisa excused herself and retired to her room.

"Would you like to watch some TV?" asked Paula.

"Yes, I would. Do you have a TV guide?"

"I think there's one on the coffee table under those magazines," said Paula.

Ace picked it up and saw that *Monk* was on the USA cable channel. "Would you like to watch *Monk* with me, Paula? We are both private detectives you know, and *Monk* is my favorite TV show."

"I have never seen it before, but I'm game." At the first intermission, Paula said, "I feel sorry for Monk. He can't help being the way he is."

"You're right, Paula. He knows he's a mess but there's nothing he can do about it. He has OCD, an obsessive compulsive disorder, a multi-faceted one of the worst kind."

After watching TV, Ace said goodnight and told Paula that he would see her at eight in the morning in the office.

Chapter 59

Tuesday morning, October 24
Day two of the trial

Ace and Paula met with Brad in his office at eight as planned. Lisa brought out some hot coffee, doughnuts, and bagels with cream cheese.

"Have either of you seen this morning's *News Sentinel*?" asked Brad.

They both shook their heads in the negative. Brad picked up the paper from his desk and told them to look at the front page.

The headline read:

> **Startling Development in the *Martin versus Adams* Trial**
>
> History may have been made in the Knox County Civil Court yesterday in the civil suit where Bret Martin is suing local attorney Bradford Adams for injuries he alleges he received in the parking garage in the building where Adams works when he was struck by his car. Adams acting as his own attorney rejected several prospective jurors because they didn't know how much money a million dollars consisted of in thousand-dollar bills. He explained to the judge (Elizabeth Robinson) that if a juror didn't know how much a million dollars was, then how could he or she possibly make a sound judgment in arriving at a decision in making a monetary award?
>
> Adams asked one of the jurors if he knew how many thousand-dollar bills it took to make a million and when

he answered negatively, he was dismissed for cause. He then announced that he intended to ask that same question of the entire jury panel. He didn't do it quite that way however, probably to keep from embarrassing the ones who didn't know the answer, instead he had everyone who did know to raise their hands. Fourteen hands went up, which meant that there were twelve people from the jury panel who didn't raise their hands, and they were dismissed for cause. These were in addition to two others that Adams had already dismissed earlier for the same reason.

Several Knoxvillians were asked for their comments regarding this case and most of them thought that future tort cases could be drastically affected by this tactic. The tort lawyers we contacted either had no comment, or they thought the mass dismissal was unconstitutional.

"If this procedure is not overturned by the higher courts, the whole tort system in this country could be in jeopardy," they said.

"What do you think that all means?" Ace asked Brad.

"I'm not sure, but we've opened up a whole can of worms. My phone has been ringing off the hook. I told Denise that I can't accept any more phone calls until the trial is over. I understand that all the major news media are coming to Knoxville to cover the trial, ABC, CBS, NBC, CNN, Fox News, and a new cable news channel, Cable News Today (CNT), and Court TV to name a few. I called Judge Robinson a little while ago and advised her of the situation. She's going to have her hands full trying to find seats for everyone."

"I think we had better get on over to the courtroom and make sure we get a seat," joked Brad. "I want you to sit at the table with me, Paula. Ace, I would like for you to get a seat in the very last row in case you need to get up and follow someone. I'll make sure a seat is reserved for you."

Chapter 60

When the three of them arrived at the courtroom around 8:00 a.m., there were so many people lined up that Brad knew that there were not enough seats for everyone. There were several reporters and cameramen there, all of them trying to get Brad to comment on the case.

"I will be glad to talk to you when this trial is over, but it would be inappropriate to do so now," said Brad. Brad knew that there were going to be some disappointed reporters when they found out that Judge Robinson was not going to allow cameras in her courtroom.

The doors to the courtroom were still locked when Brad's crew got there. About ten minutes till nine a court attendant came out and counted the first sixty people in line and let them go in along with the attorneys and their aides. The witnesses would have to wait in the hall until they were called.

The court bailiff announced that ten reporters could sit in the back of the courtroom in chairs that had been added. He picked the ten whom he thought were there first in line and let them go in. He then informed them that no cell phones or cameras were allowed.

At 9:00 a.m. on the dot, Judge Robinson walked in and sat down. The court was called to order. At about that time a couple of men in white coats came through the double doors pushing Bret Martin in a hospital bed. They pushed him up to the front of the court right in front of the judge.

"What's going on here?" demanded Brad. "This is nothing more than a theatrical attempt to garner sympathy from the jury. If he really needs to be here, can't we just roll him over in a corner somewhere, Your Honor?"

"Mr. Martin is the plaintiff in this case, Mr. Adams, and he has every right to be here, but I agree that that place is not right in front of me. Mr. Spenser, get your client moved to the back of the room where the jury won't be distracted by him."

"Yes, Your Honor," replied Spenser.

"Now that we have all settled down, you may call your first witness, Mr. Spenser."

"I call Dr. Reed Smith to the stand, Your Honor."

"Please take the stand, Dr. Smith," said the judge.

After he was sworn in, Spenser began his questioning.

"Good morning, Dr. Smith. I will be as brief as possible," said Spenser. "Were you the emergency room doctor the morning that Mr. Martin was brought to the Baptist ER?"

"Yes, I was."

"What was Martin's condition?"

"He was conscious and said he had been hit by a car."

"Was he in a lot of pain?"

"I don't know."

"You don't know! You're a doctor and you're supposed to know."

"As far as I know there is no way for a doctor to measure a patient's pain level."

"Did Mr. Martin say he was in pain?"

"Yes, he said he was in great pain."

"What did you do?"

"After he was examined he was given a shot of morphine for pain, and sent to x-ray."

"What did the x-ray show?"

"I am not a radiologist, but the number one lumbar vertebra was pushed out somewhat."

"What did you do after he was x-rayed?"

"We kept him in ER for three or four hours until a hospital room came open, he was then taken to a room, and that was the last contact I had with him."

"That's all I have of this witness," said Spenser.

"Your witness, Mr. Adams," said the judge.

"How are you this morning, Dr. Smith?"

"Very well, thank you."

"What was the date and time when Mr. Martin was brought into the ER?"

"It was approximately 9:25 a.m. on September 5 this year."

"I'll be very brief, Doctor. Did the morphine shot you gave Mr. Martin knock him out?"

"Yes, it did."

"How long did he stay that way?"

"When they came to get him to take him to the hospital room he was still out. It was around one-thirty in the afternoon when they took him to the acute care room."

"This next question is very important, Doctor. Is there any way that Mr. Martin could have made a phone call before he was taken to the hospital room?"

"That would have been impossible."

"I have just one more question, Doctor. Do you remember talking to me when I came to the ER that morning?"

"Yes, I do."

"Did I leave any information with you to give Mr. Martin?"

"Yes, you gave me your phone number and the name of your insurance company."

"Did you give this information to anyone other than Mr. Martin?"

"No."

"Then you did not give the name of my insurance company to Martin's attorney, Luther Spenser?"

"I did not."

"Thank you, Dr. Smith. I have no further questions of this witness, Your Honor."

"You may call your next witness, Mr. Spenser," said the judge.

"I call Dr. Felix Upshaw to the stand, Your Honor."

"Will the witness please take the stand and be sworn in," said the judge.

Upshaw reminded Brad of Andy Gump, a comic strip character who appeared in the newspapers many years ago. He had a huge nose with a one-half-inch-thick mustache right under it. Brad thought that the good doctor could just as well have hung a sign under it.

"What type of doctor are you?" asked Spenser.

"I'm an orthopedic doctor."

"Have you examined the victim, Mr. Martin?"

"Yes, I have."

"And what were your findings?"

"After a very through physical examination of the patient and the x-rays, it is my opinion that he will never be able to walk again."

"That's a pretty harsh diagnosis isn't it, Doctor?"

"Yes, it is. In all my years in medicine, I've never seen a condition any worse except for one of complete paralysis."

"Can you tell us in medical terms exactly what is causing the problem with Mr. Martin's back?"

"Yes. It's a severe herniated disc between the first and second lumbar vertebrae. It's one of the worst cases I've ever seen of this nature."

"Is it possible, Dr. Upshaw, that this condition could have been preexisting?"

"There is absolutely no possibility that this was a preexisting condition. I have examined the x-rays thoroughly and there is no doubt in my mind that my conclusions are accurate."

"Thank you for your expert opinion. I have one last question. Is Mr. Martin suffering any pain?"

"Yes. I would say that he is suffering great and constant pain that can only be alleviated by habit-forming prescription pain pills that he will have to take for the rest of his life."

"Is there any hope that the pain will subside?"

"Not much, I'm afraid. In cases like this, there is seldom any improvement."

"Are you absolutely sure, Doctor?"

"I would stake my reputation on it," he said. (*He has nothing to lose,* thought Brad.)

"I think that says it all, Dr. Upshaw. I have no further questions of this witness, Your Honor."

"Your witness, Mr. Adams," said the judge.

"Thank you, Your Honor," said Brad. "Dr. Upshaw—it is Doctor isn't it?"

"Yes, sir."

"Where are you from, Doctor?"

"I'm from Miami, Florida, sir."

"Did you have a good flight up here, Doctor?"

"I had a very pleasant one, sir."

"What airline did you use?"
"I flew Delta."
"Did you have a layover in Atlanta?"
"Doesn't everybody?" (There was an outburst of laughter in the courtroom.)
"I know that I always have to," replied Brad. "Where are you staying here in town?"
"At the Marriott Hotel, sir."
"That's a nice hotel, Doctor."
"Is all this questioning necessary, Your Honor?" asked Spenser.
"Try to speed thing up a little, Mr. Adams," said the judge.
"I'm sorry, Your Honor, but all this questioning will become clearer in a little while."
"Continue, Mr. Adams."
"How much are you being paid for your testimony, Doctor?"
"I object," screamed Spenser.
"What is the basis for your objection, Mr. Spenser?" said the judge.
"It's an insult to Dr. Upshaw, Your Honor."
"I'm sure he'll live through it. I'll allow it. Answer the question, Dr. Upshaw."
"I'm not sure, sir."
"Haven't you discussed it with Mr. Spenser?"
"Yes, I have, but we did not set a fixed fee."
"What you are saying is that he hired you on a contingency basis, is that correct?"
"I guess you could say that."
"How much is the contingency?"
"It's five percent, sir."
"His lawsuit is for $3 million, so if the plaintiff wins you get five percent of the loot or $150,000. Excuse me, I meant of the award judgment."
"I object to that snide remark, Your Honor," said Spenser.
"Walk softly, Mr. Adams," replied the judge.
"Sorry, Your Honor," said Brad.
"You said that you examined Mr. Martin. When and where did this take place?"

"Sunday morning in his place of residence, sir."

"And where exactly is this place?"

"Since he got out of the hospital, he's been living with Mr. Spenser. That's where I performed my examination."

"How cozy that is, Doctor, having the plaintiff and his attorney living in the same house. Is there anyone else staying there right now?"

"No. It's just the two of them as far as I know."

"You said in your testimony earlier that you found that the cause of Mr. Martin's problem was a herniated disc between the number one and two lumbar vertebrae. Is this correct?"

"Yes, sir. That is correct."

"Assume for a moment, Doctor, that if he were able, Mr. Martin would be standing up. Do you understand what I'm saying?"

"I think so."

"If he were standing up, would the number three vertebra be below or above the number one vertebra?"

"It would be below the number one vertebra."

"Are you sure?"

"Absolutely."

"We have a major problem here, Doctor. I am holding in my hand a book entitled *Anatomy* by Dr. Carmine D. Clemente of the University of California at Los Angeles. Unless he is mistaken, there is no number three lumbar vertebra in the human body. Tell me, Dr. Upshaw, do you think Dr. Clemente is wrong?"

"No, Your Honor, I misunderstood the question."

"Well, let me ask you another question and you tell me if you understand the question before you answer it. And by the way, do not address me as Your Honor, that distinction is reserved for the trial judge only."

"Yes, sir."

"The next question is fairly simple, Doctor, please let me know if you don't understand it. Here it is. Imagine Mr. Martin is still standing. Are you with me on this one?"

"Yes, sir."

"So far so good. Now would you tell me where the twelfth thoracic vertebra is located with respect to the first lumbar vertebra?"

"I'm not exactly sure, sir."

"Would you like to know? It might be helpful to you in some of your future examinations or testimonies. For your information, it's the next one above number one."

"Thank you, Your Honor."

"I really wish you would stop referring to me as Your Honor. You're going to make the judge mad at me."(There was laughter in the courtroom).

"Order, order in the court," said the judge. "Proceed very carefully, Mr. Adams."

"I'm sorry, Your Honor." (Brad thought he saw a slight smile on Her Honor's face.) "Tell me, Doctor, where did you receive your degree?"

"I received it from the Mid South Atlantic University."

"Did you bring your diploma with you?"

"Yes, sir. Here's a copy."

"Very good, Doctor. Just where is this university located?"

"It's located in Belize, sir."

"That's in Africa isn't it?"

"No, sir. It's in Central America."

"Isn't that the little country that borders Nicaragua?"

"Yes, sir."

"That's a little strange, Doctor, because my map shows that Belize borders Mexico to the north and Guatemala to the west."

"That's right. I forgot the bordering countries."

"A natural mistake, Doctor. In what city in Belize is the university located?"

"It's in the capital city, sir."

"And what might that be?"

"I don't remember, sir."

"For your information, Doctor, the capital of Belize is Belmopan. You have never been there, have you?"

"No, sir."

"Then how did you manage to get a degree from there?"

"I got it on the internet, sir."

"What did this degree cost you?"

"One thousand dollars."

"Tell me, Dr. Upshaw, how many box tops did you have to send in along with the thousand dollars?" Brad noticed that the good doctor was starting to sweat.

"Objection, Your Honor," yelled Spenser.

"The objection is sustained, Mr. Spenser, but you have made a mockery of my court by bringing in a fake expert witness. You did not do you homework. Do you have any more questions of this witness, Mr. Adams?"

"Yes, Your Honor. I would like for Mr. Upshaw to tell the court how he thought he could get away with a scam like this."

"Please answer the question, Mr. Upshaw," said the judge.

"I have a medical condition, Your Honor. I have the onset of Alzheimer's disease. It causes me to forget a lot of things."

"Are there any other symptoms of this disease, Mr. Upshaw?" asked Brad.

"There are some other side effects to it, sir."

"Would lying be one of the symptoms, Doctor?"

"Objection, Your Honor," said Spenser.

"Explain your question, Mr. Adams," said the judge.

"I was just wondering if lying was one of the symptoms, Your Honor, since this witness has committed perjury at least five times in his testimony here this morning."

"Objection, Your Honor," screamed Spenser.

"I hope that you have proof of these perjuries, Mr. Adams," said the judge.

"I do, Your Honor, and I can enumerate each one if you wish."

"That won't be necessary, Mr. Adams." Upshaw suddenly put his hand to his mouth and made a gurgling sound and indicated he needed to go to the bathroom.

"Go ahead, Mr. Upshaw," said the judge. "This would be a good time to break for lunch. It's almost eleven now. Let's all meet back here at 1:00 p.m. Court is now adjourned."

When Upshaw left the courtroom he did not go to the bathroom. He walked out of the City-County Building straight to Main Street and hailed a cab. Ace and a reporter were right behind him. Ace also hailed a cab and told the reporter to get in because they were both going to the same place.

"Where is that?" the reporter asked.

"To the Greyhound bus station where Upshaw is going," replied Ace.

They got to the bus station just in time to see Upshaw board a bus with Nashville in the destination window.

"I thought he lived in Miami," said the reporter.

"I think he just wanted the first stage out of Dodge," replied Ace.

After leaving the courtroom Brad and Paula walked across Neyland Drive to Calhouns on the Water for lunch. Calhoun's boasted of having the best ribs in the country after winning that distinction in a nationwide rib cook-off contest a few years back. Paula called Ace on his cell phone and told him to join them. He said he would be there in ten minutes.

Ace was as good as his word. He got there in a little under ten minutes. Brad and Paula were not surprised that Upshaw had skipped town. He didn't want to stick around and face perjury charges and he knew that he would not be paid, so he had nothing to lose. Brad doubted that Knox County would pursue him anyway. It would be too costly and time-consuming, and he was small fry compared to Spenser and Martin, who will both probably face perjury plus conspiracy to commit fraud charges.

"What's on the agenda for this afternoon, Brad?" asked Ace.

"I'm going to call the local insurance agent, Frank Wheeler, followed by Luther."

"I bet the sparks will start flying then," said Paula.

"I can hardly wait," said Ace.

Chapter 61

Tuesday afternoon, October 24

When Brad, Paula, and Ace had finished their lunch, they walked back to the City-County Building which was directly across the street on the other side of Neyland Drive.

They entered the courtroom and sat down and waited for the judge to appear. She came in shortly and the court was called to order.

"Did you get finished with Dr. Upshaw, Mr. Adams?" she asked.

"I think Dr. Upshaw got finished with us, Your Honor," replied Brad.

"Why do you think that, Mr. Adams?"

"Because he was seen leaving town on a Greyhound bus with Nashville in the destination window, Your Honor."

"I thought he was from Miami," replied the judge.

"He is, Your Honor. I think he just wanted the first stagecoach out of Dodge."

"Very well. Do you have any more witnesses, Mr. Spenser?"

"No, but I would like to say a few words, Your Honor, if it pleases the court."

"Go ahead, Mr. Spenser."

"I would like to apologize to the court for the conduct of my so-called expert witness. You are right, Your Honor, in saying that I did not do my homework. I made a mistake, but that does not alter the fact that we have a severely injured man lying in that hospital bed unable to walk. My client should not be penalized because of my error in judgment. That's all I have to say, Your Honor."

"Do you have anymore witnesses, Mr. Adams?"

"I would like to call Mr. Frank Wheeler to the stand, Your Honor."

"Would Mr. Wheeler please take the witness stand and be sworn in?" said the judge.

"What do you do for a living, Mr. Wheeler?" asked Brad.

"I'm the local agent for US Auto Insurance Company here in Knoxville."

"Did you receive a phone call on September 5 this year from Mr. Luther Spenser?"

"Yes, I did."

"What was the nature of that call?"

"He called and said that he had been retained by Mr. Bret Martin to represent him in an automobile accident."

"Did Mr. Spenser say in what way he was notified of the accident?"

"Yes, he said that Mr. Martin called him."

"At what time of day did you receive this call?"

"It was twelve noon."

"Are you sure?"

"Absolutely. I was just getting ready to go to lunch when the phone rang."

"I have no further questions of this witness, Your Honor."

"Do you have any questions of this witness, Mr. Spenser?"

"No, Your Honor," replied Spenser.

"You may step down, Mr. Wheeler. Do you have anymore witnesses, Mr. Adams?"

"Yes, I do, Your Honor, but first I would like to make an observation."

"Go ahead."

"Thank you, Your Honor. We have a dilemma on our hands. We have Mr. Spenser calling my insurance company at twelve noon on September 5 this year stating that Martin had called him and retained him as his attorney while he was under sedation in the hospital unable to communicate. How he knew who my insurance company was is also a mystery to me, since I only told the police and left the same information with the Baptist ER doctor to give to Mr. Martin when he woke up. How could Martin have called Mr. Spenser at twelve noon on the fifth when Dr. Reed Smith has already testified that Martin was still asleep when he was being taken to his hospital room at 1:30? I would like to call Mr. Spenser to the stand to get this mess cleared up, Your Honor."

"Will Mr. Spenser please take the stand?" said the judge.

"I object, Your Honor," said Spenser. "This is highly irregular to call the plaintiff's lawyer to testify in his own client's case."

"How long have you been practicing law, Mr. Spenser?" asked the judge.

"For almost thirty years, Your Honor."

"Then you should know that you cannot object to a judge's order. Take the witness stand, Mr. Spenser."

"Mr. Spenser, had you ever met your client, Mr. Martin, prior to September 5, this year?"

"No."

"Then how do you account for the time discrepancies in the testimony we just heard? If you have never met him before, how do you account for the fact that you are his attorney, and that he could not have hired as you told the insurance agent? In addition, how did you know with whom I had my insurance?"

"I refuse to answer under the Fifth Amendment on the grounds that it might tend to incriminate me," replied Spenser.

"I think that is a wise decision, Mr. Spenser," said Brad. "If I were your attorney that would be my exact advice to you. I have no further questions of this witness, Your Honor," said Brad.

"Be seated, Mr. Spenser," said the judge. "If it wasn't for jeopardizing Mr. Martin's case, I would jerk you off this case in a heartbeat. Do you have any more witnesses, Mr. Adams?"

"Yes, Your Honor, I would like to call Dr. Heinz Mueller."

"Would the witness please take the stand?"

"You were Mr. Martin's attending physician while at Baptist. Is this correct, Dr. Mueller?"

"Yes, sir."

"What was his condition when you first saw him?"

"He was awake and said that he was in a lot of pain and couldn't walk."

"Was he paralyzed?"

"No. I checked his reflex actions in his lower body and they were normal."

"Did that seem unusual to you that his reactions were normal, but he was unable to walk?"

"It did seem somewhat unusual."

"Do you have an opinion as to the seriousness of Mr. Martin's injuries?"

"Yes, I do."

"Would you mind telling us what that opinion is, Doctor?"

"For obvious reasons, I would rather not."

"I understand, Doctor."

"I object," screamed Spenser.

"What are you objecting to now, Mr. Spenser?" asked the judge.

"This is nothing more than a sneaky way of getting the doctor to say that he thinks my client is faking, Your Honor."

"Your objection is overruled, Mr. Spenser," said the judge. "The doctor has a right to an opinion. That's what we pay doctors to do all the time."

"Did Martin require a lot of pain-killing injections?" asked Brad.

"We don't normally give shots for pain unless it's in the ER, or under very severe conditions."

"What do you do for pain?"

"It has been found that it is better to let the patient determine when he needs the medication."

"How does that work?"

"We hook up the medication intravenously so that the patient can push a button each time he thinks the pain gets too great. It has been found that a patient will use less of the painkiller by this method."

"What type of medication were you giving him?"

"We were giving him morphine."

"And how did he do with his consumption of the morphine?"

"Exceptionally well, he only used about one tenth of what I would have expected someone in his condition to use."

"Did you draw any conclusions from this?"

"It made me think that maybe Martin's pain wasn't as bad as he thought it was."

"Did you prescribe any painkiller medicine for him when he was discharged from the hospital?"

"No, I did not."

"And why did you not prescribe any?"

"I didn't think he needed any."

"Thank you, Doctor, I have no more questions of this witness, Your Honor."

"Would you like to cross-examine this witness, Mr. Spenser?"

"No, Your Honor."

"The witness may step down. Do you have any more witnesses to call, Mr. Spenser?"

"No, Your Honor."

"How about you, Mr. Adams?"

"Yes, Your Honor, I would like to call Dr. Roger Kennedy."

"Would the witness please take the stand?"

"How are you today, Doctor?"

"I'm fine, thank you."

"What type of doctor are you, sir?"

"I'm a radiologist, sir."

"What does a radiologist do, Doctor?"

"I read and interpret x-rays."

"Where did you go to medical school, Doctor?"

"I graduated from Vanderbilt."

"Did you happen to bring along any documentation to that effect?"

"Yes, I brought my diploma with me."

"May I see it?"

"Certainly," he said, as reached into his briefcase and handed it to Brad.

"This looks and feels like real sheepskin, Dr. Kennedy. It has a real good feel about it. Is it real?"

"I think it is," he said.

Spencer was seeing red. "Objection," he screamed. (Luther had always been jealous of Brad going all the way back to college. Brad always received A's and B's without much apparent effort while he himself struggled and cheated to maintain a C average. *I've finally got you now, Brad Adams,* he thought. *You are going to be disbarred.*)

"What are you objecting to this time, Mr. Spenser?" asked the judge.

"I'm objecting to this whole charade that is going on in your courtroom, Your Honor."

"What charade are you talking about, Mr. Spenser?"

"I'm talking about that phony doctor on the witness stand with that phony sheepskin diploma pretending to be a radiologist, Your Honor."

"If he's not a radiologist, what is he?" asked the judge.

"He's a bit actor from California playing the part of a radiologist, Your Honor, and I can prove it."

"What is your proof, Mr. Spenser?" asked the judge.

"I have it from reliable sources that his real name is Malcolm Sanders and he is being paid $10,000 for his bogus testimony."

"You had better check your sources a little closer," said the judge. "I happen to know Dr. Kennedy personally. We even go to the same church. You need to sit down and cool off after you apologize to Dr. Kennedy for your wild and baseless accusations." Spenser apologized to the doctor and took his seat with a bewildered and sheepish look on his face. (Everyone in the gallery was laughing.) Brad thought he saw a slight grin on the judge's face.

"Continue on with your questioning, Mr. Adams," said the judge.

"If I may, Your Honor, I would like to give this witness a rest and recall him later on in the trial. I'm sure that he is a little flustered from these wild accusations that have been thrown at him. I apologize for my opponent's wild outburst," Brad said to Dr. Kennedy.

"Very well, you may step down, Dr. Kennedy. Will you be calling any more witnesses in this trial, Mr. Spenser?"

"No, Your Honor."

"Do you have anyone else to call, Mr. Adams?"

"Yes, Your Honor. I would like to call Bret Martin."

"Do you foresee a lengthy interrogation of Mr. Martin?"

"Yes, Your Honor, I do."

"Then I think it would be best to adjourn for the day and continue at nine in the morning. Court is dismissed."

Chapter 62

Wednesday morning, October 25
Third day of the trial

Ace and Paula met with Brad in his office at 8:00 a.m. as planned and had the usual doughnuts and coffee.

"Take a look at the *Knoxville News Sentinel* headline this morning," said Brad. It read:

Expert Witness Skips Town, Spenser Takes Fifth

All the reporters who converged on Knoxville for the *Martin versus Adams* civil trial were not disappointed in yesterday's session. Someone said the trial had more wrinkles than Tim the Tool Man's suit in a bag. Under intense questioning by Brad Adams, Dr. Felix Upshaw, the expert witness for Martin, evidently got so rattled that he left the courtroom during the lunch break and hopped a bus to Nashville. Brad Adams was relentless in his questioning of Mr. Upshaw and got him to admit that he got his doctor's degree on the internet from somewhere in the country of Belize. The witness was supposed to return after lunch for more questioning by Adams, but he apparently got cold feet.

The trial was full of surprises. One of them was when Adams called Martin's lawyer himself to the witness stand to testify. There seemed to be a discrepancy in the chain of events surrounding just how Martin could have called Spenser and retained him as his attorney when he was under sedation at Baptist Hospital at the time in question. Spenser refused to testify and invoked the Fifth Amendment.

A short while later during the trial while Adams was questioning a local radiologist by the name of Roger Kennedy, Spenser jumped up out of his chair and accused the doctor of being a phony. Judge Robinson admonished Spenser, and had him apologize to Dr. Kennedy. She also informed Spenser that she personally knew Dr. Kennedy. She informed him that they both attended the same church.

Brad, Ace, and Paula left and walked the short distance from Brad's office to the courtroom for the third day of the trial. The court was called to order and the judge told Adams to call his witness.

"I call Mr. Bret Martin to the stand, Your Honor."

"OK, Mr. Adams, but first let me ask you a question. What happened between yesterday and today that would require you to have your left arm a sling?"

"It's just a minor sprain, Your Honor, but I thought it would be best to immobilize it."

"I see, Mr. Adams. How long do you think that you will have to wear it?"

"I don't think I will need to wear it for more than few days, Your Honor."

"Do you think you might be able to remove it at the end of this trial?"

"I certainly hope so, Your Honor."

"Very well. Mr. Martin, please take the witness stand."

"Since the witness is in the hospital bed and won't be able to sit in the witness stand, I wonder if we could roll him up in front of your bench and have him face me, Your Honor," said Brad. "I would like for him to look me in the eye while I question him."

"It is so ordered," said the judge. He was rolled and placed where he was facing Adams.

"Is there a hand crank on that contraption, Mr. Martin, so that you can be raised up high enough that I can see you?"

"Yes, there's one on the right side."

Brad asked the attendant to crank it up. "If you feel any pain, Mr. Martin, just let us know. That's good," said Brad, "that's high enough. How are you feeling today, Mr. Martin?" asked Brad.

"Not very well I'm afraid. I'm about the same."

"Do you feel up to answering a few of my questions?"

"I'll try," he said.

"Are you in any pain?"

"Yes, I am in quite a bit of pain, sir."

"Have you taken any pain medication since you got out of the hospital?"

"Yes. I have to take it every day."

"What doctor prescribed it for you?"

"I am not sure, sir."

"You're not sure? Mr. Martin, you're under oath here. What medication are you taking, and where did you get it?"

"I am taking morphine and Mr. Spenser got it for me."

"Is he a medical doctor?"

"I don't think so."

"Did you give a prescription to Spenser for him to get the medicine for you?"

"No."

"Then how do you think he got it?"

"I don't know. You'll have to ask him."

"How often do you need to take a pain pill?"

"About every four hours."

"You're going to be here for more than four hours today. Did you bring any of those elusive pain pills with you?"

"No."

"Would you like a bullet to bite on if your pain becomes unbearable?"

"Objection, Your Honor," screamed Spenser.

"Be careful, Mr. Adams," said the judge.

"I'm just trying to be helpful, Your Honor. Let's move on, Mr. Martin. Can you walk?"

"No. I cannot."

"Have you taken any steps at all since 9:00 a.m. on September 5 this year?"

"No, sir."
"Are you a Knoxville native?"
"No."
"Where are you from?"
"Originally I'm from Los Angles, California."
"Where did you live most recently before coming to Knoxville?"
"I lived in Las Vegas, Nevada."
"What did you do there?"
"I worked in construction doing roofing and sheet rock installation."
"Did you do any other type of work in LA?"
"Just a few odd jobs, nothing much else to speak of."
"Did you do any other type of work in Vegas?"
"No, sir."
"Had you ever met your attorney, Mr. Spenser, prior to coming to Knoxville?"
"No, sir."
"This next question is very important and I want you to think about it very carefully before you answer it. Did you contact Mr. Luther Spenser to represent you in this case prior to twelve noon on September 5, 2006?"
"No, sir."
"Then how did he come to be your attorney?"
"He contacted me."
"When and where?"
"He came to see me at Baptist Hospital the day of my accident, around seven in the evening during visiting hours."
"How did he get your name?"
"I don't know. You'll have to ask him."
"Weren't you curious?"
"No. To tell the truth, I was still somewhat out of it at that time."
"How did you end up in Knoxville? Did you know anyone here?"
"No, I heard that there was a lot of construction work in Knoxville and I thought I could get a good job here. I didn't know anyone here before I got here."
"When did you arrive here?"
"I got in here on August 31 this year."
"Were you able to find any work here?"

"I really hadn't gotten around to that."

"Do you have a car?"

"No, sir."

"Then what were you doing in the parking garage of the BB&T Bank Building at nine in the morning on September 5 of this year?"

"I was retrieving a car for a man I met."

"What man?"

"I don't know his name"

"Where did you meet him?"

"I ran into him as I was coming out of the YMCA where I was staying."

"Are you telling this court that a complete stranger came up to you on the street and asked you to get his car out of the parking garage?"

"Yes, sir."

"That's a little hard for me to swallow, Mr. Martin. I can't believe that a reasonable man would trust a complete stranger with his car."

"Objection, Your Honor," yelled Spenser. "Mr. Adams is impugning the character of my client."

"Objection sustained," said the judge. "Move on, Mr. Adams."

"Yes, Your Honor. Did he give you the keys to his car?"

"Yes, he did."

"Was it a bunch of keys or just the car key?"

"It was just the car key."

"Did the key have the remote opener with it, or was it just a single key?"

"It was just a single key."

"What did you do with the key?"

"I put it in my right front pocket."

"Did this man pay you any money up front for picking up the car?"

"Yes, he gave me a ten-dollar bill and said he would give me ten more when I brought him his car."

"What did you do with the ten spot?"

"I put it in my pocket with the key."

"Where were you supposed to deliver the car?"

"I was supposed to take it back to the YMCA."

"What was this man supposed to be doing while you retrieved his car, twiddling his thumbs?"

"I don't know?"

"What did this man look like?"

"He was a Caucasian man about five foot ten with a medium build and brown hair."

"Let me see if I got this right. He was a white man of average height, average weight, and average hair color. I think I passed him in the hall three times coming into court this morning." (There was uproar in the courtroom.)

"Order in the courtroom," said the judge. "One more outburst like that, and I'll clear this courtroom."

"Did this man tell you where the car was parked?" asked Brad.

"Yes. He told me it was in the parking garage beneath the BB&T Bank Building on the corner of Main and State streets."

"Did he tell you exactly where in the garage it was parked?"

"He said it was on level three."

"Did he describe the car or give you the license number?"

"He said the car was a black 2005 Chevrolet Impala."

"What was the purpose of the ten-dollar bill the man gave you?"

"It was to pay me for getting his car just like I told you."

"Is that all the money he gave you?"

"That's what I just told you."

"I was just wondering if you were going to retrieve the car and crash through the barrier gate and skip out without paying the parking fee."

"Oh, I just remembered. He gave me another ten to pay for the parking."

"How convenient. Did he also give you the parking ticket?"

"Yes."

"What did you do with the other ten and the parking ticket?"

"I put them in my pocket with the key and the money."

"I see, Mr. Martin, but I don't understand how you were going to find the right car among all the other black cars on level three unless the man told you the slot number of the parking space?"

"I remember now, he told me that it was parked in slot number 319."

"You are wrong, Mr. Martin. Unless they have painted slot numbers on the walls since I parked there this morning, there are no slot numbers."

"I object, Your Honor," shouted Spenser. "That was entrapment if I ever saw it."

"Overruled, Mr. Spenser. Your client painted himself into this corner and he is going to have to get himself out of it."

"We have a major dilemma here, Mr. Martin."

"What is that?" he asked.

"In addition to the lie you just told this court there seems to be a huge discrepancy in your tale. I mean story."

"What discrepancy is that?" he asked.

"I have a list of all the possessions you had on your person when you were admitted to Baptist, and several items that you told this court that you had, are missing."

"What is missing?"

"There are two 10-dollar bills, a car key, and a parking ticket. How do you account for the loss of these items, Mr. Martin?"

"They must have been knocked out of my pockets when you hit me," he said.

"I don't think that kite will fly, Mr. Martin. You would stand a better chance of getting struck by lightning in church on Christmas day in a leap year than anything being knocked out of your right front pocket. And, in addition, the police were at the scene in minutes and did not find any of those items. Is that the best story that you can come up with?"

"The people at Baptist Hospital must have stolen those things," said Martin.

"I don't think so, Mr. Martin. I don't believe that someone would steal a key to who knows what, along with a parking ticket, and take two 10-dollar bills, and leave three 20s. That's too much of a stretch. Let's get on with the questioning, Mr. Martin. I notice that you are in a hospital bed here today. Do you have a hospital bed at Mr. Spenser's house?"

"No, I sleep in a daybed."

"You stated that you were unable to walk. How do you use the bathroom?"

"I have to use the bedpan."

"Who is your nurse?"

"I don't have one."

"How do you manage all day when Mr. Spenser is at work?"

"Mr. Spenser comes home two or three times a day to check on me, and I can also call him if I need him."

"How convenient, Mr. Martin. Let's move along, we still have a long way to go. Do you like movies, Mr. Martin?"

"I object," said Spenser. "I see no point to this question."

"Explain, Mr. Adams," said the judge.

"It will become very clear where I am going shortly, Your Honor."

"Continue," said the judge.

"I am going to give you the names of six movies and I want you to tell me if you have ever heard of any of them. Do you understand?"

"Yes, sir."

"I will list them as follows:

1. *Shootout in the Black Hills*
2. *The Sheep Herder*
3. *The Paid Killer*
4. *Ride into the Sunset*
5. *The Gunslinger from El Paso*
6. *The Scam*

"Do any of these movies ring a bell, Mr. Martin?"

"A couple of them sound familiar," he said.

"They should all sound familiar, Mr. Martin, because you played in each one of them." (There were murmurs of surprise in the courtroom.)

"Objection," screamed Spenser. "What is Mr. Adams trying to drum up now?"

"Overruled. You may continue, Mr. Adams."

"I want you to think very carefully, Mr. Martin, before you perjure yourself any further. I wouldn't be asking you a question like I just asked you unless I already knew the answer. Do you understand the severity of perjury?"

"Yes, sir."

"I am going to ask you another question. Did you have a role in any of these movies?"

"Yes, sir, I had a part in all of them."

"What kind of parts did you play?"

"I was a stuntman in them." (There were some oohs and aahs in the gallery.)

"Order in the court," said the judge.

"Your Honor, I would like to ask you to recess this trial for the rest of the day if I may?" said Adams.

"For what reason, Mr. Adams?"

"I was expecting a FedEx package this morning containing the videotapes of the six movies I just mentioned, along with some other evidence, Your Honor. The local movie rental stores did not stock them, so I had to order them on eBay."

"I'm afraid that my court schedule will not allow that, Mr. Adams. As soon as this trial is over I have another one scheduled."

"When I agreed to an early trial, Your Honor, I made it very clear that there would be a problem getting all my evidence in time, and Mr. Spenser agreed to let me introduce new evidence during the course of the trial."

"Be that as it may, Mr. Adams, I have no choice in the matter."

"Thank you, Your Honor," said Brad. About that time the door guard stuck his head in the door and said that Mr. Adams' secretary was here with a FedEx package for him. *She's right on time, just as we scheduled it*, thought Brad.

"Very well, bring it in. I guess that solves both our dilemmas," said the judge. "I think this would be a good time for a lunch break; it's been a long morning and it's almost eleven. Lets all meet back here at 1:00 p.m. Court is now adjourned."

Chapter 63

Wednesday afternoon October 25

"The court will now come to order," said the judge. "Before we broke for lunch, you had some new evidence to introduce, Mr. Adams. You may do that now."

"Objection," yelled Spenser.

"What are you objecting to, Mr. Spenser?" said the judge.

"I'm talking about discovery, Your Honor, or the lack of it. I'm objecting to this evidence being presented right near the end of the trial that I have not had a chance to look at."

"Mr. Spenser, you, and I, and Mr. Adams sat in my office a few days ago and you agreed to this very thing. You were in such a rush to get an early trial date that you may have jeopardized your own case. Would you like to come up and examine the new evidence now?"

"No, Your Honor," said Spenser.

"The objection is then overruled. Present your evidence, Mr. Adams."

"Thank you, Your Honor. I don't intend to show all these six movies to the court, but I would like to show about a five-minute clip of one of them, but first I have a couple of before and after pictures."

"Would you like to examine this evidence before it is presented to the jury, Mr. Spenser?"

"I don't think it would do me any good, Your Honor," said Spenser.

"I have here two letter-size pictures that have the date and time printed in the lower right-hand corner that I would like to present to the court, Your Honor."

"Let me look at them first, Mr. Adams," said the judge. Brad handed her the pictures. She looked at them and asked Brad where they were taken.

"The first one was taken at Baptist Hospital at the time Mr. Martin was being discharged. The second one was taken about thirty minutes later in the driveway of Mr. Spenser's home as Martin got out of Spenser's van. In the first picture you can see Martin being loaded into the back of Spenser's van and placed on a mat. In the second picture you can see Martin walking up the sidewalk to Spenser's house. I also have a movie of this if you would like to see it," said Brad.

"I think I've seen enough," said the judge as she handed the pictures to the court attendant and told him to pass them to the jury. "Mr. Martin, I want you to get up out of that hospital bed right now and go sit in the witness chair. If you need any help I will call in a couple of strong men to assist you. Do you have any problems with that?"

"No, Your Honor," he said, as he proceeded to the chair.

"Would someone get that contraption on wheels out of my courtroom?" asked the judge. "Mr. Spenser, you and your client have made a mockery of my court and caused a lot of wasted time and money to be needlessly spent, not to mention the useless hospital bill you may have run up. Who's going to pay for all those expenses? You may continue questioning your witness, Mr. Adams."

"Thank you, Your Honor. If it's OK with you, I think I'll take off my sling. My arm feels much better now."

"I think that would be a good idea, Mr. Adams. You can begin your questioning now."

"I am going to ask you a question that I already know the answer to, Mr. Martin. Do you understand what I'm saying?"

"Yes."

"Good. Do you know a man in Las Vegas by the name of Lamont Brown?"

"My client pleads the fifth, Your Honor," said Spenser.

"Who is testifying here, Mr. Spenser, you, or your client? You have the right to advise him, but not to answer the question for him. The witness will decide whether to answer the question," said the judge.

"I will answer the question, Your Honor. Yes, I know Mr. Brown," said Martin.

"In what capacity do you know him?"

"We worked at the same place in Vegas."

"And where did the two of you work?"

"At the MGM Grand Hotel in Las Vegas."

"What did Mr. Brown do there?"

"He was head of security."

"And what did you do there?"

"I was a dealer at a blackjack table."

"Where is all this senseless questioning going, Your Honor?" Spenser asked.

"Explain, Mr. Adams," said the judge.

"I believe that my next two questions will clear things up, Your Honor."

"While you were dealing blackjack did you ever have Mr. Luther Spenser playing at your table?"

"Objection," screamed Spenser.

"Objection is overruled. Answer the question, Mr. Martin."

"Yes. Mr. Spenser played at my table."

"On how many occasions did he play?"

"He played many times during a several-month period."

"How was his luck?"

"Pretty good the first couple of trips. He won quite a bit of money during that period."

"Do you know how much he was up?"

"I think it was around half a million dollars."

"What happened after that on his other trips to Vegas?"

"He started to lose."

"Were you the dealer when he started to lose?"

"No. I had quit my dealer's job by then."

"Why did you quit?"

"Luther and I became good friends while he was winning big, and he asked me to quit and be his aide."

"Why did he need an aide?"

"I'm not sure, but I think it fed his ego."

"I see. What happened when Mr. Spenser started losing?"

"He couldn't afford to pay me anymore and they wouldn't give me my job back. Luther had gone back to Tennessee, so we just drifted apart."

"How much money did Mr. Spenser lose at the blackjack table?"

"I heard from the staff at MGM that he lost close to a million and a half." (There was a lot of noise from the gallery.)

"Order in the court," said the judge.

"Whose idea was it to pull off this phony accident scam?"

"It was Luther's idea. I really did come to Knoxville looking for work and I called Luther to see if he knew of a good job I could get. He was flat broke and his business had declined because of all the time he had spent in Vegas and he was desperate. He knew that I used to be a stuntman and that's how he came up with the idea. He told me it would be a piece of cake."

"That's a damn lie," screamed Spenser.

"You're already skating on thin ice in my courtroom, Mr. Spenser, and if I hear one more curse word out of you, I'll have you gagged. Would you like you take the witness stand and refute his testimony?" asked the judge.

"No, Your Honor."

"Then be quiet, Mr. Spenser."

"I have no more questions of this witness, Your Honor. I would now like to show the five-minute clip of the movie titled *The Scam*," said Brad. "There is no doubt that the stuntman in this scene is Bret Martin as you will see in the credits at the end of this clip because he is the only stuntman in the movie."

"Very well," said the judge.

The TV and VCR were set up and Brad ran the tape. He explained that the movie was almost identical in its setting as it was in the parking garage of the BB&T bank. In both cases the driver was turning a corner when a man ran into the windshield of the car and fell to the concrete. He also pointed out that the victim in both cases were the one and the same, Bret Martin. "But there is one big difference between the two so-called accidents," he pointed out. "In the movie version, Mr. Martin was actually injured and had to be admitted to the LA General Hospital because of a back injury. That's the injury that showed up on the Baptist Hospital x-rays that our good Dr. Upshaw swore was not a preexisting condition. One part of the evidence that was delivered by FedEx is a copy of the LA General Hospital x-rays that were taken on July 17, 1999, the day of his accident. The testimony regarding these x-rays were the reason I had Dr. Roger Kennedy on the witness stand before he was falsely accused by

Luther Spenser of being a phony. He was going to testify that the injury to Mr. Martin was preexisting. I don't believe I need to call him now with all other evidence that has been presented. I have no further questions of this witness, Your Honor."

"Very well," she said. "Do you have any other witnesses, Mr. Spenser?"

"No, Your Honor."

"How about you, Mr. Adams, do you have anything else?"

"I'm finished, Your Honor," said Brad.

"Very well, we will now present closing arguments. You may go first, Mr. Spenser."

"I have no closing remarks, Your Honor."

"Very well, you may make your closing remarks, Mr. Adams."

"I would like to thank everyone associated with this trial. I think it has been a fair trial and well conducted," said Brad.

"I wanted this trial so that I could vindicate myself and at the same time expose the two people who tried to extort money out of me and my insurance company. My associates and I did a tremendous amount of investigative work to unravel the conspiracy that went on in this scam. The plaintiff has confessed to this scam and implicated his own attorney. They have both committed perjury in this trial and they will have to pay the consequences. I trust this jury, which I consider to be one of the most enlightened ones ever empanelled in a civil case, to come up with a just verdict. I have nothing further, Your Honor."

"Very well, the jury will now make their way to the jury room. Your first order of business will be to elect a foreman," said the judge. "As soon as this has been accomplished, I want to know whom you elected. Just go to the door of the jury room and notify the guard and he will notify me.

"Everyone else may now leave the courtroom," said the judge. They all started to leave with the reporters leading the way.

Brad called Ace and Paula together and suggested that they all go a block down the street to Pete's Café and get a bite to eat while they were waiting on the jury verdict. He called Denise at his office and asked her to come to the courthouse and wait on the verdict. "Call me on my cell phone if anything at all develops," he said. "I don't think the jury will be out much more than an hour."

The three of them walked the block to Pete's Café that is owned by a Greek-American, but the food is more American than Greek.

"How do you think it went?" Brad asked them.

"I think you kicked some butt," replied Ace. "I could hardy contain myself when Spenser accused Roger Kennedy of being a phony."

"I think you have personally made an impact on the future of all civil lawsuits," said Paula.

"That it something that is long overdue," replied Brad. "By the way, there is one thing that's still bothering me."

"What is that?" asked Ace.

"How did Luther know who I had my car insurance with?"

"Do you shred all your bills at home?" Ace asked.

"No, I don't."

"There's where the problem lies," Ace replied. "A good garbage scrounger can find out all he needs to know by sifting through your garbage."

"I will certainly shred everything in the future," said Brad.

"What do you think will happen to Spenser and Martin?" asked Ace.

"For starters, neither of them will pass go. I think the judge will have both of them arrested and sent straight to jail. I also see both of them charged with conspiracy to commit fraud. I think that Luther will be disbarred and I think both will be tried, convicted, and will spend time in prison."

The waitress appeared and took their order just as Brad's cell phone rang. It was Denise, who called to inform him that the jury had elected Richard Washington its foreman.

He announced the news to Ace and Paula.

"That sounds like good news to me," said Ace. "Washington seemed to me to be one of the most levelheaded jurors on the panel."

"I don't think we could have picked a better one ourselves," said Brad.

They finished their sandwiches and their second cup of coffee. It had been a little over an hour since the jury convened. Brad thought they should have reached a verdict by now. Just at that moment Denise called again. "I don't know what this means, Mr. Adams, but the jury just informed the judge that they have reached a decision but can't decide on the amount. The judge has given them until 6:00 p.m. to arrive at a decision or they will have to come back tomorrow."

ACE SLEUTH, PRIVATE EYE

Brad looked at his watch. It was now 4:00 p.m. The jury had two more hours to arrive at an award.

Brad informed Ace and Paula of the quandary.

"What do you think it means?" asked Paula.

"It looks to me like we ended up with an O. J. jury," replied Brad. "I don't understand what's going on. I thought I was making good eye contact with most of them. Just look at all the evidence. I'm really concerned."

"It ain't over till the fat lady sings," said Ace.

"I didn't see any fat ladies in the courtroom," said Brad.

"I think we must be missing something here," said Ace.

"I wish I knew what it was," replied Brad. "I think we need to pay our bill and head back up to the courthouse."

They walked the block back up Main Street to the courthouse and it was swarming with reporters. They had also gotten the word.

The three of them sat around and fiddled their thumbs until around five-thirty when it was announced that the jury had reached a decision. Brad, Ace, and Paula took a seat at Brad's table and a multitude of people just pushed past the door guard and filled the courtroom to overflowing. The judge just tolerated the situation because there wasn't much that she could do about it anyway. The jurors all returned to the courtroom and took their seats.

"I was informed that the jury had arrived at a decision but could not decide on the amount of damages," said the judge. "Is that correct, Mr. Foreman?"

"Yes, Your Honor," replied Richard Washington.

"What is the amount of the monetary award that was decided?" she asked.

"Two million dollars," the foreman replied. There was an outburst in the courtroom that took almost a minute to quiet down.

"You were interrupted by the gallery, Mr. Foreman. Did you have anything else to say?"

"Yes, Your Honor, I wanted to say that the $2 million is the amount of the award to the defendant, Mr. Adams, one million each from Mr. Spenser and Mr. Martin respectively."

Several reporters left the courtroom in a rush as the entire gallery stood and applauded. The judge finally got everything back to order and had some questions of the jury.

"Is the decision unanimous, Mr. Foreman?"

"Yes, it is, Your Honor," he replied.

"I would like to see a show of hands by the jury to confirm the decision," said the judge. Every one of the jurors raised their hands.

"Do you realize, Mr. Washington, that this jury has just rendered a decision the likes of which has never been rendered before today? Do you and the jury realize the significance of this decision they have just made?"

"Yes, we do, Your Honor," replied Washington. "We were just following your instructions to the jury. We considered it our duty to find the damages and make the award accordingly. We found that Mr. Adams had been damaged by the lawyer and his client."

"The jury has spoken," said the judge. "Will the two officers in the rear of the courtroom take Mr. Spenser and his client into custody and charge them with perjury, for starters? You may also want to get the DA to look into charges of conspiracy to commit fraud. Court is adjourned. I would like to see Mr. Adams in my chambers now."

Before going into the judge's chambers, Brad shook hands with each of the jurors and congratulated them on their verdict. He especially thanked Richard Washington for his leadership as foreman of the jury.

Brad told Ace and Paula that he would like to take them out for dinner around eight tonight. "I will call you," he said. He then walked into Judge Robinson's office wondering what this was all about.

Chapter 64

Wednesday, October 25, 6:00 p.m.

"Come in, Mr. Adams," said Judge Robinson. "I just wanted to talk to you for a few minutes. I would like to say that this is one of the most enjoyable trials over which I have ever presided, and if you ever tell anyone I said that, I will hold you in contempt."

"That wouldn't be all bad, Your Honor," said Brad.

"Do you like being held in contempt, Mr. Adams?"

"If you take away the last two words, I wouldn't mind it at all."

"Are you flirting with me, Mr. Adams?"

"I have a first name, Your Honor," said Brad.

"So do I, Brad," she replied. "Let me ask you a question. As Jay Leno frequently says, what was that all about in there yesterday?"

"Are you talking about Luther's wild accusations?"

"Yes."

"Ace and I discovered a bug in my conference room which we suspected was placed there by Spenser. We just had a little privileged conversation, and I guess he overheard us."

"That was very clever of you, Brad."

"I have to give Ace the credit for that. I just wanted to remove the darn thing."

"Let me ask you another question, Brad. Why did you wait to submit those before and after pictures of Spenser and Martin leaving the hospital near the end of the trial when they were taken weeks before? Haven't you ever heard of discovery?"

"About that, Your Honor, my detective, Ace Sleuth, took those pictures with his cell phone and then lost his cell phone. He looked everywhere for that phone and just found it this morning."

"Where did he find it, Brad?"

"It had fallen down between the front seat and the console in his Mustang. He had to put his brakes on real hard this morning, and that darn thing slid out from under the seat right at his feet."

"Do you happen to have any beachfront property in Arizona that you would like to sell me along with that tall tale, Brad?"

"You really know how to hurt a guy, Your Honor."

"That's water under the bridge now, Brad. What are you thoughts on the verdict?"

"I was pleasantly surprised by it, but as far as money goes, it is a moot point. Neither of those two charlatans has a penny to their name. I have never heard of a jury making an award to the defendant before, but I can see the logic in it. If this decision is not overturned by some liberal judge, there could be far-reaching effects in future civil cases. If the tort lawyers know that they might end up owing money themselves there may be a lot fewer baseless civil suits filed. It would probably eliminate the frivolous ones altogether."

"I think you are right, Brad, but if Spenser and Martin are as broke as you say, I don't think either of them will file an appeal. It's awfully hard to file an appeal from a prison cell. I think they both have a lot more on their minds right now than filing an appeal against a jury award which they will never pay. Do you think Spenser has any malpractice insurance?"

"What insurance company in its right mind would insure Luther, Your Honor?"

"Good point, Brad. By the way, you may call me Elizabeth outside the courtroom, but don't ever call me Liz, that name makes me feel old."

"OK, Elizabeth, we're going to have a party at Club LeConte Saturday night and I would be honored for you to come as my guest. No, make that my date." (Club LeConte is a private club on the top floor of the First Tennessee Bank Building, Jake Butcher's building. It was the first of the two gleaming towers.)

"I will come on one condition, and that condition is, that you do not refer to the party as a victory party. I don't want it to look like you and I were in cahoots during the trial."

"Good, I think I can manage that," said Brad. "We plan to start around seven-thirty. I can come by your house and get you about seven." Brad got her address and home phone number. "I'll see you then," he said.

"Before you leave, I would like to talk to you about how I run my courtroom. Did you know that being a judge could be one of the loneliest professions in the world, Brad?"

"I haven't really thought about it, but I can see where that might be possible."

"You have probably heard what they call me outside the courtroom, haven't you?"

"I'm afraid I have," replied Brad.

"There's a reason for that. Every schoolteacher will tell you that if you don't get control of your classroom the very first day of school, you're going to have problems all year. I don't want my courtroom to become like Judge Ito's, where OJ's Dream Team controlled it."

"I've heard some people refer to them as the Scheme Team," said Brad.

"Like the time they schemed up the false charges against the LA police, accusing them of framing O. J. without one scintilla of evidence? I can't understand why any person who calls himself a judge would allow something like that to go on in his courtroom."

"Nothing much surprises me what occurs in courtrooms these days. Some of the judges are actually making the laws rather than interpreting them," said Brad. "Is there anything else we need to talk about?"

"Nothing that I can think of," said Elizabeth. "I'll see you Saturday."

Chapter 65

Wednesday, October 25, 6:30 p.m.

As soon as Brad left the judge's office, he called Ace and told him that he would meet him and Paula at the Copper Cellar Restaurant on the strip around 7:30 p.m. The portion of Cumberland Avenue near the UT campus is affectionately referred to as the "Strip." Brad had also called Denise and the four of them met there at the appointed time.

After they were seated Brad asked Denise what had been going on at the office since she had returned there around 4:45 from the courtroom.

"The phone has been ringing off the hook," she said. "I stayed there until 6:30 and came straight here. You've had calls from *The News Sentinel,* the *Washington Times,* ABC, NBC, CBS, CNT, Fox News, and Court TV. They all wanted an interview with you."

"I think we've opened up a whole can of worms," said Brad. "I have been giving serious consideration to going back to work on a full-time basis."

"What type of work?" asked Ace.

"I would like to defend civil lawsuits that I consider to be frivolous, or ones that offer no proof of wrongdoing on the part of the defendant. A case in point would be a case like mine but, without the scam. If Martin had actually been injured by my car through no fault of my own, I don't believe I should have to pay him damages. There are a lot of cases out there like that, and if I am going to undertake this, I am going to need some help, namely you and Paula," he said to Ace. "And of course I'll always need Denise. She's my right hand, so to speak."

"She could also be your left hand if it ever needs to be put it back in that sling," joked Ace.

"The purpose of that sling, Ace, was to draw attention away from Martin in that hospital bed. I would like for both of you to come and work for me full-time," said Brad. "Do either of you have any problems with that?"

"Not me," said Ace. "I was just wondering where my next job was coming from."

"I have no problems either," said Paula. "I'd love to work for you."

"Come in tomorrow and we can work out the salaries, benefits, holidays, etc. How about the lease on your office, Ace? I will pay any remaining rental that you may owe."

"Not to worry," said Ace, "I have just been paying by the month anyway."

They finished their dinner and left. Ace took Paula back to her car at BB&T where she had left it.

"You won't believe what Lisa will be doing Saturday night, Ace."

"Studying, I suppose," he said.

"No, she has a date, her first," said Paula.

"Well, good for her," said Ace. "Is he a nice boy?"

"He's a straight-A student just like Lisa, and seems to be very levelheaded," said Paula.

"I knew a man once who was levelheaded," said Ace. "Tobacco juice ran out of his mouth equally on both sides."

"Would you get serious for a minute, Ace?" asked Paula.

"Sorry, I just couldn't pass that one up," replied Ace. "I'm very happy for Lisa. I've got to get going now. I'll see you in the office in the morning. I love you." They embraced and departed with a kiss.

Chapter 66

Thursday morning, October 26

The headlines for the *Knoxville News Sentinel read*:

Jury in Martin-Adams Case Awards Defendant $2,000,000

The Martin-Adams civil trial has been full of surprises, but the last day of the trial takes the cake. Martin's lawyer and Martin himself were both arrested, placed in handcuffs, and taken to the county jail and charged with perjury, and may end up being charged with conspiracy to commit fraud. Probably the most unusual aspect of the trial was when the jury foreman, Richard Washington, announced the verdict that awarded $2 million to the defendant, Brad Adams. No one can ever remember this happening in a civil trial before. The plaintiff and his lawyer were each assessed $1 million.

Mr. Washington has become somewhat of a celebrity himself along with the defendant, and lawyer, Brad Adams. Washington has been invited to appear on The HHH Talk Radio Show. (The HHH talk show is an extremely popular talk show in east Tennessee and three surrounding states. It is hosted by a popular Host by the name of Hallerin Hilton Hill). Almost all the major news media have representatives in Knoxville, and the local hotels and restaurants are doing a booming business.

After finishing reading the paper, Brad called Ace into his office to sit down and have a cup of coffee. "I talked to you and Paula yesterday about coming to work for me full-time. I have already set you up in a corner office, and I would like for you to start as soon as possible if $75,000 per year plus amenities is acceptable to you."

"That's the perfect amount," replied Ace. "I now will be making as much as my friend Lamont, who is the security head for the MGM Grand."

"I have already got a lawsuit lined up for you; however, it will take place in Nashville. I hope that you don't mind traveling."

"I love traveling as long as I know that I can always come back to Knoxville," said Ace.

"There is one other thing, Ace," said Brad, as he handed him an envelope. "This is a bonus for the great work you did on my case."

Ace opened the envelope and found a $5,000 check. "I know exactly what I'm going to spend this on," he said, "a ring for Paula. Thanks a lot, Brad, I really appreciate this."

"Don't thank me, thank US Auto Insurance Company. Denise is working up their bill right now. It comes to around $200,000. By the way, when are the two of you getting married?" asked Brad.

"I don't know exactly. I need to discuss it with Paula, but we would like to get married before the end of the year."

"I'm pretty sure that David and Jennifer will be getting married somewhere in that same time frame. What would you say to a double ceremony at the First Baptist Church where I go, if I can arrange it?"

"I don't know, Brad, Paula kind of had her heart set on Temple's Feed Store in Sevierville, but I believe I can talk her out of it. The double ceremony sounds fine."

"We could have the reception at Club LeConte," said Brad. "Would you like for me to see what times it is available?"

"Yes, why don't you do that?"

"I think I have someone who could perform the ceremony," said Brad.

"Who?" asked Ace.

"Elizabeth Robinson."

"Do you mean Judge Beno?"

"She's an entirely different person outside the courtroom, Ace. I'm taking her to Club LeConte Saturday night as my date."

"She is a very attractive woman, Brad."

"I don't have anything else now, Ace. Do you have anything?"

"No, but if you can spare me for a little while, I need to go to my bank and the jewelry store."

"Very well. Please send in Paula as you leave."

Brad asked Paula to come in and sit down. "I just wanted to talk to you about your job here, Paula. Do you like your new office?"

"Yes, I like it a lot. I even have a window."

"How does $50,000 a year sound to you, Paula?"

"It sounds too good to be true. That means that I can give up my job at the Copper Cellar and be home with Lisa at night."

"Good, there are some things that go along with it such as paid holidays, hospital insurance, and a 401K pension plan which I will match with what you put in up to ten percent of your salary."

"I couldn't ask for anything better than that, Brad."

"You will be my assistant, Paula. You will know everything I'm doing and be able to speak for me in my absence."

"I will certainly do my best to handle that responsibility, Brad."

"Good, I'll go over the new case that I have accepted in Nashville. I don't think that you will be required to do much traveling, but Ace will have to do some. I just got through talking to Ace about maybe having a double wedding ceremony for you and him, and David and Jennifer."

"That sounds super," said Paula.

"Do you have any objections with having the ceremony performed at the First Baptist Church, Paula? I will try to get Elizabeth Robinson to perform the ceremony."

"None whatsoever," she said. "I would be honored for her to do it."

"When I asked Ace that question he said that you had your heart set on Temple's Feed Store in Sevierville."

"I think I can forego that this one time, Brad."

"How would you feel about having the reception at Club LeConte?"

"I would love it, Brad. Are we still on for the Saturday night party there?"

"Yes, it starts at seven-thirty."

"We'll be there with bells on," said Paula.

Chapter 67

Saturday evening, October 28
Club LeConte

Ace and Paula arrived at the club at seven-thirty and found that everyone else was already there. They were all in the room that Brad had reserved for them. Brad would later reserve the entire club for the wedding reception. He was there with Elizabeth, Denise, her husband Mark, and David and Jennifer.

Jennifer came up to them and was smiling from ear to ear. "How good to see you again, Dr. Zachary," she said.

"As I live and breathe, if it's not Nurse Jones. How good it is to see you again. I believe you know my future wife, Paula."

"I believe we've met. Do you remember my future husband, David?"

"Yes. I believe we've met. When are you two getting married?"

"That's what we wanted to talk to you and Paula about," said Jennifer. "David and I both like the idea of a double marriage ceremony, and we would like to see if we can agree on a mutually acceptable date. David has some news for us."

"I will be moving back to Knoxville at the end of November," said David. "I have found that I can conduct my business from anywhere in the country with today's technology, and there's no place I would rather live than Knoxville. I am a UT graduate and I love Tennessee football, the Lady Vols basketball, and I'm beginning to love the men's basketball now that they have a great coach. In addition, I don't believe I will miss the Atlanta traffic jams."

"That is great news," said Paula. "Jennifer and I have become good friends and I was afraid I was going to lose her to Atlanta."

"Why don't we try to settle on a date for the weddings?" said Ace. "Brad has given us some dates when he can book Club LeConte. Does anyone have a problem with Saturday December 16?"

"I think that would be a good date," said David and Jennifer.

"No problem for me either," said Paula.

"Then all we have to do is see if it's OK with Elizabeth," said Ace.

The four of them walked over to Brad and Elizabeth and informed them of their decision. They both were agreeable to the date. "It's settled," said Brad. "I'll make all the arrangements."

Jennifer called Ace to one side and asked him if he would give her away at the wedding.

"I would hate to give you away, Jennifer, I would much rather keep you. Just kidding, I would be honored to give you away. I will finally get to be your father."

"I love you, Ace," said Jennifer. "You will always be a daddy to me."

"There is one thing though I wish you would do for me," said Ace.

"What is that?" replied Jennifer.

"I wish that you would notice Paula's engagement ring before she pops a gasket."

"I will on one condition."

"What is that?" asked Ace.

"That somebody notices mine."

"Let me see," said Ace. "Pardon me for being so unobservant. That's a beautiful ring. It must be at least two carats. I'll tell you what we need to do to rectify everything, Jennifer."

"What do you have in mind, Ace?"

"Let's walk over to where Paula and David are standing and put on a little act." Ace explained to Jennifer how it would play out.

They both walked over to them and got into conversation with them, and Ace looked at Jennifer's left hand and explained in a loud voice, "Is that a new ring, Jennifer?"

"Yes," she said as she looked at Paula, and said in a surprised voice, "Paula! You have one too. How beautiful it looks on you."

After a half hour of socializing, Brad had them all sit down so he could talk to them before the dinner started.

"As you all know, my phone has been ringing off the hook since the trial, I have had to turn down three civil cases in the last two days. They were too far away, and besides, I had already accepted one in Nashville. The Nashville case involves a pilot who was performing stunts in an airplane that was not designed for stunt flying. The instruction manual distinctly points out that his plane should not be used for stunt flying, however the pilot's lawyer claims that since the warning was not stamped somewhere on the plane that the aircraft company is liable. The pilot ended up with permanent injuries and will be confined to a wheelchair for the rest of his life. Unlike Bret Martin, this man's injuries are real."

"I thought all planes that were designed for stunt flying had some sort of marking on the plane somewhere," said Ace.

"They do have a marking for the stunt planes on their rudders, but there is no marking on the plane he was flying that states it is not qualified for stunt flying."

"Isn't that stretching things quite a bit, Brad? It's sort of like trying to prove a negative," said Ace."

"His lawyer said the pilot didn't know anything about the markings on the plane in the first place."

"Isn't that going to be a tough case when they roll the man in on a stretcher?" asked Ace.

"It's not going to be an easy case. They're suing for $5 million. The pilot was a wealthy man with a good income, and they will be suing for loss of wages in addition to pain and suffering. It's not right for a company to be sued when they are not at fault. If I win the case for them, they still lose. The airplane company will be out the cost of the trial plus all my fees. This will be a tough case, but if I can get an intelligent jury, I believe we can win it. I had a 'make it go away' clause inserted in the contract with the stipulation that if we get the lawsuit withdrawn, our company would receive ten percent of the lawsuit amount. That would be $500,000 in this case."

"Who is our client, Brad?" asked Ace.

"The company is Allison Aircraft, a manufacturer of small planes."

"Has a trial date been set?" asked Paula.

"The trial date has not been set, but I believe it will start sometime after the first of the year. There is one other thing I would like to say before we eat. I have been invited to appear on the *Dave Michaels* talk show on CNT Wednesday of next week."

"Way to go," said Ace.

"I would like for you to get started on the Nashville thing Monday, Ace. See me in my office at 9:00 a.m. I would now like to propose a toast to the two couples who are getting married. My very dear friend and date has graciously agreed to perform the ceremony, which she has informed me, would be her first. Would anyone like some champagne?"

Chapter 68

Monday, October 30

Ace entered Brad's office and Brad had Denise bring them both a cup of coffee.

"I want to bring you up to speed on the Nashville case, Ace," said Brad. "I have a copy of the lawsuit that was filed in the Davidson County Court. It states that one John Stanley was flying out of the Nashville Air airport on October 1, 2006, and he was flying an Allison single-engine Eagle that crashed when a portion of the wing broke off, causing the pilot to crash into a cornfield, where he received permanent and disabling injuries. His lawyer is a man by the name of Fletcher Collins whom I've never heard of. I had Denise make you a copy. That's the gist of the lawsuit except for a lot of legalese which I'm sure you're not interested in."

"It looks like I need to take a trip to Nashville and the sooner the better," said Ace.

"I'll have Denise make a plane reservation for you," said Brad.

"I think it would be better if I just drove down there myself. "It's only a three-hour drive, and I wouldn't have to rent a car when I got there."

"Good point," said Brad. "When can you leave?"

"I don't think right now would be too soon," said Ace.

"Good hunting. I know you'll do a good job."

"I'm on my way as soon as I stop by and tell Paula," said Ace.

Paula was busy at her desk when Ace informed her of his trip. "Be careful. I'll miss you," she said.

"Would you mind doing me a favor, Paula?"

"Look on your computer and get the address and phone number for Nashville Air?"

It took her about a minute to come up with an address and phone number.

Ace told her he loved her, kissed her goodbye, and took the elevator to the parking garage, retrieved his car, and headed west on I-40. It was 9:30 a.m. when he left the parking garage. He had not had breakfast so he stopped in Harriman at the Cracker Barrel and ate some country ham and eggs. As he was returning to his car after he had eaten, he happened to notice a bumper sticker on an old beat-up pickup truck with the ugliest dog he had ever seen standing up in the bed. Ace had remembered seeing a bumper sticker once on an old beat-up car that read: "MY OTHER CAR IS A ROLLS ROYCE." This was a bumper sticker along the same lines, but with a twist. It read: "MY OTHER DOG IS A LHASA APSO." After taking a picture of the bumper sticker with his cell phone, he drove from there directly to the Nashville Air Airport utilizing his GPS which told him every turn to make.

He arrived there at twelve noon Central time having gained an hour when he crossed the central time zone in Cumberland County.

The airport was rather small with only a small staff working there.

Ace walked up to a lady working behind a desk and asked her if they gave flying lessons.

She told him he needed to see George Wilson, who was working in the hanger which she pointed out to him. Ace walked into the hangar and went up to the only person in the hangar. The man appeared to be about forty-five years old and in good condition. He looked to be about six feet tall weighing around 200 pounds. Ace was happy to see that he was wearing a Tennessee Vol cap.

"I'm Ace Sleuth from Knoxville, Tennessee, and I'm glad to see that you are a Big Orange fan."

"Hi, I'm George Wilson. Are you here to take flying lessons?"

"No, I'm here on business. Do you know a man named John Stanley?"

"Yes, I gave him flying lessons a couple of years ago, why do you ask?"

"His attorney has filed a lawsuit against Allison Aircraft whom my employer, Brad Adams, represents."

"Is that the same Brad Adams that won that scam lawsuit last week in Knoxville?"

"He's the one and the same."

"Is John suing because of the airplane accident he had?"

"Yes, he's suing for $5 million," said Ace. "What kind of student was he?"

"He was very cocky and I always had to hold him back. He was always wanting do a loop in my plane. What in the world is the basis for the lawsuit?"

"His attorney claims that Stanley didn't know that the airplane he was flying was not rated for stunt flying."

"He should have known that. Every stunt plane has a distinctive marking on the rudder."

"That's what I thought," replied Ace.

"In addition, that very question was on the test he took to get his license. If I remember correctly, the test showed a picture of the symbol and the student had to identify it, and he got it right."

"Could I get a copy of that test?"

"I believe I can come up with one."

"Do you keep copies of all the old tests?"

"Yes, we keep them for five years here and then send them to Nashville."

"I may have to subpoena his actual test," said Ace.

"I don't think that would be a problem, Ace."

"How often did Stanley fly?"

"He flew about once a week."

"Did he always fly alone?"

"Most of the time he did, but a couple of times he brought a woman along, whom I suspected was not his wife."

"What made you think that?"

"The way they talked and looked at each other."

"Do you know her name?"

"I heard John refer to her as Sheila a couple of times."

"Do you happen to have the phone number of Mr. Stanley?"

"I believe I have it here somewhere, if not, I can look it up in the directory. Here it is."

"George, I can't begin to tell you how much you have helped me. Do you ever go to the UT football games?"

"It's so hard to get tickets that I mostly watch them on TV."

"How would you like to go to UT-LSU game on November 4 and sit in Brad's sky box?"

"Are you kidding me, Ace? I can't think of anything else I would rather do. By the way, that name Ace rings a bell. Are you the guy who got carjacked in Knoxville and got the prep's picture trapped inside your car?"

"That was me, George. Take my phone number and call me a few days before the game. We can put you up in a hotel if you like. It's all on us."

"Thanks, Ace. If you need for me to testify in the trial just let me know."

"I don't think there will be a trial, George, but thanks anyway."

Ace got in his car and drove toward Nashville, about twenty miles to the southwest. He dialed John Stanley's home phone number and a woman answered. "Is John there?" asked Ace.

"He's still at the office," she said.

"Could I have his office number please?"

"What's this all about, and who are you?"

"My name is Dr. Wallace Proctor and I've been retained by John's attorney, a Mr. Fletcher Collins, as an expert witness in his forthcoming lawsuit. I need to go over some things with him before the trial."

"I think John mentioned something about an expert witness," she said, and then gave him the work number.

"Thank you very much, Mrs. Stanley."

As soon as he had hung up, Ace dialed the new number, and a female voice informed him that this was the office of John Stanley. "Who should I say is calling?" she asked.

"Tell him that it's his expert witness, Dr. Wallace Proctor." She passed him right through.

"Dr. Proctor, I've been expecting your call," said Stanley.

"Good, Mr. Stanley. We need to get together as soon as possible because my schedule is very tight."

"I am free right now. Where would you like to meet?"

"I'm staying here at the Sheraton Nashville Downtown Hotel on Union Street. Are you nearby?"

"I can be there in twenty minutes."

"Are you able to drive?"

"Yes, I manage pretty well, everything considered. I have a special car with all the necessary gadgets on the steering wheel. I also manage to get in and out of the car by myself."

"Good. I will be waiting on you in the main lobby and I'll have on a name tag."

"Good. I'll see you shortly," said Stanley.

The good man was right on time, and he had no trouble locating Ace. Mr. Stanley was a rather good-looking man who probably stood about five feet eleven before his accident. He had a full head of hair sprinkled with a little gray, but there was something about the man that seemed a little shady to Ace.

"Why don't we step into the bar around the corner so we can find a quiet place to talk?" said Ace.

"Good idea," said John.

They both sat down and ordered a drink.

"I will come right to the point, Mr. Stanley. I am truly sorry for your accident, but it is not the fault of Allison Aircraft. My name is not Dr. Proctor, but Ace Sleuth, and I work for the man who is defending Allison Aircraft, the company you are suing. I really don't think this lawsuit was your idea. Were you approached by a tort lawyer about this case? Did he instigate this lawsuit? I don't believe that you should be the only one to shoulder the blame, I think your lawyer is just as guilty as you are for filing a phony lawsuit."

"What are you talking about? Are you daft?"

"I'm talking about you doing stunts in a plane that you knew wasn't designed for that type of flying."

"I didn't have any information to the contrary."

"I have a witness who is willing to testify otherwise."

"This meeting is over right now, Mr. Sleuth," he said, as he got up and started to leave the bar.

"Hold on a second, Mr. Stanley. Do you know a man by the name of George Wilson?"

"Yes."

"Well, he's willing to testify in court that there was a question on your pilot's test relating to the stunt marking on aircraft, and that you answered it correctly."

"That's only his word against mine," he said.

"I'm afraid that there's more to it than his word against yours, Mr. Stanley. Copies of all pilot tests are kept on file for five years. We can and we will subpoena that test if we have to go to trial. Am I making myself clear?"

"You don't scare me."

"Have you ever heard of a lawyer by the name of Brad Adams? He can't wait to get you on the witness stand."

"Was he the one who got all that publicity in Knoxville recently?"

"He certainly is. In that case, both the lawyer and the client ended up in jail and will probably spend at least ten years there. In addition, each one of them was assessed a million dollars for trying to scam Mr. Adams. It's going to be a whole different ball game out there, John, as a result of this lawsuit. Tort lawyers and their clients who try to manipulate the system are going to be held responsible for their actions. You and your lawyer could actually be found to be causing financial damages to Allison Aircraft, and you and he could be out millions yourselves. If the jury finds fraud both of you could go to jail. The days are over when lawsuits can be filed for any flimsy reason with impunity."

"You're just trying to scare me off."

"Did you see the transcripts of the trial in Knoxville? Brad Adams would chew you up and spit you out on the witness stand. If you've got any secrets such as a girlfriend named Sheila, or Alice, etc, I guarantee you that it will come out at the trial. You are playing with fire, John. I work full-time for Brad Adams now and I really believe he would rather go to trial with this case after he's seen all the evidence I've uncovered. He charges $500 per hour and he's not going to be too happy to lose all that money he would make on this case. He had so much fun in his last trial that I'm not sure I can talk him out of this one. He hates injustice so much that he refused to stop the trial in Knoxville. He had more than enough evidence to stop the trial in its tracks, but he wanted to punish the lawyer and his client. He only has to ask you one question when he gets you on the witness stand and the ball game is over."

"What question is that?"

"The question is: 'Did you know that the plane you crashed while doing stunts was not qualified for that type of flying?' If you answer 'No,'

Brad will pull out the copy of your pilot's test and you will be charged with perjury. If you answer 'yes,' the judge will throw out the case. You're in a lose-lose situation, John. I tell you what I'm going to do. I'm going to do you a favor. I'm going to give you until tomorrow at this time to drop this case, or it's out of my hands."

"You're bluffing."

"Why don't you test me? You have until tomorrow by, let me see," as he looked at his watch, "make that 5:15 p.m. central time. Until then, ciao for now."

Ace got a motel room for the night and slept soundly. He got up the next morning and drove the twenty-five or so miles on I-40 east to Lebanon and had breakfast again at a Cracker Barrel Restaurant. Lebanon is the headquarters and the home of the Cracker Barrel Restaurant chain and the first Cracker Barrel Restaurant. Ace remembered eating at the original one several years ago, but found out that it was no longer in use. After eating he took I-40 east for the trip back to Knoxville. He had an idea. He dialed 702-555-5555 on his cell phone.

"MGM security," the familiar voice said.

"Lamont, how are you doing?"

"I'm just fine, Ace, I read about the big case in Knoxville. Way to go."

"Thanks. I just wanted to call and tell you that I didn't have to use the VCR tapes you gave me."

"That's good news, Ace. I'm relieved to hear that. I stuck my neck way out on that one. What else is new?"

"Paula and I have set the date for our wedding. It's going to be December 16 at the First Baptist Church in downtown Knoxville. It's going to be a double ceremony with Brad Adam's son, David, marrying a girl named Jennifer, whom I knew twenty years ago and have just met again. It's a long intriguing story, but she has asked me to give her away at the wedding."

"Do you still want me for your best man, Ace?"

"I certainly do, Lamont. Would you like for me to make reservations for you here at the Marriott?"

"I can handle that from this end a lot better, and get a good discount in the process. The offer is still open on the honeymoon deal here at MGM."

"We graciously accept, Lamont. Come a couple of days early and I'll show you around."

"I'll try to do just that, Ace. I'll let you know in plenty of time."

"Good. I'll pick you up at the airport in my '76 Mustang."

"Keep in touch, Ace."

Ace arrived in Knoxville around 1:00 p.m. He parked in the parking garage of the BB&T, and took the elevator to the twenty-fourth floor. Brad was in his office when Ace walked in.

"Sit down, Ace, I have some great news. The Nashville lawsuit has been dropped."

"I thought it would be, Brad, but it didn't come cheap."

"How much is it costing us?"

"Well, in addition to my expenses, you will have to allow one George Wilson to occupy two of your sky box seats for the UT- LSU game, and maybe a night or two in the Marriott."

"How did you manage that, Ace?"

"If I told you, I would have to kill you."

"Do you realize that you just cost me a bundle in lost fees at $500 per hour?"

"That should be no problem for a moneybags like you; besides, what about the 'make it go away' clause and the $500,000?"

"Well, there is that," said Brad.

Chapter 69

Wednesday, November 1

The Dave Michaels Show

"Good morning, Brad," said Dave. "Let me tell the radio audience a little bit about you.

"My guest today is Bradford Adams, who is an attorney from Knoxville, Tennessee, where he has just won one of the most talked-about trials since the O. J. Simpson one. Tell us about it in a nutshell, Brad."

"On September 5 of this year a man hit the windshield of my car as I was rounding a corner of the parking garage beneath the building where I work. He fell to the concrete floor and ended up in the hospital claiming to be in severe pain and unable to walk. I suspected it was a scam from the beginning, which turned out to be true. With some excellent detective work by my investigator, Ace Sleuth, we were able to find more than enough evidence to stop the trial, but I wanted to go to trial to exonerate myself, and at the same time, make sure that the crooked lawyer and his client went to jail. It turned out that the client was a former stuntman and he and his lawyer had met at a blackjack table in Vegas."

"Tell the audience the unusual aspects of the trial, Brad."

"There are so many twists and turns I don't quite know where to start. The plaintiff's attorney in this case had hired a quack doctor, whom we later found out got his doctorate degree on the internet from a place in Belize. He ended up skipping town when he was excused to go to the bathroom and hasn't been heard from since. I got the lawyer for the plaintiff on the witness stand and got him to commit perjury and take the fifth. We had so much evidence against the two of them that we didn't even have to use all of it. Under intense questioning of the plaintiff, I got him to admit that the whole so-called accident was a scam from the word go. He came in the courtroom in a hospital bed claiming to be unable to walk and ended up getting out of the bed and walking to the witness chair on orders from the judge."

"Tell us about the jury selection process and the unusual verdict from the jury."

"I didn't want a bunch of undereducated jurors judging me, so I came up with a plan to dismiss them for cause."

"Tell us about that."

"It's really very simple. I just asked them if they knew how much money a million dollars was. I specifically asked them how many thousand-dollar bills it took to make a million. About half of them didn't know, and they were dismissed for cause."

"Why do you think the judge went along with this?"

"Because she is a fair-minded judge," said Brad. "I explained to her that I didn't think it would be fair for someone to sit on a jury trial for $3 million when they had no idea how much a million dollars was. She agreed."

"What about the jury's verdict?"

"The jury verdict was one of the most amazing things about the trial. The jury found for the defendant, namely me, in the amount of $2 million, one million each from each the lawyer and his client."

"Had this ever happened before?"

"Not that I have been able to determine."

"How do you feel about the tort system in our country today, Brad?"

"Dave, I think it's a disaster. In my opinion, we have a model-T Ford held together by rusty baling wire."

"Why do you say that?"

"Look at the system right now. Any tort lawyer can sue anybody for any reason with impunity. In some class-action suits he can also pick the venue. In some of these cases the lawsuits are nothing more than legalized extortion."

"Those are pretty harsh words, Brad."

"Sometimes harsh words are needed. We can't keep going down this bumpy road, It's costing the American taxpayers billions and billions of dollars in insurance and medical costs annually in order to let some greedy tort lawyers fly around in their private jets. It's almost like winning the lottery for them."

"How much money do you think we could save if we reduced the number of tort cases?"

"If we cut the number of lawsuits in half, I believe we could lower car and hospitalization insurance by at least twenty-five percent, and malpractice insurance by more. In addition to the insurance savings, I believe much more money could be saved by cutting down on unnecessary costly medical procedures that are performed by doctors and hospitals for fear of being sued if they miss something in their examinations."

"That makes a lot of sense to me, Brad. What changes would you make if you had a chance?"

"First I would make the loser of the lawsuit pay. When I say pay, I don't just mean the court cost, I'm talking about defense lawyer fees, lost time for everyone involved, and any other fees, such as paying for investigations. I'm talking about the loser paying for everything associated with the defense of the case. I believe this loser pay scenario would cut the cases by much more than fifty percent. I also believe that the lawyer bringing the suit should be held equally responsible with his client and each made to pay half of all expenses associated with the lawsuit. If the lawsuit is valid in the first place, there should be no problem with someone who has a legitimate claim from getting justice."

"What are some cases that you think were unfounded?"

"One situation comes to mind but it never went to court because it was a scam. I would have loved to have defended that one in court. It was the one where a woman claimed to have found a finger in her chili at a fast-food restaurant. My first question of the witness when she got in the chair would be: 'Tell me, Miss Jones, exactly how you have been damaged by finding this finger in your chili? Did you have a heart attack that has affected your health? You look pretty healthy to me? Tell me precisely how you were affected.' The only person who suffered injury in this case was the poor man who lost his finger. It seems to me that a lot of people take great pleasure in seeing successful companies have to shell out money. The American people end up paying higher prices for many goods and services because of these types of lawsuits."

"What are some other steps you would recommend regarding tort cases?"

"I would do away with class-action suits altogether and the pathetic television ads that go along with them. They evidently want the people who see the ads to go out and buy the product and get in on the lawsuit. The more the merrier, the more the money it seems to me. When a diet drug was under a class-action lawsuit, and the venue selected was a poor county in Mississippi where many of the people were undereducated, a local pharmacist reported that a woman came in to get a prescription filled for the diet drug and she only wanted two of the thirty pills the prescription called for, evidently just enough to get in on the lawsuit. Are we insane to put up with a system like this, Dave?"

"We must be or we would do something about it."

"Did you know that just a threat of a lawsuit can send a company or an individual into a panic? Sometimes when a victim of a lawsuit wins the case, they still lose. They have to spend a lot of money hiring lawyers and investigators. They should be compensated for these expenses and lost time, not to mention their mental anguish."

"I agree with you completely, Brad. What are some of the other steps that you would take?"

"I would like to see a review board made up of judges and some well-respected businessmen in the community to screen all civil cases to determine if they are court worthy. This might eliminate half of the cases. I think that in every civil case the burden should be placed on the person bringing the suit to prove that the defendant was at fault in the case. They should also have to prove negligence on the part of the defendant. I knew of a man a few years back who was driving down the street within the speed limit when a young man, who was in a fight in a pool room, ran out right in front of the man's car and was killed. The driver's insurance company paid an amount they thought would be cheaper than going to court, and the man was left with a blemished record through no fault of his own. This is unfair."

"Is there anything else you would recommend?"

"Yes, I would do away completely with punitive damages which can triple the amount of the award. I don't know who came up with this crazy idea, but whoever it was needs to watch out for the guys in the white coats.

ACE SLEUTH, PRIVATE EYE

A tort lawyer can get some of these jurors so aroused that it's just a roll of the dice what kind of judgment they might come up with. I don't want people like that determining how I may be required to live the rest of my life, rich, poor, or in between. It's a scary thing. Let me give you an example where people want to be rewarded for their ignorance and stupidity. Let's take the case of the proverbial step ladder. Have you ever noticed all the warning signs on a step ladder? You can hardly read the brand name for all the other stickers on it. I don't think it does any good anyway because some tort lawyer wheels an injured man on a stretcher into the courtroom who looks like death warmed over and the jury can't keep their eyes off him. We find that this man was injured when he fell off a step ladder that was in perfect working condition. He was injured because of his own carelessness and he should not be rewarded for it at the expense of an innocent company. Most times the jurors vote with their hearts instead of their brains. This case should have never made it to court. I believe that the only way the injured person should win in this case is to prove that the ladder was defective when it came from the factory. If the ladder had become unsteady because of neglect and misuse, then the ladder company should not be held liable. It is the responsibility of the owner to take good care of his tools and equipment and to use common sense when working with them. Personal responsibility is the name of the game in my opinion."

"Do you have any other recommendations, Brad?"

"I have just one. I would like to see attorney advertisements of all kinds eliminated. I don't believe that any professional should have to advertise unless it's a young professional just getting started in business. The professional organizations at one time disallowed advertising until a federal judge ruled it unconstitutional."

"What are your plans now that your lawsuit is out of the way, Brad?"

"I plan to work full-time defending what I consider to be unfounded lawsuits. I hate injustices, whether it is the defendant or the plaintiff who is being wronged, and I will do my best to right these wrongs."

"I don't believe I would want to go up against you in a court of law, Brad. I would like to thank you for coming on my show and educating my audience and me on the tort system in this country."

"It has been my pleasure, Dave. Thanks for having me."

Chapter 70

Friday morning, November 3

Brad had returned from his appearance on the *Dave Michaels Show* and had asked Ace to meet him in his office first thing Friday morning. Paula was also in attendance.

"You did a bang-up job on Dave's show, Brad," said Ace.

"Thanks. What I wanted to talk to you about is a civil trial going on here in Knoxville that involves a woman by the name of Hillary Jenkins. She claims she suffered debilitating neck injuries when a local resident by the name of Clifford Owens hit her car from behind in the West Town Mall parking lot as he pulled in behind her. She claims that she was getting ready to pull out of the parking space when he hit her. Owens claims that she actually backed into his car after he had just parked and was getting ready to get out of his car. He said his engine was not even running."

"It sounds a lot like she said, he said," replied Ace.

"Exactly, Ace, but I'm afraid that the jury might lend more credence to the 'she said' part. Here's what we have. Owens' defense lawyer, Preston Woods, just suffered a mild heart attack and will be laid up for a couple of months. I have been asked to take over the case in midstream. Owens doesn't want another lawyer provided by the insurance company because he doesn't think they did a thorough enough investigation. If I don't take it the case it will have to be continued at a later date and started all over. Owens is anxious to go forward, and I would like to get your opinion on this matter, Ace."

"I say go for it."

"How do you feel about it, Paula?" asked Brad.

"I agree with Ace," she said.

"Then it's agreed," said Brad. "Jenkins' attorney is a man from Lexington, Kentucky, by the name of Roland Frazier, and I don't know a thing about him. The trial judge is named Walter Sears, and from what I've heard, is a fair man.

"The trial was just getting started when Woods had his heart attack. The jury is in place and the trial resumes Monday, November 13. We have a lot of work to do and a short time in which to do it. Here's what I want each of you to do.

"Ace, I want you to find out all you can about their expert witness, a doctor by the name of Winston Collier. I want you to also get the local address of Hillary Jenkins and see what you can dig up at her residence. I think her address is in this pile of paperwork that they gave me.

"Paula, I want you to go through this pile of paperwork and let me know if you find anything you think I should know about. I also want you to get on the internet and find out all you can about Hillary Jenkins. Find out if she is a Knoxville native, where she works now, and any other jobs she has had in the past. I want anything at all that you can find out about her. See if you can dig up anything at all about Dr. Collier, such as where he's from, so that we can give Ace a starting point. Are there any questions from either of you?"

"Not for now," they both said.

"Well, let's make some hay then. By the way, there is one thing I almost forgot to tell you two. Owens was driving a 2007 Mercedes S550 when this all went down. I don't believe it was a coincidence that he was driving an expensive car. I don't believe in coincidences."

As soon as they left, Brad called Denise and had her set up a meeting with Owens. He then dialed his old friend, Roger Kennedy, the radiologist.

"It's me again," said Brad. "You may not want to speak to me after your ordeal in court last week, but I just took on a case that needs your expertise again."

"To tell you the truth, Brad, I rather enjoyed that little fiasco at the trial. What do you have for me this time?"

Brad brought Roger up to speed on how he had gotten the case. "I need for you look at some more x-rays. This time they are in the neck area."

"I'll be glad to take a look, Brad. Just bring them over."
"When would be a good time for you, Roger?"
"Any time today is fine with me."
"I'll be over in thirty minutes," said Brad.

Chapter 71

Roger was waiting when Brad walked into his office. Brad explained about the accident in the West Town Mall parking lot as he handed him the x-rays.

Roger studied them for a few minutes and asked Brad when the accident had taken place.

"I don't have the exact date before me, but it couldn't have been more than three months ago."

"Then this neck injury is preexisting," said Roger.

"Are you certain?"

"Yes, it takes a certain amount of time for an injury of this type to heal as the x-rays show here."

"Could you testify to that in court?"

"Yes, I could."

"Roger, I have something to ask of you, and it won't hurt my feelings if you say no. I paid you for your testimony in my trial."

"Yes, you did, Brad, and if I may say so, you paid me quite well. What are you getting at?"

"I want to ask you to testify in this case pro bono, and I'll tell you why; your testimony will add a lot of credence to our case. What do you say?"

"I think it would be great, Brad. I can't wait to see the look on the lawyer's face when I answer the question. You know, Brad, I think that it is only right that I testify pro bono, as you lawyers call it. I never did get around to testifying in your first trial if you remember?"

"Yes, it almost slipped my mind. I never did recall you after that fiasco with Luther Spenser, did I? Thanks a lot, Roger. I'll be in touch with you about the date and time."

"Glad I could be of help, Brad."

Ace put on his homeless outfit and headed for the garbage cans belonging to Hillary Jenkins at a rented little house at a street a block off Broadway in North Knoxville. He didn't mind that it was broad daylight. If they caught him all they would do is tell him to leave. It only took him a minute to determine which can was hers, and less time than that to gather all the paperwork he found and place it in a plastic bag. He could sort it out at his office.

He returned to his office and started going through the stuff. The first things he noticed were a couple of envelopes that had been forwarded from her previous address in Cincinnati. There were some other items such as bills and bulk mailings, but Ace was more interested in the previous address which he copied to his little black book.

He had just changed into his normal working clothes when the phone rang. It was Paula calling.

"What's up, baby doll?"

"I thought you might be interested to know that Dr. Collier was employed at Charity Hospital in Cincinnati up until a year ago."

"That's great, Paula. How did you find out?"

"If I told you, Ace, I would have to kill you."

"It looks like I need to make a trip to Cincinnati pretty soon, Paula, and I think it would be better if I drove. It's only about a five-hour trip, and I can leave about eight in the morning. Is Brad in?"

"Yes, do you want me to put you through to him?"

"I would appreciate it."

"How you doing, Ace?" asked Brad.

"Pretty good, Brad," said Ace. He then filled him in on all he had found out and the Cincinnati trip.

"Could you come by the office for a few minutes and pick up a credit card that Denise is holding for you? I would like for you and Paula to start using credit cards as much as possible. It provides better records, and besides, I get back up to five percent of everything that's spent."

"That sounds like a win-win situation to me."

Ace had a few things to do first. He made up six different ID cards and laminated them. He didn't know exactly what he would need in Cincinnati so he made an AMA card for an orthopedic surgeon by the name of Barry King, and for an attorney at law by the name of Albert

Hefley. He also made one for a Medicare official from Columbus, Ohio, along with the three others. He also made up a business card for each of the ID cards.

Ace got in his Mustang and went by the office and picked up the credit card, kissed Paula goodbye, and then drove by his domicile and picked up a few clothes. He then got in his car and headed west on Kingston Pike to the Joseph A. Banks clothing store. He had already found a good use for his credit card.

He was greeted by a male clerk as soon as he walked through the door.

"How may I help you?" he asked.

"I would like a good-quality business suit that is neither too conservative nor too flamboyant. I want something in between."

"I think I have just the suit you are looking for. Come this way please."

He showed Ace a three-piece which looked good to him, but it wasn't exactly what he wanted.

"Do you have something similar without the vest?"

"Yes, I believe I do." He then showed Ace a similar "vestless suit" with a price tag of $700.

He tried on the coat, which fit perfectly, but the pants were about an inch too big in the waist.

"No problem sir," he said, as he marked the pant length. "We can take in the waist. Would Wednesday of next week be satisfactory?"

"No, I must have the suit today, preferably within the next hour."

"I'm afraid that is impossible, sir."

"Then I'm afraid it is impossible for me to purchase the suit," said Ace.

"Let me check with our tailor. I'll be right back."

He came back in a couple of minutes.

"Would you mind waiting about forty-five minutes, sir?"

"I think I can manage that." When the clerk brought the suit, Ace made good use of his new credit card.

Chapter 72

Monday morning, November 6

Ace hit the road to Cincinnati in his 1976 Mustang turned on the radio and heard a very pretty song entitled "Eighty Acres of Stars," which he thought was well delivered. The DJ announced that the recording was by Annie Sims, an up-and-coming country singer. Ace expected that he would be hearing more about her. She sounded country with a touch of class. He wondered if this was the same Annie who used to play the piano and sing at the Regas Restaurant. *Probably not,* he thought. (But Ace was wrong.)

Ace arrived in Cincinnati five hours later. The first thing he wanted to do was to look up the address where Hillary Jenkins had lived just a few months back. He purchased a city map to use in conjunction with his GPS. He liked to know what section of the city he was in. He had no trouble finding her house. It was a small two-bedroom house not far from the Cincinnati Reds' Great American Ball Park. He got out of the car and knocked on the door. A heavy-set woman in her fifties came to the door.

"My name is Kennedy Fields and I'm looking for Hillary Jenkins," he said.

"She don't live here no more," the woman said.

"When did she move?"

"About three months ago."

"Did you know her?"

"No, she moved out before I moved in."

"Who lives in the house next door?"

"Her name is Edith Smith."

"Do you think she knows her?"

"I would think that she does."

"Do you know if Edith is at home?"

"I think so. I just saw her a few minutes ago."

"Thanks, I'll go talk to her."

"Why do you want to see her?"

"She was left a small sum of money from a distant relative she probably doesn't even know exists, and I'm trying to get it to her."

"I don't know exactly where she moved to, but maybe Edith can help you."

"Thanks a lot." Ace left and walked over to the house next door and knocked on the door.

A middle-aged woman with a sprinkling of gray in her brown hair came to the door.

"My name is Kennedy Fields and I was just next door looking for Hillary Jenkins, and found out that she had moved. The lady next door said you might be able to tell me how to get in touch with her."

"Come in, Mr. Fields, and have a cup of coffee with me. My name is Edith Smith and I was just wondering how I was going to spend the next few minutes. What do you take in you coffee?"

"Cream and sugar please," said Ace.

"How may I help you, Kennedy?"

"Miss Jenkins was left a small sum of money by a distant relative and I'm trying to find her to give it to her."

"How small a sum is it?"

"I guess it's OK for me to tell you. It's a little over $5,000."

"That seems like a lot of money to me, but that would be peanuts to Hillary."

"Why do you say that?"

"Because of the million dollars she won for her part in a lawsuit over her accident."

"When did this accident take place?"

"I think it was a little over a year ago"

"Did you know her well?"

"I knew her pretty well up to the time she had the accident and had to go to the hospital."

"What happened to her?"

"She had a neck injury in a car wreck."

"Did the trial take place here in the city?"

"Right here in Hamilton County."

"When was this?"

"I think it was about six months ago."

"When did she move?"

"About a month after the trial. I never saw her much after she won all that money. I think it went to her head and she thought I wasn't good enough for her."

"Do you know where she moved to?"

"I think it was somewhere farther down south."

"If I can't locate her, the money will revert to the state, so I'll keep looking a little while longer. Thanks for your information. The coffee was delicious."

"I wish you could stay a little longer, Kennedy, but if you got to go, you got to go."

"I wish I could spend more time talking to you, Edith; I've really enjoyed our conversation. You have been very helpful to me." Ace left and headed straight to the Hamilton County courthouse.

Ace passed through the metal detectors that are commonplace in all courthouses since 9/11, and headed for the circuit court clerk's office. He walked up to the young lady at the reception desk and introduced himself and asked her if he could see the trial records of a civil lawsuit brought by Hillary Jenkins.

"I don't see why not," she said, "it's public record. All you have to do is go to the internet and type in the names, and you get the information instantly."

"I might have a problem there because I don't know all the names, just Hillary's."

She looked the case up and found the docket number and asked Ace if he would like to get a copy of it.

"That would be great," he said.

"There is a ten-dollar fee for the copy."

"No problem," said Ace.

She hit some keys on her computer and walked across the room to a high-speed printer and the trial papers were there waiting on her.

Ace got the papers, found a seat in the waiting area, and took a look at the trial papers. The first name that jumped out at him was the name of the expert witness in the case, Dr. Winston Collier, the same one in the Knoxville case. *Well, well, well,* he thought, *what an interesting development this is.* He also noted that the start date of the trial was June 26, 2006. His next stop was to find a nice motel where he could change into his $700 suit and have a place to spend the night. He found a nice Hampton Inn Motel which offered a full free breakfast and checked in. He quickly changed into his new suit and headed for Charity Hospital.

Ace parked his car and walked up to the receptionist's desk in the lobby and asked her to direct him to the hospital administrator's office. She sent him down the hall to Room 101 and he asked the young lady at the desk if Mr. Willard Simpson was in. Ace looked very businesslike in his new suit.

"Whom shall I say would like to see him?"

"Tell him it's Lawrence Miller from the regional Medicare office in Columbus," said Ace.

She buzzed his office and told Ace to go right in.

"Thank you," he said, and walked in to see a man of around sixty and a little overweight with intelligent eyes.

"How may I help you, Mr. Miller? Do you have any identification?"

"Certainly, Mr. Simpson," said Ace, as he showed him his freshly laminated ID.

"I wish I was here under more pleasant circumstances, Mr. Simpson, but sometimes we don't get to do what pleases us."

"What is the problem?"

"Sir, we have had several complaints from some of our Medicare patients who have been in your hospital concerning overcharges on their bills."

"What type of overcharges?"

"They claim that there are charges for procedures that were not performed, and there were items or services on their bills that they did not receive."

"I know, Mr. Miller, that sometimes our people doing the billing get a little aggressive, but we do our best to keep it under control."

"I'm sure you do, Mr. Simpson, but there is another problem here at your hospital that involves one of your doctors."

"Who is that?"

"He is a doctor by the name of Winston Collier."

"Dr. Collier no longer works here."

"And why is that?"

"I'm afraid that I cannot reveal that information, Mr. Miller."

"When did he leave the hospital?"

"He left almost a year ago."

"Did he leave of his own accord?"

"I'm afraid I can't answer that, Mr. Miller."

"I see. Well let's get back to the overcharges again. I think I may have to institute an investigation into the overcharges. I would hate to see your hospital blacklisted by Medicare."

"What do you want to know about Dr. Collier?"

"I want to know all the details. If he is unsuitable to be a doctor, I want to remove him from our Medicare list."

"We have had a problem with him for many years. We thought he performed way too many operations, and not very good ones at that. His malpractice insurance rates went through the roof, and we couldn't afford the payments. In addition, we were afraid of lawsuits against him and the hospital."

"Did he find a position at any other hospital?"

"I don't think so. I saw in the paper where he was an expert witness in a few civil lawsuits."

"What is his area of expertise?"

"He is an orthopedic surgeon."

"Could you give me the exact date that he left the hospital?"

"Yes," he said, as he called his secretary and asked her to have the information ready for him on his way out.

"Thanks a lot, Mr. Simpson. I wish you would take a close look at your billing department and try to keep a closer rein on them."

"I certainly will, Mr. Miller. I want to maintain a good working relationship with Medicare. I think Judy will have that information for you."

The secretary handed Ace the information and he noticed that Collier's last day at the hospital was November 23, 2005.

The next morning after a good breakfast in the motel, Ace made the return trip to Knoxville.

Chapter 73

Tuesday morning, November 7

Ace met with Brad and Paula in the office to inform them of his findings in Cincinnati.

"This puts a whole new light on the trial," said Brad. "I don't believe Owens' insurance company spent a penny on an investigation."

"I don't think so either. What do you have in mind, Brad?" asked Ace.

"I want to settle out of court."

"Do you think that's wise?" asked Paula.

"Sit back and watch. See if you can get in touch with Hillary's lawyer, Mr. Roland Frazier, in Lexington, and see when he can meet with us here in my office."

"What reason do you want me to give him for the meeting, Brad?"

"Tell him we want to settle out of court. That should get him down here in a New York minute. That's all I have for now."

Paula got Mr. Frazier on the phone and he said he would meet them in Brad's office at 9:00 a.m. tomorrow.

The next morning Brad, Ace, and Paula where having their morning coffee in the small, previously bugged, conference room when Denise brought in the lawyer.

"Have a seat, Mr. Frazier. I'd like for you to meet my assistant, Paula Novak, and my investigator, Mr. Ace Sleuth. Ace just got back from Cincinnati yesterday where he found some information that seriously affects this trial."

"What kind of information?"

"I'll let Ace here fill you in on that."

"I found that a trial that took place in Cincinnati on June 26 this year that was just a dress rehearsal for the one here in Knoxville."

"What are you talking about?"

"Well, the defendant is the same and her injury is identical to the one she's claiming here, and to top it all off, the expert witness is the same."

"Are you kidding me?"

"I have a transcript of the trial right here. I've even made you a copy."

"I want to say right off that I knew nothing about this," said Frazier.

"We didn't think you did, Roland. That's why we called you in without the two co-conspirators being invited."

"There is more," said Ace. "Your expert witness was fired from Charity Hospital in Cincinnati for performing excessive operations and not performing them very well at that."

"What is the next step?" Frazier asked. "Your assistant Paula said that you wanted to settle out of court?"

"That's right. Let's take a look at what happens if we go to court," said Brad. "Your client and expert witness are both going to have to commit perjury or take the fifth when I face them with this evidence. I don't believe either of these alternatives will be acceptable to you. It means that you will have a 'lost case' on your record, and in addition, you will not receive a dime for your services."

"I see your point. What do you recommend?"

"My client has been damaged by these two characters and I want him compensated accordingly. I want you to tell them that the amount of compensation required is $500,000 from each of them."

"That's nothing more than blackmail."

"Do you mean it's kind of like some of the lawsuits you tort lawyers file?" said Brad. "I just call it settling out of court."

"I'm not sure I can get them to go along with this."

"I think they will jump at the chance when you explain the alternatives to them."

"What are the alternatives?"

"Five to ten years in jail for conspiracy to commit fraud. I have a respected radiologist here in Knoxville who is willing to testify that Hillary's neck injury is preexisting, and if that isn't enough, the copy of the trial transcript will seal the deal. The trial starts Monday of next week and if I don't hear back from you by Friday noon of this week, I'm going to turn the transcript over to the Knox County DA."

"I will do my best to convince them."

"I would suggest that in the future you do a little investigation of your own before you take on a case. Do you tort lawyers just take the word of any Tom, Dick, or Harry that walks through your door? It only took my investigator one day to gather all the information he gave you. If you have any trouble convincing those two yahoos, just let me have a go at them. They both have the money. Hillary won $1.5 million in her Cincinnati trial suit, of which she got two thirds, and Dr. Collier should have a bundle on ice from all those operations he did. I would like the money in a cashier's check please."

"I will get back to you," said Frazier.

"Thanks for your cooperation," said Brad, as Frazier walked out of the office.

"Paula, I want to draft up a document for Denise to type up. Word it something like this. Title it: 'OUT OF COURT SETTLEMENT IN THE CASE OF HILLARY JENKINS VERSUS CLIFFORD OWENS.' Make the body of the document read as follows: 'The sum of $1 million is hereby received as an out-of-court settlement in the lawsuit of Hillary Jenkins versus Clifford Owens for his out-of-pocket expenses, lost time, and mental anguish caused by the false lawsuit filed against him by the parties mentioned above.'" Brad then called Denise into his office.

"I also want you to draft the following checks and date them November 13:

1. $666,667 to Mr. Clifford Owens
2. $333,333 to Mr. Bradford Adams
3. $25,000 to Mr. Ace Sleuth
4. $10,000 to Miss Paula Novak
5. $5,000 to Miss Denise Davis

"The last three checks are bonuses for a job well done."

"I really appreciate this, Brad. You are an honest man, you know."

"Why is that, Paula?"

"You could have kept the whole million and Owens would have been happy just to get out from under the lawsuit."

"It never entered my mind, Paula."

"I also want to thank you," said Ace. "This money could make us a down payment on a house of our own."

"Denise, I would like for you to set up a meeting with Mr. Owens at his convenience. Just tell him it's very important; I want to surprise him with the news."

"Mr. Adams, I don't know how to thank you for the bonus," said Denise.

"You earned it, Denise. I would also like for you to summarize the entire bill for the Martin trial and get it to me for my signature. I then want you to send it to the local US Auto claims agent, Mr. Charles Nelson. You can get his address out of the phone book."

Chapter 74

Friday morning, November 10

Brad has just got into his office. The million-dollar check for the out-of-court settlement had been delivered by FedEx on Thursday. Brad's phone rang.

Brad picked it up. "What is it, Denise?"
"Mr. Owens is here to see you."
"Send him in."
"Come in, Mr. Owens. Good to see you again."
"Your secretary said that you had some very important news, what is it?"
"We have reached a settlement in your case, Clifford."
"That doesn't sound like very good news to me, Brad."
"Maybe this will help you to understand it a little better," said Brad, as he handed him a $666,667 check made out in his name.
"Are you playing a joke on me, Brad?"
"I never joke where money is involved, Clifford."
"What can I say? How can I ever thank you?"
"You don't have to thank me, Clifford, because I also got a check, my one third of the million-dollar settlement."
"How did you manage that, Brad?"
Brad explained all the particulars as he handed him a copy of the settlement. "I think this will explain it all."
"I don't know how I can ever repay you, Brad. Do you have any idea what a $5 million lawsuit can do to a man? I haven't had a good night's sleep since this thing was filed against me."
"That's what I call mental anguish, Clifford, and it's the main reason that you're being compensated."

"I will be in your debt forever, Brad," said Clifford, as he shook Brad's hand firmly on his way out.

This is one part of my job that I really enjoy, thought Brad, *I've got one more phone call to make,* he thought, as he dialed Roger Kennedy.

"This is Brad Adams calling. Would you put Mr. Kennedy on the phone please?"

Roger answered the phone, "How can I be of help, Brad?"

"You know I asked for your help twice but I never seem to be able to take advantage of it."

"What do you mean, Brad?"

Brad filled him in on the whole deal, the fraud, the out-of-court settlement, and the amount of the settlement.

"It looks like justice triumphed again, Brad, I am glad that I was available just the same."

"You really helped me more than you know just by telling me that Hillary Jenkins' injury was preexisting."

"Call me anytime, Brad."

"You do the same, Roger."

Chapter 75

Saturday, December 16
The Wedding

Lamont had come to town a couple of days prior to the wedding. Ace and Paula gave him the grand tour by showing him around town and a tour of The Great Smoky Mountain National Park. Later that evening they dined at the Open Hearth Restaurant in Gatlinburg.

Ace had also taken Lamont to a University of Tennessee basketball game where there were 25,000 screaming fans in attendance.

During the past month, Brad had taken on another civil case that he considered to be unfounded, and he and his staff had been pretty busy. Brad had Paula and Denise in charge of making all the wedding preparations. He had already rented the entire facilities of Club LeConte for the reception. No money was to be spared in the quality of the food being served at the sit-down dinner for 250 invited guests.

The wedding was scheduled for 6:00 p.m. at the First Baptist Church, only a block west of Brad's office on Main Street. Ace was giving away Jennifer in her and David's wedding in addition to getting married in the dual wedding, himself. It was decided that Ace would walk Jennifer down the aisle and then stand beside Paula during the ceremony. Lisa was Paula's maid of honor, and Lamont was Ace's best man. Brad's was David's best man and Jennifer had chosen a coworker from Baptist as her maid of honor. There were several ushers and bridesmaids in attendance.

There were 250 invited guests along with some reporters from the *Knoxville News Sentinel*.

The wedding got underway with Elizabeth Robinson performing the ceremony. This was all new to her and she did a commendable job of performing the ceremony of marrying both couples at the same time without repeating the words for each couple. After the wedding the married couples were driven the single block to the First Tennessee Bank Building in a horse-drawn carriage, while the attendees all walked.

Brad had hired a "big band" to play at the reception which specialized in contemporary music, but the music had the big band sound.

Jennifer and David walked up to Ace and Paula, and Ace said, "Why, if it isn't Nurse Jones. What a pleasant surprise?"

"I really appreciated you walking me down the aisle, Dr. Zachary, but there was just one thing missing."

"What was that?"

"Your stethoscope."

"Sorry about that. I usually carry it with me."

"Ace, I just want to thank you. If it hadn't been for you, I never would have met David."

"All's well that ends well," he said.

About that time Lisa walked up and kissed Ace on the cheek, and said, "Welcome to the family, Daddy. Do you mind if I call you Daddy?"

"I wouldn't have it any other way," said Ace. "What a change a day makes," said Ace, "yesterday I didn't have a single daughter, and today I have two."

"While you two lovebirds are on your honeymoon, what am I going to do for math problems, Ace?"

"Not to worry. This problem I'm giving you is older than my and your ages combined, Lisa, but it's a good one. I am leaving you this problem written on the outside of this envelope with the solution sealed inside. The problem is not a math one, but is one of logic. There are three men lined up in a row, each facing forward where each of them can only see the man in front of them. The man in back can see the two men in front of him and the man in the middle can only see the man in front of him and he can't see either one of the other two. There are two red hats and three white ones. The hats are randomly placed on the heads of the three men while they are all blindfolded. The blindfolds are then taken off and each one is asked what color hat he is wearing. They ask the man in the rear, who can see what color hats the two men in front of him are wearing, and he says that he doesn't know. They ask the man in the middle, who can see only what color hat the man in front of him is wearing, and he also says that he doesn't know. When they ask the man in front, who can't see what color hat either of the other two men is wearing, he tells them what color hat he himself is wearing. What color hat was the front man wearing, and how did he know? The answer is sealed inside the envelope, which I know you won't need to open. Put yourself in each of the men's shoes as they each answer the question. Also assume that each one of the men is intelligent and have given thoughtful consideration to the problem and to their answer."

It was now time to eat.

There was a choice in the food selection between lobster, prime rib, or filet mignon, or a bit of all three. Champagne was flowing in a continuous stream along with all sorts of expensive wines.

After everyone had eaten, Brad stood up and made a toast to the newlyweds, and announced that he and Elizabeth would be getting married in March of the coming year.

Ace and Paula spent their wedding night at the Marriott and left the next morning for a week in Vegas.

David and Jennifer flew out the same day for a week in Cancun, Mexico.

Lisa left the reception with her aunt, with whom she was staying, until Paula and Ace returned from Vegas. It was Sunday and she took another look at the math problem, which she hadn't been having much luck in solving. *I've got to try another approach,* she thought. *I've been trying to picture what each man saw. Maybe I need to concentrate on what they didn't see,* she thought. When she did this the answer became clear as a bell. If the man in the rear saw two red hats then he would know he was wearing a white. So he didn't see two reds. The middle man didn't see a red hat on the man in front or he would have known that he couldn't also be wearing a red one. So if he didn't see a red hat he had to see a white one. That meant that the man in front was wearing a white hat.

Chapter 76

Monday, December 25
Christmas Day

Ace and Paula returned from their honeymoon on Sunday the 24 and Brad had closed the office until Tuesday, January 2, 2007.

He met with Ace and Paula on January 2 to discuss what was on the agenda for the next several weeks.

"I received a check from US Auto for a little more than 200 grand. They got off easy. I didn't bill them for all of my hours, which at $500 per hour, could have shot the bill up $25,000 more. I could have billed them for 250 hours, but I only billed them for 200.

"It looks like we are going to be busy for the coming year. We have had to turn down several civil cases. I am only going to take on the cases that appear to be blatantly absurd or baseless."

"What is our next case?" asked, Ace

"It is a case where a pizza delivery boy for one of the countries largest pizza companies ran over a pedestrian who walked in front of his car. In the first place, I don't believe the boy was at fault, and secondly, I'm not sure if the delivery boy is an employee of the pizza company that is being sued, or whether he is a self-employed person driving his own car. That legal question will have to be determined.

"Later I want to discuss with both of you about some sort of profit-sharing plan. I will get back to you in about thirty days on that matter. Before we get started back to work, are there any questions?"

"Do you think you have made a difference in future civil court cases?" asked Ace.

"I think that 'we' may have made a difference, you, Paula, Denise, and me. Only time will tell. If now some of these tort lawyers will start investigating some of their clients before they file the lawsuits, we could probably eliminate a lot of legal time-wasting.

"I wish we could get all the frivolous suits thrown out before they ever get to the court level. I would also like to see the jurors in these suits be made up of sensible and intelligent persons and I think I may have plowed some new ground in this area. I would also like to see the envelope pushed a little like it was in the Bret Martin case where the jury found damages for the defendant. I believe that jury did this country a service by sticking its neck out like it did. That took intelligence and courage on their part. I don't believe it is the function of the civil courts to try to provide compensation to all parties that have suffered disabling injuries just because they are injured. I think that in the past a lot of the injured were awarded large sums of money without any proof whatsoever of fault on the part of he defendant. We need to prevent this from happening in the future, but we also need to be very careful that we don't throw out the baby with the wash and not provide justice to the many deserving plaintiffs in the civil suits."

"What would you like to see happen in the area of tort reform?" asked Paula.

"It's very simple, Paula, I would like to see justice for all."

Epilogue

Luther Spenser was convicted of perjury and conspiracy to commit fraud and was sentenced to ten years in prison. In addition he was disbarred for life from practicing law in the state of Tennessee.

Bret Martin was tried and convicted of the same crimes as Spenser, but because of his cooperation and testimony, he received a lighter sentence of five years in prison. The young man who tried to carjack Ace's Mustang received a three-year prison sentence.

A little over two months after returning from their honeymoons, Paula and Jennifer both announced that they were pregnant. They were both hoping that their babies would be born on the same day. Lisa was tickled to death that she was going to have a sibling. Jennifer seemed more excited than any of them because she had always regretted that she never had a baby by her first husband, Scott. Ace just seemed to be in a daze.

David moved back to Knoxville and he and Jennifer purchased a condo overlooking the Tennessee River just few hundred yards from Brad's office, the Women's Basketball Hall of Fame, and the Marriott Hotel.

Ace and Paula purchased a home in the West Knoxville subdivision of Glen Cove. It's only about fifteen minutes from their office.

Brad and Elizabeth after a beautiful wedding ceremony in March, and a honeymoon in Europe, moved into Brad's condo.

The good doctor Felix Upshaw was never heard from again, and Brad thought that this was for the better.

Brad thought he was seeing some slight changes in the tort system, but he realized that we still have a long road ahead of us to achieve justice for all.

Also available from PublishAmerica

THE MAGIC COTTAGE

by Hannah Greer

Eight-year-old twins Asa and Prentiss Fallmark are spending the summer with their grandparents. Grammy and Papa set a goal for the month-long vacation: the twins are to investigate and stretch their imaginations without the use of television, electronic gadgets, or radio. Each morning, the siblings board their "imagination transporter" at the top of a hill adjacent to their grandparents' home. The twins have remarkable adventures in the land they call Serendipity where they "build" the magic cottage and meet many new friends who provide them with mystical gifts. The children become integral parts of exciting experiences in which they must use their minds and imaginations to overcome conflict. Scientific studies they learned in school develop special meanings as they explore Serendipity. Hints occur throughout the story that the grandparents know more about Serendipity than the children realize. Could it be that Grammy and Papa have magical powers?

Paperback, 132 pages
5.5" x 8.5"
ISBN 1-60672-190-9

About the author:

Hannah Greer has embraced writing since she was a child. As an educator and founder of an experiential school, she guided underachievers to utilize their imaginations. Teaming up with her illustrator sister, Tica Greer, a new series of books based on exciting adventures, *The Velvet Bag Memoirs*, has been born.

Available to all bookstores nationwide.
www.publishamerica.com

Also available from PublishAmerica

HOTEL TRANSYLVANIA

by Michael T.G. Yepes

This is a novel about exiles, refugees and immigrants. The time is the early 18th century; the scene is Paris. The location is a gambling establishment of dubious reputation—the Hotel de Transylvania. Situated on the Seine embankment, across the Louvre, a group of Hungarian expatriates support themselves on their good looks, charm, guile and political connection. This establishment is run by the grey eminence of the Abbé Brenner, under the protection of the exiled Prince of Transylvania. This is the story of the denizens of that hotel from 1713 to 1717. It is about being a foreigner, yet crafty and adaptable; it is about entering a new social environment, and succeeding or failing in Europe's most glamorous and exciting city. And it is also a reflection on a society that was rapidly emerging from the rigid rule of Louis XIV to the expanding freedoms under the Orléans regency. In the background, there is the still-smouldering conflict between the Jesuits and Jansenists. The sacred and the profane, constantly juxtaposed and confronting each other, in an environment of fabulous wealth and painful poverty—and four young men absorbing it all.

Paperback, 210 pages
5.5" x 8.5"
ISBN 1-4241-5219-4

About the author:

Michael T.G. Yepes was born in Budapest, Hungary, and came to the U.S. in 1956, after the Hungarian Revolution. He had received his secondary and college education in Budapest, and graduated from Medical School in San Francisco. A life-long interest in history and literature lead him to the California Missions, and eventually to the Jesuits on the California Peninsula. M.T.G. Yepes is married and lives with his wife in West Los Angeles. They have three adult children and 7 grandchildren.

Available to all bookstores nationwide.
www.publishamerica.com